Charles Dickens, Richard Herne Shepherd

The Plays and Poems of Charles Dickens

Vol. 1

Charles Dickens, Richard Herne Shepherd

The Plays and Poems of Charles Dickens
Vol. 1

ISBN/EAN: 9783337367053

Printed in Europe, USA, Canada, Australia, Japan

Cover: Foto ©Andreas Hilbeck / pixelio.de

More available books at **www.hansebooks.com**

THE

PLAYS AND POEMS

OF

CHARLES DICKENS

WITH A FEW MISCELLANIES IN PROSE

NOW FIRST COLLECTED

EDITED PREFACED AND ANNOTATED

BY

RICHARD HERNE SHEPHERD

IN TWO VOLUMES

VOL. I.

LONDON
W. H. ALLEN & CO. 13 WATERLOO PLACE S.W.
PUBLISHERS TO THE INDIA OFFICE
1885

CONTENTS.

INTRODUCTION.

OF the five plays now collected in these volumes, the first three were written by Charles Dickens for the St. James's Theatre under Braham's management and lesseeship. *The Strange Gentleman, The Village Coquettes,* and *Is She his Wife? or Something Singular!* appeared successively at that theatre between Michaelmas of 1836 and Easter of 1837, with more or less of applause and success, and were published separately in pamphlet form soon after their performance.

1. The earliest of these three St. James's pieces was *The Strange Gentleman,* first performed on Thursday, September 29, 1836. The plot was founded on one of the *Sketches by Boz,* " The Great *The Strange* Winglebury Duel," and it will not be an *Gentleman.* uninteresting task to the reader to compare the different treatment in the sketch and in

+

the play. The plot of the story is further complicated in the drama by the addition of two young ladies and their lovers. Altogether, it contains a greater number of whimsical mistakes and perplexities than even Goldsmith's *She Stoops to Conquer;* the second title of which, had it not been appropriated, would have suited *The Strange Gentleman* exactly. It consists of "the mistakes of a night," at an inn on the North road; where the various personages, arriving with separate objects, are led into a series of misconceptions as to each other's identity and purposes. The Strange Gentleman himself, whose object is to escape the direful consequences of a challenge from his rival, and who is heard of by the other travellers as they arrive, without being seen by them, is supposed by each to be the person whom each expects to meet. An elderly and wealthy spinster takes him for the lordling on whom she is going to bestow herself and her fortune by a trip to Gretna; and a runaway damsel imagines he is her lover with whom she is about to take a similar flight. During the *imbroglio* that ensues, the Strange Gentleman never comes in contact with the persons who by seeing him could discover the mistake; and the

denoûment is effected by the spinster seeing at last
that the Strange Gentleman is not Lord Peter, and
by the young lady seeing that he is not her lover.
Making allowance for the antecedent improbability
(which is quite within the bounds of conventional
stage licence) of so many persons casually meeting
at an inn under such peculiar circumstances, the
incidents which arise out of their rencontre are
ingeniously contrived, follow each other very easily,
and produce some exceedingly grotesque situations.
The dialogue is lively, rapid, and full of smart and
pointed allusions.

Harley, who appeared on this occasion for the
first time at the St. James's Theatre, was a capital
Strange Gentleman. His suspicions, perplexities,
and terrors, kept the audience in a constant roar
of laughter. He was well seconded by Gardner,
in the one-eyed Boots,—a prominent character in
the drama as well as in the original Sketch. Mrs.
Penson personated to the life the bustling landlady
of the St. James's Arms, displaying nearly all the
arch vivacity that made her so delightful a *soubrette*
a quarter of a century before. The two Miss
Smiths—nieces of the famous Kitty Stephens, afterwards Countess of Essex—made a most successful

debut. They spoke elegantly and intelligently, and displayed much merit as singers. Their reception was most flattering, and they soon became general favourites. Madame Sala, mother of the since famous journalist, George Augustus Sala, also made a favourable impression ; and Forester played the young lover much better than such parts are generally played. Altogether the piece was entirely successful. It had an immediate run of fifty nights, nor was it even then finally withdrawn, but was reproduced at intervals on several occasions in the course of the following year (1837), when it was published in a pamphlet of forty-six pages by Chapman and Hall, with a frontispiece by Phiz (Hablot Browne),* the illustrator of Pickwick and of *Sunday under Three Heads.*

2. On Tuesday, December 6, *The Strange Gentleman* was replaced by the Comic Opera, in Two Acts, of *The Village Coquettes.* The music of the songs was composed by John Hullah, then a

---

* An admirably executed facsimile reprint of *The Strange Gentleman* (*minus* the frontispiece) has for some time been in private circulation. It is so cleverly reproduced as to be almost indistinguishable from the original edition, and has, we believe, more than once, been fraudulently passed off as such upon unwary collectors.

young man almost unknown to fame. Harley again played one of the leading parts in a manner which won for him Dickens's grateful and graceful acknowledgments in a Dedication. Whether considered with regard to its dramatic or musical *The Village* qualities, this opera is of a very uncom-*Coquettes.* mon character, and has no resemblance to the trumpery *libretti* in vogue at the time. It is a light and elegant comedy, in which a great deal of gaiety and humour are blended with scenes of great interest, and many sweet and natural touches of tenderness and feeling. The music is admirably in accordance with the subject,—simple, unaffected, and full of beautiful expressive, English *John* melody. While Hullah has given this *Hullah's music.* character to his airs, he has imparted to them much of the grace of the Italian school,—of the great masters of a former age ; and in the richness of his accompaniments and the skill and ingenuity of his concerted movements, he has shown his command over the resources of modern harmony. " Mr. Hullah," says a newspaper notice of the time, " has received his education in the Royal Academy of Music, and does infinite honour to his *Alma Mater.* We are sure, however, that some of the most remarkable features of his musical character must be ascribed to self-tuition ; for his style never could be so deeply imbued with the spirit of Purcell and the great old English masters, had not the bent of his own genius directed him to a course of study very different from the fashionable routine of the day."

The scene of *The Village Coquettes* is laid in an

Plot of *The* *Village* *Coquettes.* English village, and the incidents are supposed to have happened about a century and a half ago. The piece opens with the representation of a farmer's rick-yard, in which a number of work-people are engaged in the concluding labours of the harvest, and welcoming the harvest-home with a gay round and chorus. From a dialogue which ensues between John Maddox, farmer Benson's principal servant, and Martin Stokes, a small farmer, full of self-importance and bustle, with a wondrous skill in discovering when there is " something wrong " in the concerns of his neighbours, it appears that there is something wrong in the attentions paid to farmer Benson's daughter Lucy, and his niece Rose, by Squire Norton, the Lord of the Manor, and his friend, the Honourable Mr. Sparkins Flam. The Squire

and his friend enter from shooting. Mr. Norton
contrives to have a few moments' conversation with
Lucy; from which it appears that, though her
heart remains full of affection for her rustic lover,
she is dazzled by the addresses of the Squire. The
Squire joins the farmer and his friends in drinking
a glass to the harvest-home, and the scene concludes
with an animated drinking-song, sung by him, with
a chorus. George Edmunds, the lover of Lucy,
then appears in the fields, musing on his unhappi-
ness. He is lingering in hopes to meet with Lucy,
when Rose makes her appearance. This damsel,
on her part, is expecting to meet her admirer, Mr.
Flam, and is anxious to get Edmunds away.
While he is earnestly inquiring about Lucy,
Maddox enters, and soon afterwards Flam. There
is an admirable scene of coquetry on the part of the
little flirt, impertinence on that of the coxcomb,
and sturdy spirit on that of the honest peasant.
Flam plays the bully, and attempts to strike
Maddox with the butt-end of his fowling-piece;
but the blow is parried by Edmunds, who departs
with Maddox, after contemptuously upbraiding
Flam with his treachery and cowardice. Flam vows
revenge; and then succeeds in persuading his

simple mistress that the affair was all a joke. The
scene ends with a lively and clever duet between
them. The old farmer, at last, becomes acquainted
with the intimacy between the Squire and his
daughter, by means of the busy Mr. Stokes, who
no less eagerly gives the same information to young
Benson, the farmer's son. The Squire arrives at
the farm, and is boldly taxed by the young man
with his conduct, and threatened with the consequences of pursuing it. The Squire, left alone,
stifles the compunctious visitings of his conscience,
and resolves to persist in his design. He is persuading Lucy to elope with him, when they are
surprised by old Benson, who gives vent to
indignant reproaches. The Squire endeavours at
first to conciliate him ; but, stung by the bitterness
of his language, tells him his lease is expired, and
orders him to quit the farm. The farmer's friends
and servants crowd upon the stage, and the first
act is terminated by a well-wrought and agitated
finale.

In the second act Mr. Flam is lounging over his
breakfast on the morning after the above events,
when a letter is put into his hands from a London
attorney, demanding immediate restitution of a sum

of money which he had unfairly won by cheating at play. Dismayed at this communication, and the threat of exposure by which it is accompanied, he resolves on exerting himself to aid the accomplishment of the Squire's designs on Lucy, in order to obtain such a recompense as may relieve him from his dilemma. His meditations are interrupted by the entrance of the Squire in an altered mood, stung with remorse for his conduct towards Lucy, and his cruelty towards her father. While he is expressing these feelings of contrition to the astonished Flam, Lucy and Rose are announced as wishing to speak with him. Flam retires; and Lucy's eloquent appeal to Mr. Norton's principles and generosity completes his conversion. Flam, ignorant of this change, determines to carry off Lucy during the harvest-home entertainment to be given at the Hall that night; and sits down to apprise Norton of his design, and to write to his London correspondent promising immediate payment of the money demanded of him. He writes the note to Norton, but is prevented from writing the other, and hastily encloses in an envelope the letter he has received from London instead of that which he has just written to Norton, putting his

note to Norton in his pocket.   Martin Stokes, who
has learned that Flam has been inquiring for a
trusty person to do a piece of secret service for
him, presents himself as that person, and is engaged,
by a promise of reward, to have a chaise and four
in waiting at ten o'clock.   The conversation being
carried on in hints and innuendoes, Stokes naturally
enough supposes that Rose is to be the victim of
this intended abduction, and hastens away to paralyse her and her lover John Maddox by this
tremendous disclosure.   After some scenes, in
the course of which everything is put to rights
between the Squire and the farmer's family, and the
lovers are reconciled to their repentant fair ones,
all parties are assembled in the ball-room at the
Hall, with a large concourse of country people.
While a merry country dance is going forward a
scream is heard from the garden, and all is confusion.   In a few moments Edmunds enters from
the window, bearing Lucy insensible in his arms ;
and Flam, with his clothes torn and his face disfigured, is led in by Maddox and Stokes.   Suspicion
immediately falls on the Squire as the prompter of
the deed, which he indignantly disclaims.   Flam,
finding himself given up, asserts that he acted

under the Squire's instructions, and appeals for the truth of his charge to a letter in the Squire's own pocket. Mr. Norton produces the letter of the London attorney, from which he has just learned the base character of his *friend ;* and Flam retires in confusion and disgrace, leaving the Squire and his guests in harmony and happiness. The festivities are resumed; and the piece is rounded off by a repetition of the jovial chorus with which it opened. The drama is worthy of being judged by stricter rules of criticism than are usually applied to musical pieces. The plot is clear and well conducted, and the incidents sufficiently probable, with the exception of Flam's blunder in sending to Norton the letter which leads to his exposure, and the facility with which he is led to entrust his plot to Martin Stokes. The first of these may be excused by the conventional licence of the stage ; but the second betokens a degree of *greenness* not at all natural to a thorough-paced knave like Flam. The characters are well varied and supported, the dialogue is lively and vigorous, and the musical part of it contains some poetry such as opera-composers seldom meet with. Dickens has treated the character of Lucy with much skill and delicacy.

She is weak enough to be led away by the vanity of an inexperienced country girl ; yet she is so candid and ingenuous, so full of tenderness for the man whom she has wronged, so conscious and heart-stricken in the midst of her folly, that she never ceases to be amiable and interesting. Even when at length she yields to the insidious addresses of the Squire, and accepts what she believes to be an offer of his hand, she is driven to it by hasty resentment and wounded pride on hearing that Edmunds has cast her off as unworthy. Miss Rainforth was an excellent representative of this interesting character. Her appearance was most engaging, her acting full of intelligence and feeling, and her singing graceful, expressive, and beautifully chaste. Her fine song, "Love is not a feeling to pass away," was a model of pure and simple singing, without the introduction of a note that did not appear to be the spontanteous effusion of feeling. Her song, in the second act, "How beautiful at eventide," is an impassioned composition, and enabled her to display not only the extent of her vocal attainments, but the strength of her expression. Miss Julia Smith gave full effect to the light-hearted simplicity of Rose, and sang the song, " Some folks who have grown old and sour," and the flirting duet with Flam, with a most amusing playfulness, and great beauty of voice and execution. Braham gave the part of the Squire the easy good-humour that belongs to it. He sang as if he had been appearing for the first time in a new piece of his friend of the olden time, Storace; and felt, doubtless, how much of the spirit of that time was in the music he was singing. His song, or rather soliloquy, " The Child and the Old Man," displayed his matchless power of making music the language of deep and passionate thought; but even this was hardly so remarkable as the ballad already referred to, and to which he gave a charm which is quite indescribable. Bennett, as Edmunds, acted with great good sense and propriety, and sang beautifully, especially in the ballad of " Autumn Leaves," which speaks the very language of grief. Barnett's Flam was a little too studied and formal, though, on the whole, a clever and effective per-formance. Parry, in the part of young Benson, had not an important share in the business of the drama. He contributed much, however, to the effect of the concerted music, and sang a ballad, " My Fair Home," with much sweetness. The

2 *

finest acting in the piece was that of Strickland
in Old Benson. It was a fine and powerful picture
of the feelings of a father outraged in the tenderest
point. Gardner in John Maddox, gave to the life
the blunt plainness of the English peasant; and
though last, not least, Harley, in Martin Stokes,
kept the audience in an unceasing roar of laughter.
The getting-up of this Opera did the highest honour
to Braham's management. It was complete in
every part. The scenery and decorations were
singularly beautiful and splendid, and the whole
of the performers were accurately attired in the
costumes of the earlier part of the last century.
The orchestra did full justice to the airy and
elegant overture, and to the accompaniments
throughout, and the choruses and concerted pieces
were smoothly and correctly sung. A passage for
five voices especially, in the finale, entirely without
instruments, in the style of a glee, had so charming an effect that an *encore* burst at once from
every part of the house. On the whole, it is not
too much to say that no English musical piece
equal to *The Village Coquettes* had appeared
since *The Duenna*. Its success was assured and
triumphant. At its conclusion Mr. Hullah, being

loudly called for, appeared before the curtain amidst thunders of applause, in which Braham, at one of the wings, warmly joined. A cry was then commenced of " Boz," which instantly resounded from every part of the house, and was continued until Charles Dickens also came forward, and was received with equal cordiality.

The following letters of Dickens to Mr. John Hullah, the composer of the music to *The Village Coquettes*, appear in the recently-published collection of Dickens's Letters :—

Furnival's Inn,
Monday afternoon, 7 o'clock,
1836.

My DEAR HULLAH,

Mr. Hogarth has just been here, with news which I think you will be glad to hear. He was with Braham yesterday, who was *far more full* of the opera than he was; speaking highly of my works and " fame " (!), and expressing an earnest desire to be the first to introduce me to the public as a dramatic writer. He said that he intended opening at Michaelmas; and added (unasked) that it was his intention to produce the opera within *one month* of his first night. He wants a low-comedy part introduced—without singing—thinking it will take with the audience; but he is desirous of explaining to me what he means and who he intends to play it. I am to see him on Sunday morning. Full particulars of the interview shall be duly announced.

Perhaps I shall see you meanwhile.*

Petersham, Monday evening,

DEAR HULLAH,   1836.

Since I called on you this morning I have not had time to look over the words of "The Child and the Old Man." It occurs to me, as I shall see you on Wednesday morning, that the best plan will be for you to bring the music (if you possibly can) without the words, and we can put them in then.† Of course this observation applies only to that particular song.

(margin:) Charles Dickens to John Hullah.

Braham having sent to me about the farce, I called on him this morning. Harley wrote, when he had read the whole of the opera, saying:—"It's a sure card—*nothing wrong there*. Bet you ten pound it runs fifty nights. Come; don't be afraid. You'll be the gainer by it, and you mustn't mind betting; *it's a capital custom*."‡ They tell the story with infinite relish. I saw the fair manageress, who is fully of Harley's opinion; so is Braham. The only difference is, that they are far more enthusiastic than Harley—far more enthusiastic than ourselves even. That is a bold word, isn't it? It is a true one, nevertheless.

---

* *Letters of Charles Dickens*, vol. iii. p. 2.
† *Vide infrà*, p. 219, *note*.
‡ The phrases italicised are playful adoptions of two favourite expressions of Martin Stokes, the character which Harley played in *The Village Coquettes.*—ED.

"Depend upon it, sir," said Braham to Hogarth yesterday, when he went there to say I should be in town to-day, "depend upon it, sir, that there has been no such music since the days of Sheil, and no such piece since *The Duenna.* Everybody is delighted with it," he added, to me to-day. "I played it to Stansbury, who is by no means an excitable person, and he was *charmed.*" This was said with great emphasis, but I have forgotten the grand point. It was not, "I played it to Stansbury," but "I sang it—*all through* !!!"

Charles Dickens to John Hullah.

I begged him, as the choruses are to be put into rehearsal directly the company get together, to let us have, through Mrs. Braham, the necessary passports to the stage, which will be forwarded. He leaves town on the *8th of September.* He will be absent a month, and the first rehearsal will take place immediately on his return; previous to it (I mean the first rehearsal—not the return) I am to read the piece. His only remaining suggestion is, that Miss Rainforth will want another song when the piece is in rehearsal—"a *bravura*—something in the 'Soldier Tired' way." We must have a confab about this on Wednesday morning.

Harley called in Furnival's Inn, to express his high delight and gratification; but unfortunately we had left town. I shall be at head-quarters by 12, Wednesday (noon).*

The following was written on the Sunday following the first performance of the piece:—

---

* *Letters of Charles Dickens,* vol. iii. pp. 3–4.

Furnival's Inn, Sunday Evening,

MY DEAR HULLAH,   [December 11, 1836.]

Have you seen *The Examiner?* It is rather
depreciatory of the opera; but, like all inveterate critiques
against Braham, so well done that I cannot help laughing
Charles   at it, for the life and soul of me. I have seen *The*
Dickens
to John   *Sunday Times, The Dispatch,* and *The Satirist,*
Hullah.   all of which blow their critic trumpets against
unhappy me most lustily. Either I must have grievously
awakened the ire of all the " adapters " and their friends,
or the drama must be decidedly bad. I haven't made up
my mind yet which of the two is the fact.

I have not seen the *John Bull* or any of the Sunday
papers except *The Spectator.* If you have any of them,
bring 'em with you on Tuesday. I am afraid that for
" dirty Cummins' " allusion to Hogarth, I shall be reduced
to the necessity of being valorous the next time I meet
him. *

The Village Coquettes, although preceded by
The Strange Gentleman on the stage, was the first
written and the first published. It was written,
as we gather from the Preface, in 1835, and
published as a pamphlet, with the author's full
name on the title-page, by Bentley, a few days

---

* *Letters of Charles Dickens,* vol. iii. pp. 1–2. The reference
in the concluding sentence is to a foul-mouthed criticling
in the *Weekly Dispatch,* who had had recourse to "the
blackguard's loaded bludgeon of personalities."—ED.

before Christmas 1836.* A copy sent to John
Forster was the means of first bringing Dickens
into personal communication with his future
biographer. Seven of the Songs were issued
separately with Hullah's music.

· This piece, like its predecessor, had a fairly
long run, till it gave way in its turn to a third
attempt, a Comic Burletta, in one act, entitled
Is She his Wife? or Something Singular! the best,
perhaps, but hitherto the least known of· the
three. This little farce was first performed at
Is She the St. James's Theatre on Monday,
his Wife? March 6, 1837. There are only six
characters—in fact, only five with any real business.
The leading character, Felix Tapkins, was again
played by Harley, and the other principal parts by
Forester and Halford,† Gardner, Miss Allison, and

---

* A so-called "facsimile reprint" of *The Village Coquettes*
has been issued by the original publishers, since Dickens's
death ; but its value is greatly impaired by gross inattention
throughout to textual accuracy.

† Forester was the original Lovetown, but was replaced
by Halford. The minor part of Lovetown's servant, who
has only a few words of announcement to utter, does not
appear in the cast, and was probably taken by any supernumerary ready at hand.

Madame Sala. Harley's benefit took place on the evening of Monday, March 13, when he made his appearance for the seventh time in the little farce, and received a most cordial welcome from the audience. He afterwards appeared in the character

Comic Song by Charles Dickens, written for Harley.

of Mr. Pickwick, and sang a comic song, written for him by Boz, giving an amusing description of a Blackwall whitebait dinner. He excited roars of laughter by the manner in which he *looked* the character and gave the humorous points of the song. Of this comic song I have been unable to find any trace, nor can I decide with certainty for how many further nights the burletta ran; but a play-bill now lying before me announces its performance for the *nineteenth* time, on Tuesday, April 25, 1837.

The original edition of *Is She his Wife?* was, like the two former pieces, printed at the time. It is, however, among the *rarissima* of modern literary curiosities, being in fact what French bibliographers call "introuvable." The only copy I have succeeded in tracing (and that has now perished) was purchased from the collection of the late Mr. Thomas Hailes Lacy, the famous theatrical bookseller. It became the property of

Mr. James R. Osgood, of the firm of Osgood and
A lost literary rarity. Co., of Boston, U.S.A., who fortunately
preserved the text for us by issuing an
American reprint of it in 1877. But the original
copy was destroyed in the fire which burned
Messrs. Osgood's business premises in December
1879.* Another remarkable circumstance is that
this little piece appears to have been unknown to
or forgotten by Mr. Forster, who makes no allusion
direct or indirect to its existence throughout the
whole of his biography of Dickens. Meantime
the question of authorship, apart from internal
evidence, is otherwise established by the discovery
of the contemporary play-bills which describe *Is
She his Wife?* as " an original Comic Burletta,
in One Act, *written by Boz.*"

These are the only three dramatic pieces, acted
and published, of which Dickens was the sole author.
Some trace remains in his correspondence of
negotiations with Braham, or of overtures indirectly
conveyed through Harley, for a fourth piece. But
for one reason or another the proposal fell through,

---

* Readers desirous of fuller particulars on this subject
are referred to a paper by the present writer entitled " A
Lost Work of Charles Dickens," published in *The Pen*,
October 1880, pp. 311–312.

and Dickens's connexion with the St. James's Theatre henceforth ceased. A letter of Dickens's to Harley on this subject runs as follows:—

48, Doughty Street,

MY DEAR SIR,   Saturday Morning.*

I have considered the terms on which I could afford just now to sell Mr. Braham the acting copyright

Charles Dickens to J. P. Harley.
in London of an entirely new piece for the St. James's Theatre; and I could not sit down to write one in a single act of about one hour long, under a hundred pounds. For a new piece in two acts, a hundred and fifty pounds would be the sum I should require.

I do not know whether, with reference to arrangements that were made with any other writers, this may or may not appear a large item. I state it merely with regard to the value of my own time and writings at this moment; and in so doing I assure you I place the remuneration below the mark rather than above it.

As you begged me to give you my reply upon this point, perhaps you will lay it before Mr. Braham. If these terms exceed his inclination or the ability of the theatre, there is an end of the matter, and no harm done.

Believe me ever faithfully yours,
CHARLES DICKENS.†

---

* This letter is otherwise undated; but as Charles Dickens did not remove from Furnival's Inn to 48, Doughty Street, until March 1837, it cannot have been written until after the production of *Is She his Wife?*

† *Letters of Charles Dickens*, vol. i. p. 5.

Dickens had not yet, however, abandoned all idea of continuing to write for the stage. In the winter of 1838, he was trying his hand at a farce for Macready, to be produced at Drury Lane. It is in the month of November 1838, presumably, that he thus addresses Macready on the subject:—

Doughty Street,

My DEAR MACREADY,   Monday Morning.

I have not seen you for the past week, because I hoped when we next met to bring *The Lamplighter* in my hand. It would have been finished by this time, but I found myself compelled to set to work first at " Nickleby," at which I am at present engaged, and which I regret to say —after my close and arduous application last month— I find I cannot write as quickly as usual. I must finish it, at latest, by the 24th, and the instant I have done so, I will apply myself to the farce. I am afraid to name any particular day, but I pledge myself that you shall have it this month, and you may calculate on that promise. I send you with this a copy of a farce I wrote for Harley when he left Drury Lane, and in which he acted for some seventy nights. It is the best thing he does. It is barely possible you might like to try it. Any local or temporary allusions could be easily altered.

Believe me that I only feel gratified and flattered by your inquiry after the farce, and that if I had as much time as I have inclination, I would write on and on and

Charles Dickens to Macready.

on, farce after farce, and comedy after comedy, until I
wrote you something that would run.

P.S. For Heaven's sake don't fancy that I hold *The
Strange Gentleman* in any estimation, or have a wish
upon the subject.*

The farce of *The Lamplighter* was, in a few

The Lamp-
lighter.

weeks, duly finished, read by the author
to the actors according to custom, and
put into rehearsal. The piece, however, does not
seem to have found favour with the company, and
the following is Dickens's magnanimous reply to
Macready's appeal for permission to withdraw it.

48, Doughty Street,
My dear Macready,　　　　December 13, 1838.

I can have but one opinion on the subject—with-

Charles
Dickens to
Macready.

draw the farce at once, by all means.
I perfectly concur in all you say, and thank
you most heartily and cordially for your kind
and manly conduct, which is only what I should have
expected from you; though, under such circumstances, I
sincerely believe there are few but you—if any—who
would have adopted it.

Believe me that I have no other feeling of disappointment connected with this matter but that arising from
the not having been able to be of some use to you. And
trust me that, if the opportunity should ever arrive, my

---

* *Letters of Charles Dickens,* vol. i. p. 16.

ardour will only be increased—not damped—by the result of this experiment.*

The unfortunate *Lamplighter* was accordingly withdrawn and never acted. The stage copy, however, written in the fair clerkly hand of a copyist, came into possession of the late Mr. John Forster, and forms part of the priceless collection of books and manuscripts bequeathed by him to the nation and deposited in the South Kensington Museum. Rescued from the clutches of *fainéant* librarians† and flunkey officials, it is now presented here in its

The Lamplighter's Story. proper sequence among Dickens's other dramatic writings, together with the story from the *Pic Nic Papers* into which he turned

---

* *Letters of Charles Dickens*, vol. i. p. 17.

† The Forster Collection has now been for six years in the possession of the South Kensington authorities; and no Catalogue adequate or inadequate has appeared up to the present time. The loose list compiled by Mr. Forster's secretary in his lifetime, and printed for private reference (conveying but a very faint notion of the hidden treasures of the Collection), is the sole catalogue available, and even that can only be consulted on the premises. Of the Dyce Collection, an ill-digested, incomplete, and grossly inaccurate Catalogue—full of blunders for which a schoolboy would be whipped—was issued at a prohibitive price, after a delay of years, in two cumbrous volumes. The room provided for the accommodation of readers is capable of seating some six, or at most eight, persons; in the winter months this room is closed at four o'clock, and in the summer at five; and the use of ink is forbidden.

it two or three years afterwards, and which has never been included in any Collected Edition of his Works. The reader will find a comparison of the two versions—of the dramatic and the narrative treatment of it—not without interest.

And here may be said to close the first epoch of Dickens's career as a dramatist. His two remaining attempts as a playwright were made at a much later period of his life, and in conjunction with other writers.

The one-act farce entitled *Mr. Nightingale's* *Mr. Night-* *Diary* was the joint work of Charles *ingale's* *Diary.* Dickens and Mark Lemon, and was written for the performances of "The Guild of Literature and Art," and privately printed in the year 1851,—a tiny pamphlet of twenty-six pages, a copy of which is preserved in the Forster Collection at South Kensington.* Dickens himself played the part of Gabblewig, with all the numerous transformations and metamorphoses it involved, while Mark Lemon, his coadjutor, took the part of Slap. The piece was first performed at Devonshire House, on Tuesday, May 27, 1851.

---

* *Forster Catalogue*, p. 185. Bound up in a volume of ten Plays, of which "Not so Bad as we Seem" is the first, and "Mr. Nightingale's Diary" the second.

"A stage play, however slight," writes the late Mr.

R. H. Horne, who was one of the Company of the Guild, "devised and written by the combined humour and skill of two such admirable amateur actors and popular writers as Charles Dickens and Mark Lemon, could not fail to be peculiarly interesting; how much more so when we know that the characters introduced on the scene were expressly invented and adopted with a view to the special histrionic talents of the two eminent persons who enacted the piece, and when we also know but too sadly that neither of them can ever again be seen in any earthly form. This very amusing production was written for the after-piece to Lord Lytton's comedy of *Not so Bad as we Seem,* and was acted for the first time at Devonshire House, on the night which inaugurated the series of amateur performances in aid of the fund proposed to be raised for the foundation of 'The Guild of Literature and Art.' It was never published, and a few copies only were printed and circulated among the members of the 'Guild.' But, like the possessors, they have all drifted away on the surges of time, and whoever would revert to the piece has very little chance of getting any copy, or fragment of a copy, to assist his memory.

"The plot was so very slight as scarcely to merit the name, but the principal characters were of a kind never to be forgotten. These were eleven in number, of which Mark Lemon personated three, Dickens five, and Augustus Egg one—and a very remarkable one it was. The remaining characters are of little moment, and, in

I. 3 +-

truth, we forget who it was that played Mr. Nightingale.* The reader will bear in mind that the Queen, the
Prince Consort, and most of the Court were present, her
Majesty and *suite*, who had retired for some refreshment
after the performance of the comedy, having returned to
their places. The Duke of Devonshire was ' all smiles '
at our success thus far. It was quite delightful to see
any man so happy. And with regard to the audience,
nearly all of whom were members of the highest circles
as to rank, and also, perhaps (at any rate in the eyes of
Douglas Jerrold, who repeatedly declared it aloud behind
the scenes), as to female beauty, most truly might it be
said, that they all came *pour assister* on this our all-
important first night, and constituted, therefore, the best
possible audience that could be desired."†

An anonymous writer in *Macmillan's Magazine*
(January 1871) thus describes a later representation of the farce:

The farce of *Mr. Nightingale's Diary*, the joint production of Dickens and Mark Lemon, which followed Mr.
Mr. Nightingale's Collins's play of *The Lighthouse*, at Tavi-
Diary. stock House, was well calculated to exhibit
the versatility of the principal actor. Dickens played
one Mr. Gabblewig, in which character he assumed four
or five different disguises, changing his dress, voice, and

---

* Mr. Dudley Costello.—Ed.
† *Gentleman's Magazine*, May 1871, pp. 660–661. "Bygone
Celebrities," by R. H. Horne. § *Mr. Nightingale's Diary*. In
his subsequent account of the piece Mr. Horne appears to have
been betrayed by lapse of memory into many inaccuracies.

look with a rapidity and completeness which the most practised "entertainer" might envy. This whimsical piece of extravagance had been before played by the same actors in the performances for the benefit of the Guild of Literature and Art, but has never been printed, except privately for the use of the original actors. What portions were contributed by the joint authors respectively we can only surmise; but there were certain characters and speeches which bore very clearly stamped upon them the mark of their authorship.*

It was on the eve of his second visit to America that Dickens assisted in dramatising his Christmas story of *No Thoroughfare*, written conjointly and in nearly equal portions with Mr. Wilkie Collins, to form the Christmas number of *All the Year Round* for 1867. It was dramatised by Mr. Collins chiefly. But, in the midst of all the

No Thorough-fare.

work of preparation for departure, Charles Dickens gave minute attention to as much of the play as could be completed before he left England. It was "the only story," says Mr. Forster, "he ever helped himself to dramatise."† The incidents are considerably changed in the

---

* "Mr. Dickens's Amateur Theatricals : a Reminiscence."
—*Macmillan's Magazine*, January 1871, p. 210.
† *Life of Charles Dickens*, vol. i. (1872), p. 119.

drama, notably the scene in the monastery (Act V.),*
following Obenreizer's treachery on his fellow-
traveller which concludes the Fourth Act; and
the whole episode of Joey Ladle's courtship of
Sally Goldstraw, and his admiration of her
"beautiful language,"† is absent in the narrative
and peculiar to the play, and contains some highly
felicitous and characteristic Dickensian touches.
The play was produced at the Adelphi Theatre
during Dickens's absence in the United States.
It was first performed on Boxing-night of 1867,
Mr. Fechter taking the part of Obenreizer and
Mr. Webster that of Joey Ladle.

Some allusions to the piece and to its favourable
reception, when the news reached its absentee
author, are scattered through Dickens's correspondence from America in the early part of 1868.

---

* "The clock-lock is placed in the monastery of St. Bernard,
instead of in the house of a notary, as in the tale. The play
in some scenes departs from the story so widely as to be
entitled to rank as an entirely original production."—*Times*,
Friday, December 27, 1867.

† "Joey's muddled way of moralizing, his intense affection for Sally Goldstraw, his admiration of her 'beautiful
language,' and his ludicrous attempts to commit her sayings
to memory, relieve the somewhat sombre tone of the drama
throughout, and make the honest cellarman a personage of
much greater importance than he appears in the published
story."—*Ibid.*

From New York, early in January, he thus writes to his collaborator, Mr. Wilkie Collins:—

New York, Sunday, January 12, 1868.

First of the play. I am truly delighted to learn that it made so great a success, and I hope I may yet see it on the Adelphi boards. You have had a world of trouble and work with it, but I hope will be repaid in some degree by the pleasure of a triumph. Even for the alteration at the end of the fourth act I was fully prepared, for I *could not* see the original effect in the reading of the play, and *could not* make it go. I agree with Webster in thinking it best that Obenreizer should die on the stage; but no doubt that point is disposed of. In reading the play before the representation, I felt that it was too long, and that there was a good deal of unnecessary explanation. Those points are, no doubt, disposed of too by this time.*

Charles Dickens to Wilkie Collins.

To his eldest son a few days later he says:—

New York, January 15, 1868.

. . . I had previously heard of the play, and had *The Times*. It was a great relief and delight to me, for I had no confidence in its success; being reduced to the confines of despair by its length. If I could have rehearsed it, I should have taken the best part of an hour out of it. Fechter must be very fine, and I should greatly like to see him play the part.†

C. D. to C. D. jun.

---

* *Letters of Charles Dickens*, ii. 332.
† *Ibid.*, ii. 338.

To M. Charles Fechter, who played the part of Obenreizer, he writes:—

Washington, February 24, 1868.

Wilkie* has uniformly written of you enthusiastically. In a letter I had from him, dated the 10th of January, he described your conception and execution of the part in the most glowing terms. "Here Fechter is magnificent." "Here his superb playing brings the house down." "I should call even his exit in the last act one of the subtlest and finest things he does in the piece." "You can hardly imagine what he gets out of the part, or what he makes of his passionate love for Marguerite." These expressions, and many others like them, crowded his letter.

C. D. to Mr. Fechter.

I never did so want to see a character played on the stage as I want to see you play Obenreizer.†

These six pieces comprise all Dickens's extant writings for the stage. That he might have become a successful playwright, had he chosen to devote himself to the drama, seems tolerably certain: as it is, the work he actually accomplished in that kind cannot be estimated otherwise than as highly interesting and valuable, and as throwing new light on the growth and development of his genius.

---

* Mr. Wilkie Collins.
† *Letters of Charles Dickens,* ii. 362.

There are several among our foremost prose-
writers in the present century who, possessing high
imagination, and a considerable power of rhythmical
expression, have occasionally produced verse of a
high though not of the first order. Lord Macaulay's
title to fame will not rest on his *Ivry*, on his *Battle
of the Armada*, or even on his more ambitious
Lays of Ancient Rome; but one who wrote such
eloquent prose could hardly fail to write eloquent
verse. Carlyle, in spite of his untiring and energetic denunciation of modern poetry as mere
dilettantism and trifling, occasionally courted a
somewhat coy muse ; though were the original
verses and translations from the German, scattered
through his earlier writings, collected together,
they would form a volume of no mean value.
They have a wild, rugged melody of their own,
and a core of depth and significance, as have also
the occasional verses of Emerson, the sad news of
whose death just reaches England as these words
are committed to press.* The author of *Modern
Painters* might also have gained some reputation
as a poet, had he been willing to give a wider

---

* End of April 1882.

circulation to the much-coveted volume of verse in which his scattered contributions to the annuals were collected for private circulation.

The only attempt at poetry by Charles Dickens much known hitherto to the general public is Charles Dickens as a poet. the favourite song of "The Ivy Green" in the *Pickwick Papers.* This exquisite little lyric, with its effective refrain,—so often wedded to music, and so familiar to us all,—would alone suffice to show that in turning aside from prose to verse, his hand did not altogether forget its cunning. In the Comic Opera of *The Village Coquettes* there are half-a-dozen songs of almost equal tenderness and melody.

Mr. R. H. Horne pointed out many years ago* that a great portion of the scenes describing the death of Little Nell in " The Old Curiosity Shop," will be found to be written—whether by design or harmonious accident, of which the author himself was not even subsequently fully conscious—in blank verse of irregular metre and rhythm, such as Southey, Shelley, and some other poets have occasionally adopted.

---

* *A New Spirit of the Age* (Lond., 1844), vol. i., pp. 65–68.

It was chiefly in the earlier part of his career (though he never entirely abandoned the practice) that Dickens occasionally tried his hand at verse-writing. There are, as we have seen, a number of songs, humorous, satirical, and sentimental, scattered through his earlier dramatic pieces ; and to this class may be added the two songs from *Pickwick* — the far-famed "Ivy Green" and the less-known "Christmas Carol." The song written for Harley to be sung in the character of Pickwick, and describing a whitebait dinner at Greenwich, has not, apparently, been preserved.

The Loving Ballad of Lord Bateman, published in 1839, with a set of infinitely humorous illustrations by George Cruikshank, is an inimitable piece of nonsense, worthy almost to rank with Thackeray's famous improvisation of "The Three Sailors." The mock gravity of the notes adds further zest to the fun. In later editions, when the great artist's old geniality and richness of humour were frozen up by the teetotal craze, he Ballad tampered with the text of the verses and of Lord Bateman. spoilt them, tagging on some rubbish of his own at the end. In the twentieth stanza

Lord Bateman endeavours to assuage his incensed mother-in-law with these assurances :—

O it's true I made a bride of your darter,
But she's neither the better nor the vorse for me.

When Cruikshank the artist had degenerated into Cruikshank the propagandist, dreading to offend the more mealy-mouthed votaries of Exeter Hall _{Cruikshank's alterations.} by such an outrage on the proprieties, he substituted the inoffensive and colourless line—

But you'll see what I'll do for you and she;

and "took the liberty of adding three verses, to follow No. 20 (No. 21 to be omitted); to be said or sung by those parties who may approve of the alteration and addition." It is hardly necessary to assure the reader that the ballad is here restored to its original text and printed as Charles Dickens wrote it, before it was thus mutilated.

"In an utilitarian age of all other times," says Dickens himself, writing on this very subject or a kindred one, "it is a matter of grave importance that fairy tales should be respected. The theatre having done its worst to destroy these admirable fictions, it becomes doubly important that the little books themselves,

C. D. on Cruikshank's Frauds on the Fairies.

nurseries of fancy as they are, should be preserved. They must be as much preserved in their simplicity, and purity, and innocent extravagance, as if they were actual fact. Whosoever alters them to suit his own opinions, whatever they are, is guilty, to our thinking, of an act of presumption, and appropriates to himself what does not belong to him. That incomparable artist, Mr. George Cruikshank, is of all men the last who should lay his exquisite hand on fairy text. In his own art he understands it so perfectly, and illustrates it so beautifully, so humorously, so wisely, that he should never lay down his etching-needle to 'edit' the Ogre, to whom with that little instrument he can render such extraordinary justice. But to 'editing' Ogres and Hop-o'-my-thumbs, and their families, our dear moralist has in a rash moment taken, as a means of propagating the doctrines of Total Abstinence, Prohibition of the sale of spirituous liquors, Free Trade, and Popular Education. For the introduction of these topics he has altered the text of a fairy story ; and against his right to do any such thing we protest with all our might and main."*

In his later years, indeed, Cruikshank's austerity contrasted as unpleasantly with the rollicking, free-and-easy humour of his best period, as the severity of George Colman the younger, as stage-licenser, contrasted with the looseness and latitude of George Colman as playwright or *raconteur*. In the last, or almost the last, year of Cruikshank's life, the present writer was preparing a new edition, in which he endeavoured to revive the memory, of a forgotten *jeu d'esprit* written by a certain James White—*Falstaff's Letters*—dear to all lovers of Charles Lamb for Lamb's sake as well as for its own. Remembering Cruikshank's delightful illustrations to Robert Brough's *Life of Sir John Falstaff*, the thought struck him that Cruikshank might have preserved some scrap or sketch, or might without serious difficulty produce or re-furbish one, that would serve as an attractive frontispiece to White's little book in its new

---

* "Frauds on the Fairies."—*Household Words*, October 1, 1853 (vol. viii., p. 97).

shape. The suggestion was accordingly made to the enterprising and amiable publisher, who was pleased with the idea, and who, having a slight personal acquaintance with Cruikshank, wrote to him, making some overture or proposal in the matter, and sending the original edition for his inspection. In a few days came an answer from Cruikshank the veteran artist, declining to entertain and *Falstaff's* Letters. the proposal on any terms, and strongly urging his correspondent to abandon the projected reprint, as he (Cruikshank) was much shocked, in looking through the little book (herewith returned), 'Potatoes, to find that it contained——many low, prunes, and prism.' vulgar, and improper expressions. Potatoes, prunes, prism, and propriety !* It might have been possible for the once convivial Cruikshank, but it could hardly be possible for Sir John Falstaff, swaggering Pistol, Bardolph, and Corporal Nym, to " forswear sack and live cleanly."

---

* " Father is rather vulgar, my dear. The word Papa, besides, gives a pretty form to the lips. Papa, potatoes, poultry, prunes and prism, are all very good words for the lips : especially prunes and prism. You will find it serviceable, in the formation of a demeanour, if you sometimes say to yourself in company—on entering a room, for instance—Papa, potatoes, poultry, prunes, and prism, prunes and prism."—Mrs. General in *Little Dorrit* (p. 356).

Of Dickens's *Examiner* squibs his biographer
writes as follows :—

He sent me some rhymed squibs as his anonymous
Dickens's Examiner Squibs. contribution to the fight the Liberals were
then making against what was believed to be
intended by the return to office of the Tories.
I doubt if he ever enjoyed anything more than the power
of thus taking part occasionally, unknown to outsiders,
in the sharp conflict the press was waging at the time.*

It seems probable that other political squibs and
utterances in verse, prompted by the events of the
hour, were written by Dickens, and lie buried,
beyond easy reach of discovery, and possibly in
journals more obscure and less accessible than the
Examiner.

---

* Forster's *Life of Dickens* (ed. 1876), vol. i., pp. 186–187.

Another class of Dickens's poetical experiments are his Prologues,—doubly interesting to us here as akin and allied to his dramatic at-tempts. Of Dickens's Prologues, though probably more were written, only three are known to us ; the first generously volunteered to intro-duce a then new and unknown writer, Mr. Westland Marston, to the public, and spoken by Macready, who in December 1842 produced the young author's maiden play, *The Patrician's Daughter*, at Dickens's good-natured recommendation. This Prologue contains some vigorous and energetic lines, and really deserves to be remembered and preserved on its own account. The other two extant Prologues of Dickens are of considerably later date, and were written to introduce two successive plays by his friend Mr. Wilkie Collins,—" The Lighthouse," and " The Frozen Deep,"—written for the Tavistock House private theatricals.

A Word in Season and the *Hymn of the Wiltshire Labourers* are both stirring and manly protests, breathing a true Christian spirit, the one against intolerance and bigotry, the other against oppres-sion, and must have found a loyal response in thousands of honest hearts. Not *The Song of the*

Dickens's Prologues.

Shirt, nor *The Bridge of Sighs* itself, is characterised by more fervour and eloquence, by a higher enthusiasm of humanity, than the *Hymn of the Wiltshire Labourers.*

Of Charles Dickens as an actor, much were to be said, did space permit. Early in life, while still a newspaper reporter, he sought the stage as a profession, and nearly succceded in securing an engagement ; but before the negotiations came to anything, he had already turned to literature for his livelihood. When "he wrote a farce," says Mr. Forster, "by way of helping the Covent Garden manager, which the actors could not agree about, and which he turned afterwards into a story called *The Lamplighter,* he read the piece at the theatre

Charles Dickens as an actor.

before the same stage manager to whom he had written to request a very different audience in the same green-room a few years before ; and Dickens could not but fancy that into Mr. Bartley's face, as he listened to the humorous reading, there crept some strange bewildered half-consciousness that in the famous writer he saw again the youthful would-be actor."*

A tradition exists that on one occasion at least Dickens played a minor part in his own farce of *The Strange Gentleman*, in the absence of one of the regular actors ; but we are unable to vouch for the authenticity of this rumour, or to refer to any authority for it.

Of Dickens's performances during his first visit to America in 1842, his biographer has given a full and interesting account. Mr. Horne has described the performances of the Guild of Literature and Art, in which Dickens was manager and one of the chief actors, in a graphic paper, from which we are permitted to make copious extracts.

The once brilliant " Guild of Literature and Art," which commenced with the highest prospects of success,

---

* *Life of Charles Dickens*, vol. i. p. 120–121.

was founded by Sir Edward Bulwer Lytton and Charles Dickens. The former proposed to give land upon one of his estates in a locality suitable for the erection of a college, and to write a comedy, to be acted with a view to raising a preliminary fund in aid of the object in question; and, in the first instances the performers were to be celebrated authors and artists. All this was undertaken by Charles Dickens.

The artists who were engaged on Sir E. B. Lytton's Comedy of *Not so Bad as We Seem, or Many Sides to a Character*, were Daniel Maclise, Clarkson Stanfield, John Leech, Augustus Egg, Mr. Topham, Mr. Frank Stone, and Mr. Tenniel. The authors were Charles Dickens, Mark Lemon, Dudley Costello, Robert Bell, Douglas Jerrold, John Forster, Charles Knight, and R. H. Horne. Mr. Wilkie Collins and two or three others were engaged in subsequent performances; but the above list comprises all those who appeared in the first instance, when the play was represented at Devonshire House. The stage architect and machinist was Sir Joseph Paxton; and to his name, among the "past and gone," must be added that of the kind and munificent patron of the Guild, the late Duke of Devonshire.

The Duke gave the use of his large Picture Gallery, to be fitted up with seats for the audience; and his Library adjoining for the erection of the theatre.

The latter room being larger than required for the stage and its scenery, the back portion of it was screened off for a "green room." Sir Joseph Paxton was most assiduous and careful in the erection of the theatre and seats. There was a special box for the Queen. None of the valuable paintings in the picture gallery (arranged for the auditorium) were removed, but all of them were faced with planks, and covered with crimson velvet draperies. Sir Joseph Paxton arranged the ventilation in the most skilful manner; and with some assistance from a theatrical machinist, he put up all the scenes, curtains, and flies. Dickens was unanimously dubbed general manager, and Mark Lemon stage manager. We had a professional gentleman for prompter, as none of the amateurs could be entrusted with so technical, tactical, ticklish, and momentous a series of duties.

Never in the world of theatres was a better manager than Charles Dickens. Without, of course, questioning the superiority of Goethe (in the Weimar theatre) as a manager in all matters of high-class dramatic literature, one cannot think he could have been so excellent in all general requirements, stage effects, and practical details of acting and of theatrical business. Equally assiduous and unwearying as Dickens surely very few men ever were, or could possibly be. He appeared almost ubiquitous and sleepless. We had many (I really think, thirteen) rehearsals, six or seven of them after everybody knew his part, letter perfect.

Nothing could surpass the princely munificence of the Duke of Devonshire throughout this occasion, unless, indeed, it were his extreme kindness, and delicate consideration for the feelings of all the authors and artists engaged in the matter. The gates of Devonshire House were opened to our hackneys and cabriolets with all the ceremony of porters and footmen, precisely as though our vehicles had been the usual classes of courtly equipage.

4 *

A profuse and elegant cold collation (comprising every delicacy in and out of season, and the choicest wines,) was always served for the "company," behind whose chairs the Duke's own footmen in full livery ("uniform" would seem to be a more literal term, as they all wore double silver-bullion epaulettes) ; and at most of those twelve or thirteen luxurious luncheons, or *déjeûners à la fourchette*, the Duke sat down, apologizing for the very spare indulgence to which the state of his health limited him.

The principal scenes were painted by Clarkson Stanfield ; but some of them were the work of Maclise; indeed, it appeared that Mr. Egg, as well as Topham and Tenniel, gave frequent assistance, as they were all continually on the stage during the touching-up and arrangement of the scenery.

Mr. Planché was consulted about the costumes; and it was agreed that the wigs and "make-up" of faces should be as good and characteristic as possible. One military "character," not considering himself sufficiently tall for the part, had a pair of thigh boots made with cork heels four inches high.

Several amusing incidents occurred in the course of the rehearsals. The first was during the preparation of the scenic arrangements, some alteration in which was required. Sir Joseph Paxton gave his directions, and went away for a time. The hour for rehearsal had not yet come, and we were conning our parts in the green-room. Meanwhile, a tall, elderly gentleman, very plainly dressed in a suit of what looked like rather rusty black, had got upon the stage, and was lurking among the wings, now in one place, now in another, with an amiable smile upon his countenance, denoting the interest he took in the proceedings. The heavy roller of a scene was now being hoisted, and the tall gentleman in black became confused as to his whereabouts. "Now, sir!" exclaimed a voice, "do for heaven's sake keep out of the way! Do you want to get your back broke?" The elderly gentleman apologised with a deprecating bow, and immediately retired. "Who was that?" somebody inquired; but nobody on the stage at that moment knew. It was the Duke! This direful *contretemps* was speedily put to rights by the ready tact and proper feeling of our manager, and was the source of much amusement to the amiable nobleman, who warmly and humorously expressed his thanks for the timely warning. It was "set about" that the blunder had been committed by one of the stage-carpenters; but there was good reason to be afraid that it was one of *nous autres*.

Another incident, which will be regarded as rather odd and unique, may serve as material for some curious speculations as to the force of imagination, and also of the sympathy between our visual and olfactory organs. Colonel Flint, of the Guards, a bully and duellist, described in the *dramatis personæ* as a "fire-eater," was to stand with his back to the red glowing chimney-piece in "Will's Coffee House." The period is that of George the First, when it was fashionable for great bloods and bucks of the day to smoke long pipes, designated as a "yard of clay." With such a pipe Colonel Flint had duly provided himself for rehearsal; and to make his stage-business more perfect, soft-rolling clouds of smoke began to issue from the bowl, and float over the once famous coffee-room. In no time came the Manager, speaking quickly, "My dear H—— on *no* account attempt to smoke! The Queen detests tobacco, and would leave the box immediately."

"But there's no tobacco in the pipe;" replied the Colonel.

"Oh—come—nonsense."

"Look here!"—and the Colonel took out of his waist-coat pocket a handful of dried herbs. "I got them in Covent Garden market this morning, on the way to rehearsal."

"Well—we smelt tobacco the moment we came within sight of the stage," said Dickens: "the pipe must be foul."

"It is quite a new pipe!"

Mark Lemon now came up, and protesting that he also had smelt tobacco, and that the pipe must have been an old one re-burnt, to look clean, the offending clay was flung aside.

Before the next rehearsal, however, another pipe, warranted new and pure, was obtained, independent of which it was placed in the fire, and kept there at white-heat long enough to purify it ten times over, even had it been one of the unclean. Again the cloud began to unfold its volumes over "Will's Coffee-room"; and this time Sir Joseph Paxton came running from the seats in the front to the stage, declaring that the Queen so detested the smell of tobacco, that smoking must really not be attempted. Once again the Colonel protested the innocence of his pipe, in proof of which he produced a handful of dried thyme and rose-leaves from his waistcoat pocket. In vain. Sir Joseph insisted that he had smelt tobacco!—" They all smelt it! " So this second yard of clay was sent to shivers.

But the Colonel had chanced to see a " Model of the Battle of Waterloo " exhibited some years before in Leicester Square, in which the various miniature platoons of infantry, as well as the brigades of artillery, were supposed to be firing volleys, the clouds and wreaths of smoke being fragile fixtures. These capital imitations of clouds and wreaths of smoke were discovered, on very close examination, to be composed of extremely fine and thinly drawn out webs of cotton, supported on rings and long twirls of almost invisible wire, and attached at one end to the mouths and muzzles of the miniature cannon and musketry. This model for a triumph in the art of smoking a pipe in the presence of a Queen who abhorred tobacco, was now adopted by Colonel Flint, but held in reserve for the full-dress rehearsal, when there would be a preliminary audience.

He ventured to flatter himself that all these delicate considerations and assiduities would be much applauded and complimented, both by the accomplished author and the management. Far from it. No sooner was the cloud of apparent smoke perceived to issue from the pipe, than the Manager, Stage-manager, and Sir Joseph Paxton hurried together to the too assiduous Guardsman, begging him on *no* account to persist in this smoking!—or this (on examining more nearly) appearance of smoking. It would be most injudicious. The Queen would *think* she smelt tobacco, and this would be as bad as if her

Majesty really smelt it; at the same time, they added, collectively, that they themselves *had* smelt tobacco, no matter from what source, or what cause! Of course there was an end of the matter, as we were all anxious to be harmonious; and the discomfited "fire-eater" of the comedy did the best he could to bully the company in "Will's Coffee-room" with his empty-bowled and immaculate yard of clay. These minute details, however, will serve to show the pains that were taken even with the slightest parts of this performance; pains that were worthy of the *Comédie Française*.

At the full-dress rehearsal, the audience was composed exclusively of the relatives, friends, and acquaintance of the Duke of Devonshire, and of the authors and artists engaged in the performance. All went well, and the "first night" was announced. The tickets were five guineas each, and her Majesty sent a hundred guineas for her box. This night—our first—our all-important night —went off most satisfactorily. Only one little accident occurred. Every gentleman of the period, of any rank, wore a sword; the manager, therefore, intimated that as our stage was small, and would be nearly filled up with side tables and tables in front, in the conspiracy scene in "Will's Coffee House," it would be prudent and important that the swords of the *dramatis personæ* should be most carefully considered in passing down the centre, and round one of the tables in front. At this table sat the Duke of Middlesex (Frank Stone) and the Earl of Loftus (Mr. Dudley Costello), in a private and high-treasonous conversation. On the table were decanters, glasses, plates of fruit, &c. At the other table, in front, sat Mr. David

Fallen (Augustus Egg), the half-starved Grub-street author and political pamphleteer, with some bread and cheese, and a little mug of ale. The eventful moment came, when Mr. Shadowly Softhead (Douglas Jerrold), Colonel Flint and others, had to pass down the narrow space in the middle of the stage, to be presented to the Duke of Middlesex, and then, as there was not room enough to enable them to turn about and retire up the stage, each one was to pass round the corner of the table, and make his exit at the left first entrance. This was done by all with safety, and reasonably good grace, except one gentleman, who shall not be named; for as he rose from his courtly bowing, to advance and pass round, the tip of his jutting-out sword went rigidly across the surface of the table, and swept off the whole of the "properties" and realities! Decanters, glasses, grapes, a pine-apple, a painted pound cake, and several fine wooden peaches, rolled pell-mell upon the stage, and, as usual, made for the footlights! A considerable "sensation" passed over the audience; amidst which the Queen (to judge by the shaking of the handkerchief in front of the royal face) by no means remained unmoved. But Dickens, who, as Lord Wilmot, happened to be close in front, with admirable promptitude and tact, instantly called out with a jaunty air of command, "Here, drawer! come and clear away this wreck!" as though the disaster had been a part of the business of the scene, while the others *on* the stage so well managed their bye-play that many of the audience were in some doubt about the accident. When inquiry was instituted as to the culprit on this occasion, who had failed to carry his sword with due circumspection, as every one of

the " Guild " protested his innocence of the awkward fact
in question, it was presently discovered that the guilty
individual was a supernumerary lord for that scene, enacted
by a gentleman who was one of the Duke's suite.

Two other amusing incidents occurred. A number of
bedrooms had been placed at our disposal for dressing-
rooms. A certain gentleman of the " company " (the
portly and genial Mark Lemon it was whispered) had
been somewhat too long over the buttoning of a long-
flapped and stiffly embroidered waistcoat, and the call-boy
had been sent up stairs a second time from the prompter
below, to inform him that the stage would immediately be
" waiting " for him! Away ran the boy, and vanished
round a corner. In his haste, the " character " in
question took a wrong turn, and coming upon a steep
flight of stairs, down he hurried, and then down another
long flight, and presently found that he was close upon
the kitchens. Up he rushed again, and scuttled along the
gallery, till he turned into a still longer gallery, well
lighted, but vacant and hopeless. Once more he made a
turn, now wild with the thought of the stage being kept
waiting, and seeing a tall, dark figure passing the further
end, he rushed towards it—wigged, powdered, buckled,
ruffled, perspiring, maddened, and gasping out " Where—
where's the stage? " He was barely able to recognise
the Duke, who with a most delighted and delightful
urbanity, at once put him upon his right course. Another
miscalculation of time occurred, in consequence of Sir
Joseph Paxton remarking in the green-room, just after
the conclusion of the performance, that he had arranged
the Queen's chair in the supper-room, in a peculiar

manner, with exotic and other rare flowers, which had arrived that evening fresh from the Duke's gardens at Chatsworth. Colonel Flint hearing this, requested permission to see the floral throne, before her Majesty's entrance to the supper-room.

" By all means," said Sir Joseph, " but you must be very quick." Away hurried the applicant, and was speedily in the supper-room, and made his way, his stage costume notwithstanding, through a number of gentlemen in waiting, officers attired in a very different sort of uniform, footmen, &c., to their no small surprise and amusement. But the sight well rewarded the effort.

At the top of the table and furthest from the door, there was a richly-carved and cushioned chair, raised a few inches above the other chairs. It had large padded arms of figured satin and velvet, and a high back that had a carved gothic arch at the top. But very little of the chair could be clearly seen, and its outline was only indicated here and there. The whole of the back was devoted to roses, red and white, mingled with magnolias, jasmine, honeysuckle, and tuberoses; but the high arch and sides of the chair were overhung with festoons and long dripping falls and tangles of the most lovely orchidaceous and other exotic plants, and by fine trickling tendrils and dangling lines, bearing little starry flowers, and very minute and curiously-striped leaves, leaflets, and tiny fairy buds; and some of the creepers displaying little flowers and leaves that resembled a sort of floral jewellery. At the top of the arched chair back, there was a large night-flowering cereus, of most delicious and recondite perfume. (No wonder Sir Joseph was alarmed at tobacco!) The predominating colours were snow white and apple green, with a little soft azure, and a few scarlet buds, and here and there a dark Tuscany rose or two for *shadows;* the whole having been carefully selected and arranged by Sir Joseph as a suitable back ground for the dress worn by her Majesty on this, we may say unprecedented occasion. An imitation of dew-drops was achieved to a degree of perfect illusion, by means of opals and glass, as it seemed; a piece of refined ingenuity which was about to undergo a close inspection by Flint, when suddenly it was announced that the Queen was approaching the supper-room! Instantly the awakened Colonel made a dash for the open door, but it was only to encounter the bowing backs and elegantly embroidered coat-tails of gentlemen and lords in waiting, who were ushering in her Majesty! There was nothing for it but to spring aside, and range in line with the officers and gentlemen in attendance, and to " stand attention," as if on grand parade. He trusted, in the confusion of the moment, that his guardsman's uniform of the time of George I., notwithstanding the polished thigh boots and towering powdered wig, would not be observed by the Queen, with Prince Albert, the Duke, and suite attending, or following. Vain hope! The gleaming glances that passed told all; and with long rapid strides, the instant Her Majesty was seated, the anachronismic uniform made its exit at the rear of the line in which it had so unseasonably appeared *en militaire.*

After the performance, and before leaving the box, her Majesty had sent to the manager to express her gratifica-tion, coupled with the remark, " They act very well indeed." This was duly announced to the Company, when assembled for supper, and was received with great satisfaction, modest and otherwise; but Dickens went on, drily adding—"But the Queen is very kind—and was sure to say *that;*"—which very much straightened the complacent faces round the table, till they laughed at each other. Nevertheless, a few more words may be said on the subject. They really *did* act well; some, very well. When it is remembered the studious sort of men they all were, and the time, together with the great pains bestowed in all respects,—why not? The principal character, as matter of elocution, was that of *Hardman,* and the gentleman personating this rising young states-man was unquestionably one of the best private readers of the day. Then, as to acting, most of the company were practised amateurs long before this event, more especially Douglas Jerrold and Mark Lemon, who, in parts that suited them, were first-rate actors, almost equal to Dickens. The two latter were matchless in the after-piece, but the parts they played in the comedy were not in accordance with their peculiar talents. It has been said that Dickens, in private life, had very much the appearance of a seafaring man. This is quite true; and his long daily walks about London and the environs, or at the sea-side, caused him to have a very sun-burnt weather-beaten face. His full-length portrait, if truth-fully painted, might readily be mistaken for the captain of an East Indiaman. But the character and costume of " Lord Wilmot, a young man *at the head of the Mode,* more than a century ago," did not suit him, and was in fact against the grain of his nature. His bearing on the stage, and the tone of his voice, were too rigid, hard and quarter-deck-like, for such "rank and fashion," and his make-up, with the three-cornered gold-laced cocked-hat, black curled wig, huge sleeve-cuffs, long flapped waistcoat, knee-breeches and great shoe-buckles, were not carried off with the proper air; so that he presented a figure that would have made a good portrait of the captain of a Dutch privateer,* after having taken a capital prize. When he shouted in praise of the wine of Burgundy, it far rather suggested fine kegs of Schiedam. It was in *Mr. Nightingale's Diary*, which followed, that he was inimitable. Miss Mitford, being present at the performance of this some time afterwards, pronounced certain parts of his acting in this piece as something wonderful. Neither can it be said that Mark Lemon was quite at home in his part in the comedy, *viz.*, that of "Sir Geoffrey Thornside, a gentleman of good family and estate." He looked far more like a burly, wealthy Yorkshire brewer, who had retired upon something handsome. In the after-piece he could hardly have been surpassed. Yet both the last-named parts in the comedy were fairly acted. Jerrold also (a capital actor in certain parts) was hardly in his right element. The head and face of Jerrold were a good illustration of the saying that most people are like one or another of our "dumb fellow-creatures," for he certainly had a remarkable resemblance, in several respects, to a

---

* A celebrated painter is said to have made a similar remark. What would he have thought of Dickens in the above costume?—[*Note by R. H. H.*]

lion, chiefly for his very large, clear, round, undaunted, straightforward looking eyes; the structure of the forehead; and his rough, unkempt, uplifted flourish of tawny hair. It was difficult to make such a face look like the foolish, half-scared country gentleman, "Mr. Shadowly Softhead"; but he enacted the part very well, notwithstanding. As a contrast to these, Mr. Frank Stone, the painter, presented a very grave, tall, stately full-length of the proud "Duke of Middlesex," whose dignity was astonished at his wife daring to take "such a liberty" as to give him a kiss; while the "Earl of Loftus" of Mr. Dudley Costello was far too elegant for a nobleman of the court of George I., and rather resembled a highly-polished French marquis of the age of Louis Quatorze. The make-up of Mr. Egg as "David Fallen," the Grubstreet author, was such as only a fine painter could well have effected. Intellectual and refined amidst his seedy clothing; resentful of his hard lot, yet saddened by disappointment and semi-starvation, his thoughts appearing to oscillate between independence of character —his political hiring—and his hungry family in their miserable attic; such a countenance was presented as the stage has seldom seen, and is very unlikely to see again, except at rare and exceptional intervals. The Irish landlord of Mr. Fallen (Paddy O'Sullivan) was represented to perfection by Mr. Robert Bell, whose gigantic stature, long frieze coat, little bit of a hat, ragged red wig, and highly-painted smiling visage (reminding one of the *Sompnour* in the "Canterbury Tales"), gave a picture that even surpassed the effect of the rich brogue in which he blurted out the few words allotted to him. The minor parts, however, of this play have all been reduced to mere shreds in the acting copies since published. No professional actors would be at all likely to take such pains with them as were exhibited on this occasion.*

In a later paper Mr. Horne gives the following account of the farce of *Mr. Nightingale's Diary.* His recollections of the plot and characters, and his quotations of some of the speeches, written apparently from memory after a lapse of twenty years, differ considerably from the authorized privately-printed text, as reproduced in our second volume:—

The piece opened with the entrance of Mark Lemon, dressed as a German student, travelling after the manner of Wilhelm Meister on his "art-apprenticeship." The scene, however, was the private parlour of an English country inn; and it was at once discovered that the apparent student was a strolling player who had adopted that disguise in order to practise the not very uncommon, yet by no means easy, art of "living by his wits." Mark's portly figure was covered with a nankeen summer blouse, having a broad leather belt round the waist, or the place where a waist should be; and on his head he wore a German cap with a great peak, which did but

---

* *The Gentleman's Magazine,* February 1871 (quoted by kind permission of Messrs. Chatto and Windus).

little to shade his large, round, sunbrowned smiling face. On his first entrance he gave the effect of an overgrown schoolboy; but when he came close down to the lamps it was evident that he was a fully developed rogue. He wore travelling boots; a German *quersack,* or leather wallet, dangled from his belt, and he carried an unmistakable English carpet-bag, which he rapidly, and rather furtively, deposited under a table on one side of the room.

He now made a brief soliloquy, illustrated with a richly humorous expression of countenance, to the following effect:—" He was not at present a member of a company of strolling players, but he kept better company—to wit, his own—and he was now strolling, not to please others by playing for them, but to play *upon* them to please himself; and the more they paid the better *he* was pleased; *them* was his sentiments. But, at the present moment, unfortunately, he was quite out of cash, and, as was sure to happen when he was penniless, he felt more than usually hungry. For this reason he had naturally entered an inn, as the proper place for satisfying hunger; and when that sacred duty had been performed, he would consider by what means the bill was to be paid. Could any man do more?"

So saying, he seated himself at a side-table, and, after running over an imaginary larder, he resolved on ordering a good dinner, and forthwith rang the bell. As no waiter made an appearance, he rang again vigorously; and yet a third time he had to ring. The individual who then entered was greeted with a round of smiles, as well as general applause.

I.   5

"This seems rather a humble kind of an inn, my man. Is there any corn in Egypt?"

"Don't know, Sir; but we've got some *here*;—quite enough for any 'orse you may 'ire for the day."

"Ahem! You misunderstand me, young man; *I* am the horse inquiring for corn. What's the state of the larder, eh?"

"Well, Sir, there's the not werry shapely remains of a round o' boiled beef, as was 'ot the day afore yesterday; and there's the back and drumsticks of a seasonable old goose; and—and—why, Jemmy!— Jemmy Daddleham, is that you? I *thought* I know'd you!"

It turns out that Sam Weller was at one time a member of a company of strolling players, and now recognises in the German student Mr. James Daddleham, the leading tragedian of that company. Sam quickly disappears, in order to bring some refreshment for the famishing "star," who falls into a train of sentimental absurdity during his absence.

Some of the characters in this laughable piece of stage composition had no names given to them, and others had names liable to be changed with every fresh representation; and as for the dialogue, it was never twice alike, the two principals understanding each other well enough to extemporise whenever they had a fancy to do so. For this reason we have truly designated the piece a stage composition. Consequently, the printed copies (whenever a straggler may be discovered) will contain very little of what was said by these two celebrated humourists and amateurs.

Sam Weller speedily returns, bringing with him a tray. He spreads the cloth on the little side-table, and "in no time" it is seen covered with beef and bread and bottles and plates and a couple of tankards. This done, Sam seats himself at the table, opposite the eminent tragedian, who falls to with every demonstration of hunger and delight. Eating heartily, and drinking to match, always gives great pleasure to a British audience; and this most refined of audiences proved no exception. While the "star" was recruiting himself, Sam contented himself by responding to friendly pledges with the tankard, and by various amusing references to their strolling days, and to the characters impersonated by the "world-renowned" Mr. Daddleham, especially some of his tragic parts, concerning which Sam alternately flattered him with preposterous compliments, and startled him by equivocal commentaries. For instance :—

"O, Sir," said Sam, "what a 'Amlet yourn was! Shall we ever again see sich a 'Amlet?"

"You think it was good, do you, Sam?"

"Good, Sir! good's no word for it."

"Ah!" said Mr. Daddleham, with affected modesty, laying down his knife and fork, and looking down sentimentally at his portly corporation; "yes, Sam; I think there *was* something *in* my Hamlet."

"Yes, and something *of* you, too, Sir."

This ridiculous compliment to his unsuitable figure of course upset the previous eulogy. The conversation then dropped into melodrama, and Sam referred to a certain piece in which they had fought a dreadful combat together in a wood. This enlivening recollection induced

5 *

a mutual draught from the foaming tankard; and Sam, exclaiming "Ah, those wos the days, Sir—them wos!" regretted they could not fight that celebrated combat again.. Hereupon Mr. Daddleham informed Sam that it could very easily be fought again.

"When, Sir?" said Sam, eagerly.

"Now, Sam!"

"Where the place, Sir?"

"Not 'upon the heath,' but on these very boards."

"These!"

"Yes, these, Sam. Behold yonder carpet-bag, there!"

"Hah! under the table! I see it all. That bag contains—— "

"It does—it does! all the theatrical properties now left me by invidious fate."

The eminent *incog.* now rushed across to his carpet-bag, and from its well-stuffed paunch hurriedly disengaged and extracted two melodramatic short swords. Sam eagerly seized one of these weapons, and a sanguinary combat of the unique old school of popular melodrama at once commenced, in process of which every outrageous and ridiculous *stage business* of that class was carried to the utmost perfection. First, they prowled round and round each other—now darting in, very nearly, and as suddenly starting back; next a passing cut is exchanged, then two or three cuts, the swords emitting sparks, and the combatants uttering strange guttural sounds, breathing hard, and showing their teeth at each other like hungry wolves. At last they close, and strike and parry to a regular measured time, till gradually you find they are beating a sort of time very like the one known as

Lodoiska in the Lancer Quadrilles. After this they strike at the calves of each other's legs by alternate back stroke and parry, and then Sam springs upon Mr. Daddleham's left hip, and deals a succession of blows downwards at his head, all parried, of course, with ludicrous precision. Finally, the sword of Sam is passed under one of his antagonist's arms, who thereupon exhibits the agonies of being run through the body, but nevertheless comes again and again to receive the same mortal wound ; in fact, he comes, though fainter and fainter each time, till Sam is at length so exhausted with running through such a fat body that he reels backward fainting just as his antagonist falls with a last gasp and a bump upon the stage that convulses the whole audience with laughter.

After this they return panting to the table, and recruit themselves with another tankard of ale, over which some conversation takes place, introductory of the plot of the piece, such as it is, and the two quondam strollers separate. I have said that several of the characters were not named in the bills, so that we are at liberty to give them any passing name by way of identification. Even the name of Sam Weller was not given, so far as 1 remember; but nobody could doubt who it was from the first moment of his entrance. One of the characters, however, represented by Dickens was named *Mr. Gabblewig*, a capital name for an over-voluble barrister (the names, in nearly all his works, are invented with singular humour and appropriateness), but certainly of far less mark and importance in the piece than other characters he assumed.

Another of the characters played by Dickens in

this piece was a hypochondriac, for whom a certain renowned Doctor (a quack, of course) had prescribed repeated doses, day and night, of mustard and milk. The sick gentleman, seated in a great high-back, padded arm-chair, went through a rambling discourse, continually interrupted by spasmodic contortions, which he accompanied with declarations such as, " That's the mustard ! I know, by the hot, biting pang ! Ha ! that's that the milk ! I'm sure that must be the milk, by the griping ! The sour curds are now in full—Oh !—there's the mustard again !—come to—come to—come to correct the milk, as the Doctor said it would."

At this painful crisis Mark Lemon enters as the great Doctor.   His make-up is altogether admirable. Black evening dress ; with knee-smalls, black silk stockings, gilt knee-buckles, and gilt shoe-buckles ; black silk vest, with very large white shirt-frill, and a mock-diamond pin. His fingers display several mourning-rings. A high old-fashioned white neckcloth, without shirt-collar, and his hair powdered, complete his costume. He advances with a slow, soft pace, a gentle, yet somewhat pompous air, and gesticulates with his hands, occasionally patting the patient's shoulder, very much in the style of the Doctor in Punch's show, being full of ridiculous patronage and conceited paternal dogmatism. The discourse he delivers is in the following strain :—

" Yes, yes—ah, yes, my friend,—calm yourself, my *dear* sir,—be quite calm. What you are suffering from at this moment is simply the pervestigation of the lacteal mustardine panacea, acting diagonally and hydrodynamically upon the vesicular and nervine systems, and thence sympathetically upon the periosteum. But be calm—be quite calm. We shall very soon—yes—let me feel your pulse! Ah, yes very fair—three, four, five, six—my watch—my—bless my soul! I've left it at my nephew's [*Aside:* My uncle's] ; but we can count as well without it. There—that will do—keep yourself—keep yourself calm, my *dear* sir!" (Here the patient exhibited a variety of contortions.) "We shall change the medicine. We shall just order you a mild preparation of the agglomerated balsamic phenomenon, with a few grains of the carthusian pigment, and a table-spoonful every half-hour of the astrobolic decoction of tetramuncus."

Here the patient starts up in horror at the prospect of these prescriptions, and, forgetting all his ailments, rushes madly about the stage, driving the Doctor and everybody else before him in his exit.

The character that produced the greatest effect was that of a woman who had no name awarded to her in the piece, but to whom Dickens always alluded as Mrs. Gamp, although to our thinking she was not the real Mrs. Gamp, but only a near relation. Dickens's make-up in this character was not to be surpassed, unless indeed by one other which he personated, and by that of a wretched half-starved charity-boy represented by Mr. Egg. The woman, so far as I can remember, was accusing Mr. Nightingale of paternity in this matter, and she calls the boy to come forward and show himself as the living proof of her declaration. Thus summoned, a pale, miserable face, with hair cropped close, like a convict, and wearing a little round workhouse-cap, peeped forth at one wing. By stealthy degrees the object advanced in a side-long

way, half retreating at times, and finally getting behind
Mr. Nightingale's chair, and only showing himself now
and then, when lugged forth by his mother. Mr. Egg
was naturally short and attenuated, but how he contrived
to make such a skeleton-like appearance was a marvel to
all who looked upon him. Over his own face he had
literally painted another face, and one so woeful and
squalid was surely never seen before upon the stage of a
theatre. The acting was equally perfect, for not only did
he enter like "a thing forbid," but all his movements
kept up this appearance of abject self-consciousness and
furtive evasion of all eyes. He crouched down behind
or at the side of Mr. Nightingale's chair, like a starved
hound, too terrified and apprehensive even to eat if food
were offered him, and finally he skulked and bolted off
the stage at long strides, looking back as though he
expected to be shot at like some intruding reptile.
Altogether the thing was too real ; it was more painful than
amusing, or at all events pleasurable, and so far passed
the true bounds of Art. But the speech of the woman,
as delivered by Dickens, amply made up for the pain
caused by her wretched-looking boy. This speech, often
repeated afterwards, was never heard to the end, from the
incessant laughter it caused, not only among the audience,
but among all the " Guild " behind the scenes. When not
in front to hear it, we used to congregate at the wings of
the stage. It was uttered with unbroken volubility, very
nearly in the following words :—*

"Don't speak to me, sir ! now, don't go to argify with

---

* Compare with the same quotation in *Macmillan's Maga-*
zine, and with the actual printed text (vol. ii., pp. 58–59).

me! don't pertend to consolate or reason with a unper-
teckted woman, which her naytural feelings is too much
for her to support! Leave your 'ouse! No, sir, I will
not leave the 'ouse without seeing my child, my boy,
righted in all his rights!—that dear boy, sir, as you just
saw, which he was his mother's hope and his father's
pride, and no one as I knows on's joy. And the name as
was guv to this blessedest of infants, and vorked in best
Vitechapel mixed, upon a pin-cushion, were Abjalom,
after his own parential father, Mr. Nightingale, and likewise Mr. Skylark who no otherwise than by being guv to
drinking, lost an 'ole day's work at the veel-wright
business, vich it wos but limited, being veels of donkey-
chaises and goats; and vun on 'em wos even drawn by
geese for a wager, and came up the ile of the parish
church one Sunday during arternoon sarvice, by reason
of the perwersity of the hanimals, as could be testified by
Mr. Vix the beadle, afore he died of drawing on new
Vellington boots after a 'arty meal of boiled beef and
pickle cabbage to which he was not accustomed. Yes,
Mr. Robin Redbreast, I means Nightingale, in the marble
founting of that werry church wos he baptised Abjalom,
vich never *can* be undoue I am proud to declare, not to
please nor give offence to no one, nohows and noveres,
sir. No sir, no sir, I says, for affliction sore long time
Maria Nightingale bore; physicianers was in vain, and
one, sir, in partickler vich she tore the 'air by 'andfuls out
of his edd by reason of disagreement with his prescriptions on the character of her complaint; and dead she is,
and will be, as the 'osts of the Egyptian fairies, as I shall
prove to you all by the hevydence of my brother the

sexton, who I shall here perduce to your confusion in the twinkling of a star or humin hyc ! "

In the foregoing richly ridiculous speech Dickens was scarcely ever heard to its conclusion, the laughter of the audience seldom ceasing after the death of Mr. Vix by reason of his fatal new boots and too hearty meal. This woman, though designated " off the stage " as Mrs. Gamp, was evidently not that person, but another of those laughable eccentricities in which the inventive novelist delighted to indulge.

But, to conclude our account of this very curious kind of afterpiece, one more impersonation by Dickens remains to be described. It will have been noticed that the woman who discoursed so volubly and confusedly about her boy, making accusations which nobody on or off the stage can understand, announces the coming of her brother, the sexton, who is to prove something, to the confusion of everybody. And now, in a remarkably brief time after his exit as the woman, Dickens again enters as the sexton. He appears to be at least ninety years of age, not merely by the common stage make-up of long white hair, large white eyebrows, blinking pink eyelids, and painted wrinkles and furrows, but by feebleness of limbs, a body pressed down by the weight and workings of time, and suffering from accumulated infirmities. He is supported carefully by one arm, and now and then on each side, as he very slowly comes forward. The old sexton is hopelessly deaf, and his voice has a quailing, garrulous fatuity. He evidently likes to talk when an opportunity occurs, but it is quite obvious that he cannot hear himself speak any better than he can hear those who speak to him. When somebody bawls in his ear a certain question about burying, he replies in a soft, mild, quavering voice, " It's of no use whispering to me, young man." The effect of these few words was very striking, being at once pathetic and ludicrous. Tears struggled, not quite ineffectually, with laughter. This sexton is the character that Miss Mitford pronounced as something wonderful in the truthfulness of its representation. After repeated shoutings of the word " buried," he suddenly fancies he has caught the meaning, and the worn and withered countenance feebly lights up with the exclamation, " Brewed! oh, yes, Sir, I have brewed many a good gallon of ale in my time. The last batch I brewed, Sir, was finer than all the rest—the best ale ever brewed in the county. It used to be called in our parts here, ' Samson with his hair on!'—in allusion—in allusion "— (here his excitement shook the tremulous frame into coughing and wheezing)—" in allusion to its great strength." He looked from face to face to see if his feat was duly appreciated, and his venerable jest understood by those around; and then, softly repeating, with a glimmering smile, " in allusion to its great strength," he turned slowly about, and made his exit, like one moving towards his own grave while he thinks he is following the funeral of another.

With this afterpiece closed the first night's performance of the " Guild " at Devonshire House. The Duke was so delighted with our success that he proposed both the comedy and the afterpiece should be repeated. On this second night his Grace gave a magnificent ball and supper to the performers, and the whole audience. It certainly was a very brilliant scene. Some of the younger ladies amused themselves with identifying the various characters who had appeared on the stage; and this would not have been thought an easy matter, as the make-up by wigs, paint, and powder, of most of us was, we had flattered ourselves, a complete transformation.

After these two great inaugural nights, the same performances were given in the provinces, at Edinburgh, and at the Duke's mansion at Chatsworth, where the extraordinary improvements in the gardens, orchards, conservatories, and shrubberies, by Sir Joseph Paxton, so much enhanced the pleasure of the visiting amateurs. The next performances, however, immediately after those at Devonshire House, were given by the "Guild" at the Queen's Concert Rooms, Hanover Square, where they were attended by overflowing audiences. We then visited Manchester, Liverpool, Bath, Bristol, &c., meeting with great success everywhere; so much so, that Dickens announced one night after supper, and before the usual games began, that having already made £3,000, without much trouble, he thought we should continue until £5,000 was realised. With that sum he considered we should be fully justified in laying our prospectus before the public for the establishment of the "Guild of Literature and Art"—saying, "We have done thus much ourselves towards the foundation; now what will you do to help us?"

The same pieces being played at each town, and no rehearsals being required, as we had all been letter-perfect before the first night, there was plenty of leisure for private study and work of another kind,

besides visiting and amusement. It was, however, established as a rule among us, that no one should accept
an invitation to dinner or luncheon on the days when
a performance was to be given, but that we should all
dine together at two o'clock, and not sit long at table
afterwards. When the performance was over we had
supper, to which each person invited any particular
friend who was resident in that city ; and in most cases
the Mayor and other civic magnates were invited. It
was generally Dickens's custom, as he always liked to do
things on a handsome scale, to single out the principal
hotel in the place, and then take the whole hotel—at any
rate the two largest rooms, and all the beds—for the
worshipful company of the "Guild." Sometimes it
happened that we had no visitors to these supper-parties,
and the wind-up was then very apt to merge into a more
unreserved hilarity. At certain times it appeared as if
everybody was talking or laughing at the same moment ;
in fact, it certainly was so. Sitting next to Dickens
one night, and beginning to say "As for conversation "—
he suddenly exclaimed, "Impossible! it's hopeless!"—
and sank back in his chair laughing. I have alluded to
some "games" that were occasionally played among
ourselves after supper; but the reader who imagines that
whist, billiards, cribbage, chess, backgammon, or even a
"round game" was played, will by no means have hit upon
the fact. And yet, in one sense, it no doubt was a round
game, for the favourite game on these particular occasions
was leap-frog, which we played all round the supper-table.
Very much of the fun of this consisted in special
difficulties, with their consequent disasters ; for Dickens

was fond of giving a "high back," which, though prac-
ticable enough for the more active, was not easily
surmounted by others, especially after a substantial
supper; while the immense breadth and bulk of Mark
Lemon's back presented a sort of bulwark to the progress
of the majority. Now, as everybody was bound to run at
the "frog-back" given, and do his best, it often happened
that a gentleman landed upon the top of Mark's back,
and there remained; while with regard to the "high
back" given by Dickens, it frequently occurred that the
leaping frog never attained the centre, but slipped off on
one side; and we well remember a certain occasion when
a very vigorous run at it failing to carry the individual
over, the violent concussion sent the high-arched "frog"
flying under the table, followed headlong by the unsuccessful leaper. Dickens rose with perfect enjoyment
at the disaster, admirably imitating the action in panto-
mimes under similar circumstances, and exclaiming that
it was just what he expected! But the accidents attending
Mark Lemon were far more numerous, for while his
breadth and length of back were a most arduous under-
taking for any but the very long-legged ones to leap
over, his bulk and weight, when it came to his turn to
leap, were of a kind to bring down the backs of all but
the very strongest frogs.

The female characters of the comedy were enacted by
professional ladies who took private apartments in the
vicinity of the concert-room, or hall, engaged for the
"Guild," or else came down by express train on the nights
of performance. It should be explained that the "Guild"
carried their own "theatre" with them, constructed in

various parts and pieces, and made to be packed up, erected, and taken down again in a few hours—the whole being comprised in a small compass, under the arrangement of Sir Joseph Paxton and a theatrical machinist.*

In a paper entitled "Mr. Dickens's Amateur Theatricals," published in *Macmillan's Magazine* in January 1871, the anonymous writer gives an account of—

Those winter-evening festivities at the house of Charles Dickens which continued annually for several years, terminating with the performance of Mr. Wilkie Collins's drama of *The Frozen Deep*. And when he remembers the number of notable men who either shared in or assisted (in the French sense) at those dramatic revels, and have passed away in the interval, he is filled with a desire to preserve some recollections of evenings so memorable. *Private* theatricals in one sense they were; but the size and character of the audiences they brought together placed them in a different category from the entertainments which commonly bear that name; and to preserve one's recollections of those days is scarcely to intrude upon the domain of private life. The greatest of that band has lately passed away, and before him many others of "these, our actors"; and though some remain, the events of those years have, even to those who shared in them, passed into the region of history.

---

* *The Gentleman's Magazine*, May, 1871 (by kind permission of Messrs. Chatto and Windus).

"What nights have we seen at the Mermaid!" What evenings were those at Tavistock House, when the best wit and fancy and culture of the day met within its hospitable walls! There was Thackeray, towering in bodily form above the crowd, even as he towered in genius above them all, save only one; Jerrold, with the blue convex eye, which seemed to pierce into the very heart of things and trace their subtle resemblances; Leech, with his frank and manly beauty, fresh from the portrayal of "Master Jacky," or some other of the many forms of boyhood he knew so well; Mark Lemon, "the frolic and the gentle" (dear to all us younger ones, irrespective of blood-relationship, as "Uncle Mark"); Albert Smith, dropping in late in the evening after a two or three thousandth ascent of Mont Blanc, but never refusing at our earnest entreaty to sit down to the piano and sing us *My Lord Tomnoddy* or his own latest edition of *Galignani's Messenger*; Augustus Egg, with his dry humour, touching from contrast with the face of suffering that gave sad presage of his early death; Frank Stone, the kindly neighbour and friend, keen as any of us boys for his part in the after-piece; Stanfield, with the beaming face, "a largess universal like the sun," his practised hand and brush prompt to gladden us with masterpieces of scene-painting for the Lighthouse or the Ice-fields; and last,—but not here to be dismissed with a few lines only, —our bountiful host, like Triplet, "author, manager, and actor too"; organizer, deviser, and harmoniser of all the incongruous assembled elements; the friend whom we have so lately lost,—the incomparable Dickens. The very walls of that home, and the furniture which filled it, were

rich in interest and eloquent of his fame and the tribute
which it had brought him : the testimonial given him at
Birmingham ; the handsome case of cutlery sent him by
Mr. Brooks, of Sheffield (recognizant of the chance mention of his name in the pages of *Copperfield*) ; Grip the
raven, in his habit as he lived, under the glass case in
the hall ; the Chinese gong, then less common in English
houses than now, reminding the reader familiar with his
"Dickens," of that one at Dr. Blimber's which the weak-
eyed young man, to Paul's amazement, suddenly let fly
at "as if he had gone mad or wanted vengeance"; the
pictures which looked down upon us from the walls of
dining-room and staircase, Sir Charles Coldstream in his
ploughboy's disguise, or Bobadil prostrate on the couch ;
the lady in the barouche reading the current number of
Bleak House, and the curious tiger skimming the contents over her shoulder ; Dolly Varden in the wood ; poor
Kate Nickleby at work in Madame Mantalini's show-
room ; little Nell among the tombs of that old church
which in these days of restoration will soon have no
existence save on the canvas of Cattermole ;—these, and
many more such signs of the atmosphere of art and
literature in which we moved, were gathered there—
and are now scattered to the four winds.

In one sense our theatricals began and ended in the
school-room. To the last that apartment served us for
stage and auditorium and all. But in another sense we
got promotion from the children's domain by degrees.
Our earliest efforts were confined to the children of the
family and their equals in age, though always aided and
abetted by the good-natured manager, who improvised

costumes, painted and corked our innocent cheeks, and suggested all the most effective business of the scene. Our first attempt was the performance of Albert Smith's burletta of *Guy Fawkes*, which appeared originally in the pages of his monthly periodical, the *Man in the Moon*; at another time we played *William Tell*, from Robert Brough's clever little *Cracker Bon-bon for Evening Parties*. In those days there were still extravaganzas written with real humour and abundant taste and fancy. The Broughs, Gilbert à Beckett, and Planché could write rhymed couplets of great literary excellence, without ever outstepping the bounds of good taste. Extreme purists may regret that the story of the struggle for Swiss independence should ever be presented to children in association with anything ludicrous; but, those critics excepted, no other could object to the spirit of " gracious fooling " in which Brough represented William Tell brought up before Gesler for "contempt of hat"; Albert, his precocious son, resolving that, as to betraying his father, "though torn in half, I 'll not be made to split"; and when he comforts his father, about to shoot at the apple, by assuring him that he is " game," the father replying, "Wert thou *game*, I would preserve, not shoot thee." This is drollery, surely, not unworthy of Sydney Smith or Hood, and in no way to be placed in the same catalogue with the vulgarities and inanities of a later brood.

Another year found us more ambitious, and with stronger resources, for Dickens himself and Mark Lemon joined our acting staff, though, with kindly consideration for their young brethren, they chose subordinate parts.

In Mr. Planché's elegant and most witty fairy extravaganza of *Fortunio and his Seven Gifted Servants*, Dickens took the part of the old Baron Dunover, whose daughters so valiantly adopt man's attire and go to the wars; Mark Lemon contenting himself with the *rôle* of the Dragon, who is overcome by Fortunio's stratagem of adulterating the well, whither he usually resorted to quench his thirst, with a potent admixture of sherry. What fun it was, both on and off the stage! The gorgeous dresses from the eminent costumier of the Theatre Royal; our heads bewigged and our cheeks rouged by the hands of Mr. Clarkson himself; the properties from the Adelphi; the unflagging humour and suggestive resources of our manager, who took upon him the charge of everything, from the writing of the playbills to the composition of the punch, brewed for our refreshment between the acts but "craftily qualified," as Michael Cassio would have said, to suit the capacities of the childish brain, for Dickens never forgot the *maxima reverentia* due to children, and some of us were of *very* tender age: the comedian who played (in a complete jockey's suit and top-boots) Fortunio's servant Light-foot, was—we are afraid to say *how* young—but it was somewhere between two and three, and he was announced in the bill as having been "kept out of bed at a vast expense." The same veracious document represented the sole lessee and manager of the Theatre Royal, Tavistock House, as Mr. Vincent Crummles, disguising Dickens himself in the list of *dramatis personæ* as the "Modern Roscius," and Mark Lemon as the "Infant Phenomenon,"—an exquisitely conceived surprise for the audience, who by

6 *

no means expected from the description to recognise in the character the portly form of the editor of *Punch*. This time, by the way, must have been the winter preceding the commencement of hostilities with Russia, for Dickens took advantage of there being a ferocious despot in the play—the Emperor Matapa—to identify him with the Czar in a capital song, (would we could recall it!) to the tune of *The Cork Leg*, in which the Emperor described himself as "the Robinson Crusoe of absolute state," and declared that though he had at his court "many a show-day, and many a high-day," he hadn't in all his dominions "a Friday!" Mr. Planché had in one portion of the extravaganza put into the mouth of this character for the moment a few lines of burlesque upon Macbeth, and we remember Dickens's unsuccessful attempts to teach the performer how to imitate Macready, whom he (the performer) had never seen!

Another time we attempted Fielding's *Tom Thumb*, using O'Hara's altered version, further abridged and added to by the untiring master of our ceremonies. Fielding's admirable piece of mock-heroic had always been a favourite of Charles Dickens. It has often been noticed how rarely he quotes in his books, but the reader of *Pickwick* will remember how in an early chapter of that immortal work Mr. Alfred Jingle sings the two lines:—

> In hurry, post-haste, for a licence,
> In hurry, ding-dong, I come back.

They are from Lord Grizzle's song in *Tom Thumb*. Mark Lemon played the giantess Glumdalca, in an amazing get-up of a complete suit of armour and a coal-scuttle bonnet; and Dickens the small part of the ghost of Gaffer Thumb, singing his own song, on the occasion, a verse of which may be quoted, if only to illustrate the contrast between the styles of the earlier and later burlesque. In O'Hara's version the ghost appears to King Arthur, singing :—

> Pale death is prowling,
> Dire omens scowling
> Doom thee to slaughter,
> Thee, thy wife and daughter;
> Furies are growling
> With horrid groans.
> Grizzle's rebellion
> What need I tell you on?
> Or by a red cow
> Tom Thumb devour'd?
> Hark, the cock crowing,   [*Cock crows.*
> I must be going.
> I can no more!   [*Vanishes.*

Dickens's substituted lines were, as nearly as we can remember, as follows :—

> I've got up from my churchyard bed,
>   And assumed the perpendicular,
> Having something to say in my head,
>   Which isn't so very particular!
> I do not appear in sport,
>   But in earnest, all danger scorning—
> I'm in your service, in short,
>   And I hereby give you warning—   [*Cock crows.*
>
> Who's dat crowing at the door?
>   Dere's some one in the house with Dinah!
> I'm call'd (so can't say any more)
>   By a voice from Cochin China!

Nonsense, it may be said, all this; but the nonsense of a great genius has always something of genius in it.

The production next year, on the same stage, of the drama of *The Lighthouse*, marked a great step in the rank of our performances. The play was a touching and tragic story, founded upon a tale by the same author, Mr. Wilkie Collins, which appeared in an early number of *Household Words*. The principal characters were sustained by Dickens, Mark Lemon, Mr. Wilkie Collins, and the ladies of Dickens's family. The scenery was painted by Clarkson Stanfield, and comprised a drop-scene representing the exterior of Eddystone Lighthouse, and a room in the interior in which the whole action of the drama was carried on. *The Lighthouse* was performed two or three years later at the Olympic, with Robson in the character originally played by Dickens. The little drama was well worthy of publication, though by conception and treatment alike it was fitted rather for amateurs, and a drawing-room, than for the public stage. The main incident of the plot—the confession of a murder by the old sailor, Aaron Gurnock, under pressure of impending death from starvation (no provisions being able to reach the lighthouse, owing to a continuance of bad weather), and his subsequent retractation of the confession when supplies unexpectedly arrive,—afforded Dickens scope for a piece of acting of great power.*

---

* "Carlyle compared Dickens's wild picturesqueness in the old lighthouse-keeper to the famous figure in Nicholas Poussin's Bacchanalian Dance in the National Gallery."— FORSTER's *Life of Charles Dickens*, vol. iii. p. 51.

Of Dickens's acting in his own farce of *Mr. Nightingale's Diary*, the writer adds:—

One of the characters played by Dickens was an old lady, in great trouble and perplexity about a missing child; of which character (nameless in the drama) he always spoke, when he had occasion to refer to her off the stage, as Mrs. Gamp, some of whose speeches were as well worthy of preservation for droll extravagance of incongruity as the best of her famous prototype in *Martin Chuzzlewit*. In addition to her perplexity about the missing infant, she is further embarrassed as to the exact surname of Mr. Nightingale, which she remembers to be that of a bird, but cannot always refer to the correct species of that order. A quotation from memory will leave no doubt as to the fertile and singular fancy from whose mint it came* :—

"No, sir, I will not leave the house! I will not leave the establishment without my child, my boy. *My* boy, sir, which he were his mother's hope and his father's pride, and no one as I am aweer on's joy. Vich the name as was giv' to this blessedest of infants and vorked . in best Vitechapel mixed upon a pincushin, and ' Save the mother' likewise, were Abjalom, after his own parential father, Mr. Nightingale, who no other ways than by being guv' to liquor, lost a day's vork at the veelwright business, vich it was but limited, Mr. Skylark, being veels of donkey-chaises and goats; and vun vas even drawn by geese for a wager, and came up the aisle o' the

---

* Compare with the same quotation, somewhat differently given by Mr. Horne, in the *Gentleman's Magazine*.

parish church one Sunday arternoon by reason of the
perwerseness of the animals, as could be testified by Mr.
Wix the beadle afore he died of drawing on Vellinton
boots to which he was not accustomed, after an 'earty
meal of roast beef and a pickled walnut to which he were
too parjial! Yes, Mr. Robin Redbreast, in the marble
fontin of that theer church was he baptized Abjalom,
vich never can be unmade or undone, I am proud to say,
not to please nor give offence to no one, nohows and
noveres, sir. . . . Ah! 'affliction sore long time Maria
Nightingale bore; physicians *was* in vain '—not that I
am aweer she had anyone in particular, sir, excepting
one, vich she tore his hair by handfuls out in consequence
of disagreements re*lat*ive to her complaint; and dead she
is, and will be, as the hosts of the Egyptian fairies; and
this I shall prove, directly minute, on 'the evingdence of
my brother the sexton, whom I shall here produce, to
your confusion, young person, in the twinkling of a star
or humin eye!"

Scarcely had the old lady quitted the stage when
Dickens reappeared as "my brother the sexton," a very
old gentleman indeed, with a quavery voice and self-
satisfied smile (pleasantly suggesting how inimitable must
have been the same actor's manner as Justice Shallow),
and afflicted with a "hardness of hearing" which almost
baffled the efforts of his interrogators to obtain from
him the desired information as to the certificate of Mrs.
Nightingale's decease. "It's no use your whispering to
me, sir!" was the gentle remonstrance which the first
loud shout in his ear elicited; and on the question being
put whether "he had ever buried"—he at once inter-

rupted to reply that he *had brewed*; and that he and his old woman—"my old woman was a Kentish woman, gentlemen: one year, sir, we brewed some of the strongest ale that ever you drank, sir: they used to call it down in our part of the country (in allusion, you understand, to its great strength, gentlemen), ' Samson with his hair on,' "—at which point the thread of his narrative was cut short by the reiteration, in a louder key still, of the intended question in a complete form.

A third character in the farce, sustained by Dickens, was that of a *malade imaginaire*, for the time being under treatment by a new specific, "mustard and milk," the merits of which he could not highly enough extol, but which nevertheless was not so soothing in its effects but that the patient gave every minute a loud shriek— explaining apologetically, "That's the mustard!" followed immediately by a still louder one, "That's the milk!"

We are afraid to say in how many other disguises our manager appeared, but there was certainly one other, a footman or waiter, in which character the actor gave us a most amusing caricature of the manner of one of his own servants; and we remember with what glee, one night at supper after rehearsal, Dickens learned that the man in question had been heard imitating his master in the part for the amusement of his fellow-servants, in utter ignorance that he himself had sat in the first instance for the portrait.

This very clever farce might well be given to the public now that the chief actor is no more; for though the character is wholly beyond the reach of most amateurs, or even most professionals, *the piece contains dialogue full of humour peculiarly Dickensian.*

As a comedian, it is perhaps with Charles Mathews alone that we should think of comparing Charles Dickens. In repose, the walk and voice and manner of the two were much alike; though in power of facial and vocal change Dickens had great advantages; and he had further an *earnestness* quite beyond the reach of the other actor, the lack of which kept him from excelling in many characters for which in other respects he would seem to have been peculiarly qualified.

The same amazing fertility and rapidity of invention, in which Dickens stands without a rival as a humourist, often served him in excellent stead, in the sudden substitution of extempore remarks known to the professional actor as " gag." On one occasion, in a farce played after *The Frozen Deep*, one of the characters having occasion to disguise himself for the moment in the chintz cover of the sofa, Dickens suddenly observed, to the astonishment of his fellow-actors, " He has a general appearance of going to have his hair cut ! " a comparison so ingeniously perfect as to convulse everybody on and off the stage with laughter.

The success of *The Lighthouse*, performed at Tavistock House in the January of 1856, and subsequently repeated at Campden House, Kensington, for the benefit of the Consumption Hospital at Bournemouth, induced Mr. Wilkie Collins to try his dramatic fortune once more, and the result was the drama of *The Frozen Deep*, with an excellent part for Dickens, and opportunity for charming scenic effects by Stanfield and Telbin. The plot was of the slightest. A young naval officer, Richard Wardour, is in love, and is aware that he has a rival in the lady's affections, though he does not know that rival's name. His ship is ordered to take part in an expedition to the polar regions, and the moody and unhappy young officer, while chopping down for firewood some part of what had composed the sleeping compartment of a wooden hut, discovers from a name carved upon the timbers that his hated rival is with him, taking part in the expedition. His resolve to compass the other's death gradually gives place to a better spirit, and the drama ends with his saving his rival from starvation at the cost of his own life, himself living just long enough to bestow his dying blessing on the lovers; the ladies, whose brothers and lovers were on the expedition, having joined them in Newfoundland. The character of Richard Wardour afforded opportunity for a fine display of mental struggle and a gradual transition from moodiness to vindictiveness, and finally, under the pressure of suffering, to penitence and resignation, and was represented by Dickens with consummate skill. The charm of the piece as a whole, however, did not depend so much upon the acting of the principal character, fine as it was, as on the perfect refinement and natural pathos with which the family and domestic interest of the story was sustained. The ladies to whose acting so much of this charm was due are happily still living, and must not be mentioned by name or made the subjects of criticism in this place; but the circumstance is worth noticing as suggesting one reason why such a drama, effective and touching in the drawing-room, would be even unpleasing on the stage. Such a drama depends for its success on a refinement of mind and feeling in the performers which in the present state of the theatrical art, must of necessity be rarely possessed, or if possessed must speedily succumb to the unwholesome influences of that class of dramatic literature which is found to please best at the present day.

The production of *The Frozen Deep* has a literary interest for the reader of Dickens, as marking the date of a distinct advance in his career as an artist. It was during the performance of this play with his children and friends, he tells us in the preface of his *Tale of Two Cities*, that the plot of that story took shape in his imagination. He does not confide to us what was the precise connexion between the two events. But the critical reader will have noticed that then, and from that time onwards, the novelist discovered a manifest solicitude and art in the construction of his plots which he had not evinced up to that time. In his earlier works there is little or no constructive ability. *Pickwick* was merely a series of scenes from London and country life, more or less loosely strung together. *Nicholas Nickleby* was in this respect little different. In *Copperfield* there is more attention to this specially dramatic faculty, but even in that novel the special skill of the constructor is exhibited rather in episodes of the story than in the narrative as a whole. But from and after the *Tale of Two Cities*, Dickens manifests a diligent pursuit of that art of framing and developing a plot which there can be little doubt is traceable to the influence of his intimate and valued friend Mr. Wilkie Collins. In this special art

Mr. Collins has long held high rank among living novelists. He is indeed, perhaps, open to the charge of sacrificing too much to the composition of riddles, which, like riddles of another kind, lose much of their interest when once they have been solved. And it is interesting to note that while Dickens was aiming at one special excellence of Mr. Collins, the latter was assimilating his style, in some other respects, to that of his brother novelist. Each, of late years, seemed to be desirous of the special dramatic faculty which the other possessed. Dickens's plots, Mr. Collins's characters and dialogues, bore more and more clearly marked the traces of the model on which they were respectively based. It is possible, however, that another consideration was influencing the direction of Dickens's genius. He may have half suspected that the peculiar freshness of his earlier style was no longer at his command, and he may have been desirous of breaking new ground and cultivating a faculty too long neglected. His genius was largely dramatic, and it was the overpowering fertility of his humour as a *descriptive* writer which led him at the outset of his literary career to prose fiction as the freest outcome of his genius. He loved the drama and things dramatic ; and notwithstanding what might be inferred from the lecture which Nicholas administers to the literary gentleman in *Nicholas Nickleby*, he evidently was well pleased to see his own stories in a dramatic shape, when the adaptation was made in accordance with the spirit and design of the originator. Most of his earlier works were dramatised, and enjoyed a success attributable not less to the admirable acting which they called forth than to the fame of the characters in their original setting. His Christmas stories proved most successful in their dramatic shape, and it is difficult to believe that he had not in view those admirable comedians, Mr. and Mrs. Keeley, when he drew the charming characters of Britain and Clemency Newcome. His *Tale of Two Cities* was arranged under his own supervision for the stage, and he seems to have had a growing pleasure in seeing his works reproduced in this shape, for *Little Em'ly*, the latest arrangement of *David Copperfield*, was produced with at least his sanction and approval; and a version of the *Old Curiosity Shop*, under the title of *Nell*, was similarly approved by himself shortly before his death. In the present state of the stage we may well be thankful for pieces so wholesome in interest, so pure in moral, so abounding in unforced humour, as his best stories are adapted to provide.*

To the Plays and Poems, which it was our essential and primary plan to reproduce in these volumes, have been added some Miscellanies in Prose, also now first collected; none of them, we believe, unworthy of their great writer; and one of them, the earliest in date—a wise, manly and emphatic protest against Sabbatarianism—published in pamphlet form in 1836, now so rare as to be out of the reach of readers not blessed with

---

* *Mr. Dickens's Amateur Theatricals, a Reminiscence.*— *Macmillan's Magazine*, January 1871, pp. 206–215.

the purse of Fortunatus. Another, the latest in date, and written less than a year before his death, is his last casual piece of writing, and possesses peculiar interest here as an admirable and enthusiastic analysis of the acting of the friend whose performance of the part of Obenreizer, in his own drama of *No Thoroughfare*, contributed so largely to its success and won from Dickens such warm acknowledgment.

The *Bibliography of Dickens* (originally issued in 1880) which is added as an Appendix, has been carefully revised throughout and considerably enlarged, and may claim to be more accurate and exhaustive than it could be on its first appearance.

It is no part of the present Editor's duty to detain the reader from the rich feast of humour before him with any observations on the genius and career of Dickens. That task has been performed by abler pens. But the fourteen years that have elapsed since his death have in nowise diminished the fascination which surrounds his strong and energetic individuality, or the love and interest with which thousands of readers of all ages regard him. The voice we knew so well is silent for ever; but his written words, on which he might well rest his claim to his countrymen's remembrance, will still charm new readers of a later generation, and readers yet unborn. Standing on the Christmas morning after his death, as I have stood at each successive Christmas since, by his grave in Poet's Corner, beautified by loving and pious hands with flowers and immortelles, in the solemn sanctuary where, in the noontide of his creative genius, I first stood, so long long ago, with the lost and venerated father from whom, almost before the century had yet completed its earlier half, I had already caught some childish sense of the great humourist's treasure of smiles and tears, I seemed not till then fully to realize all that there was in Charles Dickens which the grave is powerless to take away.

RICHARD HERNE SHEPHERD.

5, BRAMERTON STREET,
KING'S ROAD, CHELSEA:
Christmas, 1884.

THE
STRANGE GENTLEMAN.

[*The Strange Gentleman; a Comic Burletta.   In Two Acts.
By " Boz."   First performed at the St. James's Theatre,
on Thursday, September 29, 1836.   Chapman and Hall,
186 Strand.—MDCCCXXXVII.*]

CAST OF THE CHARACTERS.

MR. OWEN OVERTON (*Mayor of a small town on the road to Gretna, and useful at the St. James's Arms*) . . . . . MR. HOLLINGSWORTH.

JOHN JOHNSON (*detained at the St. James's Arms*) . . . . MR. SIDNEY.

THE STRANGE GENTLEMAN (*just arrived at the St. James's Arms*) . MR. HARLEY.

CHARLES TOMKINS (*incognito at the St. James's Arms*) . . . MR. FORESTER.

TOM SPARKS (*a one-eyed "Boots" at the St. James's Arms*) . . MR. GARDNER.

JOHN } *Waiters at the* { MR. WILLIAMSON.
TOM } *St. James's Arms* { MR. MAY.
WILL } { MR. COULSON.

JULIA DOBBS (*looking for a husband at the St. James's Arms*) . . MADAME SALA.

FANNY WILSON (*with an appointment at the St. James's Arms*) . MISS SMITH.

MARY WILSON (*her sister, awkwardly situated at the St. James's Arms*) MISS JULIA SMITH.

MRS. NOAKES (*the Landlady at the St. James's Arms*) . . . MRS. W. PENSON.

CHAMBERMAID (*at the St. James's Arms*) . . . . . MISS STUART.

Miss Smith and Miss Julia Smith will sing the duet of " I know a Bank," in " The Strange Gentleman."

7 *

COSTUME.

MR. OWEN OVERTON.—*Black smalls, and high black boots. A blue body coat, rather long in the waist, with yellow buttons, buttoned close up to the chin. A white stock; ditto gloves. A broad-brimmed low-crowned white hat.*

STRANGE GENTLEMAN.—*A light blue plaid French-cut trousers and vest. A brown cloth frock coat, with full skirts, scarcely covering the hips. A light blue kerchief, and eccentric low-crowned broad-brimmed white hat. Boots.*

JOHN JOHNSON.—*White fashionable trousers, boots, light vest, frock coat, black hat, gloves, &c.*

CHARLES TOMKINS.—*Shepherd's plaid French-cut trousers; boots; mohair fashionable frock coat, buttoned up; black hat, gloves, &c.*

TOM SPARKS.—*Leather smalls, striped stockings, and lace-up half boots, red vest, and a Holland stable jacket; coloured kerchief, and red wig.*

THE WAITERS.—*All in black trousers, black stockings and shoes, white vests, striped jackets, and white kerchiefs.*

MARY WILSON.—*Fashionable walking dress, white silk stockings; shoes and gloves.*

FANNY WILSON.—*Precisely the same as Mary.*

JULIA DOBBS.—*A handsome white travelling dress, cashmere shawl, white silk stockings; shoes and gloves. A bonnet to correspond.*

MRS. NOAKES.—*A chintz gown, rather of a dark pattern, French apron, and handsome cap.*

SCENE.—A SMALL TOWN, ON THE ROAD TO GRETNA.

TIME.—PART OF A DAY AND NIGHT.

Time in acting—One hour and twenty minutes.

THE STRANGE GENTLEMAN.

ACT I.

Scene I.—*A Room at the St. James's Arms; Door in Centre, with a Bolt on it. A Table with Cover, and Two Chairs.* R. H.

Enter Mrs Noakes. C. DOOR.

MRS. NOAKES.

Bless us, what a coachful! Four inside—twelve out; and the guard blowing the key-bugle in the fore-boot, for fear the informers should see that they have got one over the number. Post-chaise and a gig besides.—We shall be filled to the very attics. Now, look alive, there—bustle about.

Enter First Waiter, *running.* C. DOOR.

Now, John.

FIRST WAITER (*coming down* L. H.)

Single lady, inside the stage, wants a private room, ma'am.

MRS. NOAKES. R. H.

Much luggage?

FIRST WAITER.

Four trunks, two bonnet-boxes, six brown-paper parcels, and a basket.

MRS. NOAKES.

Give her a private room, directly.   No. 1, on the first floor.

FIRST WAITER.

Yes, ma'am.

[*Exit* FIRST WAITER, *running.*   C. DOOR.

Enter SECOND WAITER, *running.*   C. DOOR.
Now, Tom.

SECOND WAITER (*coming down* R. H.)

Two young ladies and one gentleman, in a post-chaise, want a private sitting-room d'rectly, ma'am.

MRS. NOAKES.

Brother and sisters, Tom ?

SECOND WAITER.

Ladies are something alike, ma'am.   Gentleman like neither of 'em.

MRS. NOAKES.

Husband and wife and wife's sister, perhaps. Eh, Tom ?

SECOND WAITER.

Can't be husband and wife, ma'am, because I saw the gentleman kiss one of the ladies.

MRS. NOAKES.

Kissing one of the ladies!   Put them in the small sitting-room behind the bar, Tom, that I may have an eye on them through the little window, and see that nothing improper goes forward.

SECOND WAITER.

Yes, ma'am.   (*Going.*)

MRS. NOAKES.

And Tom!   (*Crossing to* L. H.)

SECOND WAITER (*coming down* R. H.)

Yes, ma'am.

MRS. NOAKES.

Tell Cook to put together all the bones and pieces that were left on the plates at the great dinner yesterday, and make some nice soup to feed the stage-coach passengers with.

SECOND WAITER.

Very well, ma'am.

[*Exit* SECOND WAITER.   C. DOOR.

Enter THIRD WAITER, *running.*   C. DOOR.

Now, Will.

THIRD WAITER (*coming down* L. H.)

A strange gentleman in a gig, ma'am, wants a private sitting-room.

MRS. NOAKES.

Much luggage, Will?

THIRD WAITER.

One portmanteau, and a great-coat.

MRS. NOAKES.

Oh! nonsense!—Tell him to go into the commercial room.

THIRD WAITER.

I told him so, ma'am, but the Strange Gentleman says he *will* have a private apartment, and that it's as much as his life is worth, to sit in a public room.

MRS. NOAKES.

As much as his life is worth?

THIRD WAITER.

Yes, ma'am.—Gentleman says he doesn't care if it's a dark closet; but a private room of some kind he must and will have.

MRS. NOAKES.

Very odd.—Did you ever see him before, Will?

THIRD WAITER.

No, ma'am; he's quite a stranger here.—He's a wonderful man to talk, ma'am—keeps on like a steam engine.   Here he is, ma'am.

STRANGE GENTLEMAN (*without*).

Now don't tell me, because that's all gammon

and nonsense; and gammoned I never was, and never will be, by any waiter that ever drew the breath of life, or a cork.—And just have the goodness to leave my portmanteau alone, because I can carry it very well myself; and show me a private room without further delay ; for a private room I must and will have.—Damme, do you think I'm going to be murdered!—

    [*Enter the three Waiters,* c. DOOR—*they form down* L. H., *the* STRANGE GENTLEMAN *following, carrying his portmanteau and great-coat.*

There—this room will do capitally well, Quite the thing,—just the fit.—How are you, ma'am? I suppose you are the landlady of this place? Just order those very attentive young fellows out, will you, and I'll order dinner.

MRS. NOAKES (to Waiters).

You may leave the room.

STRANGE GENTLEMAN.

Hear that?—You may leave the room. Make yourselves scarce. Evaporate—disappear—come.

    [*Exeunt Waiters,* c. DOOR.

That's right. And now, madam, while we're talking over this important matter of dinner, I'll just secure us effectually against further intrusion. (*Bolts the door.*)

MRS. NOAKES.

Lor, sir! Bolting the door, and *me* in the room!

STRANGE GENTLEMAN.

Don't be afraid—I won't hurt you. I have no designs against you, my dear ma'am: but *I must be private.* (*Sits on the portmanteau,* R. H.)

MRS. NOAKES.

Well, sir—I have no objection to break through our rules for once; but it is not our way, when we're full, to give private rooms to solitary gentlemen, who come in a gig, and bring only one portmanteau. You're quite a stranger *here*, sir. If I'm not mistaken, it's your first appearance in this house.

STRANGE GENTLEMAN.

You're right, ma'am. It *is* my first, my very first—but not my last, I can tell you.

MRS. NOAKES.

No?

STRANGE GENTLEMAN.

No (*looking round him*). I like the look of this place. Snug and comfortable—neat and lively. You'll very often find me at the St. James's Arms, I can tell you, ma'am.

MRS. NOAKES (*aside*).

A civil gentleman. Are you a stranger in this town, sir?

STRANGE GENTLEMAN.

Stranger! Bless you, no. I have been here for many years past, in the season.

MRS. NOAKES.

Indeed!

STRANGE GENTLEMAN.

Oh, yes. Put up at the Royal Hotel regularly for a long time; but I was obliged to leave it at last.

MRS. NOAKES.

I have heard a good many complaints of it.

STRANGE GENTLEMAN.

O! terrible! such a noisy house.

MRS. NOAKES.

Ah!

STRANGE GENTLEMAN.

Shocking! Din, din, din—Drum, drum, drum, all night. Nothing but noise, glare, and nonsense. I bore it a long time for old acquaintance sake; but what do you think they did at last, ma'am?

MRS. NOAKES.

I can't guess.

STRANGE GENTLEMAN.

Turned the fine Old Assembly Room into a stable, and took to keeping horses. I tried that too, but I found I couldn't stand it; so I came away, ma'am, and—and—here I am (*rises*).

MRS. NOAKES.

And I'll be bound to say, sir, that you will have no cause to complain of the exchange.

STRANGE GENTLEMAN.

I'm sure not, ma'am; I know it—I feel it, already.

MRS. NOAKES.

About dinner, sir; what would you like to take?

STRANGE GENTLEMAN.

Let me see; will you be good enough to suggest something, ma'am?

MRS. NOAKES.

Why, a broiled fowl and mushrooms is a very nice dish.

STRANGE GENTLEMAN.

You are right, ma'am; a broiled fowl and mush-rooms form a very delightful and harmless amuse-ment, either for one or two persons. Broiled fowl and mushrooms let it be, ma'am.

MRS. NOAKES.

In about an hour, I suppose, sir?

STRANGE GENTLEMAN.

For the second time, ma'am, you have anticipated my feelings.

MRS. NOAKES.

You'll want a bed to-night, I suppose, sir;

perhaps you'd like to see it ?   Step this way, sir,
and—(*going* L. H.)

STRANGE GENTLEMAN.

No, no, never mind.   (*Aside.*)   This is a plot to
get me out of the room.   She's bribed by somebody who wants to identify me.   I must be careful;
I am exposed to nothing but artifice and stratagem.
Never mind, ma'am, never mind.

MRS. NOAKES.

If you'll give me your portmanteau, sir, the
Boots will carry it into the next room for you.

STRANGE GENTLEMAN (*aside*).

Here's diabolical ingenuity; she thinks it's got
the name upon it.   (*To her.*)   I'm very much
obliged to the Boots for his disinterested attention,
ma'am, but with your kind permission this portmanteau will remain just exactly where it is;
consequently, ma'am, (*with great warmth,*) if the
aforesaid Boots wishes to succeed in removing this
portmanteau, he must previously remove *me*,
ma'am, *me*; and it will take a *pair* of very stout
Boots to do that, ma'am, I promise you.

MRS. NOAKES.

Dear me, sir, you needn't fear for your portmanteau in this house; I dare say nobody wants it.

STRANGE GENTLEMAN.

I hope not, ma'am, because in that case nobody

will be disappointed.   (*Aside.*)   How she fixes her old eyes on me!

MRS. NOAKES (*aside*).

I never saw such an extraordinary person in all my life.   What can he be ?   (*Looks at him very hard.*)

[*Exit* MRS. NOAKES, C. DOOR.

STRANGE GENTLEMAN.

She's gone at last !   Now let me commune with my own dreadful thoughts, and reflect on the best means of escaping from my horrible position. (*Takes a letter from his pocket.*)   Here's an illegal death - warrant;   a   pressing   invitation   to   be slaughtered ; a polite request just to step out and be killed, thrust into my hand by some disguised assassin in a dirty black calico jacket, the very instant I got out of the gig at the door.   I know the hand ; there's a ferocious recklessness in the cross to this " T," and a baleful malignity in the dot of that " I," which warns me that it comes from my desperate rival.   (*Opens it, and reads.*)   " Mr. Horatio Tinkles "—that's him—" presents his com- pliments to his enemy "—that's me—" and requests the pleasure of his company to-morrow morning, under the clump of trees, on Corpse Common,"— Corpse Common!—" to which any of the town's people will direct him, and where he hopes to have the satisfaction of giving him his gruel."—Giving him his gruel! Ironical cut-throat!—" His punctuality will be esteemed a personal favour, as it will save Mr. Tinkles the trouble and incon-venience of calling with a horsewhip in his pocket. Mr. Tinkles has ordered breakfast at the Royal for *one*. It is paid for. The individual who returns alive can eat it. Pistols—half-past five—precisely." —Blood-thirsty miscreant! *The* individual who returns alive! I have seen him hit the painted man at the shooting-gallery regularly every time in his centre shirt plait, except when he varied the entertainments, by lodging the ball playfully in his left eye. Breakfast! I shall want nothing beyond the gruel. What 's to be done? Escape! I can't escape; concealment 's of no use, he knows I am here. He has dodged me all the way from London, and will dodge me all the way to the residence of Miss Emily Brown, whom my respected, but swine-headed parents have picked out for my future wife. A pretty figure I should cut before the old people, whom I have never beheld more than once in my life, and Miss Emily Brown, whom I have never seen at all, if I went down there, pursued by this Salamander, who, I suppose, is her accepted lover! What is to be done? I can't go back again; father would be furious. What can be done? nothing! (*Sinks into a chair.*) I must undergo this fiery ordeal, and submit to be packed up, and carried back to my weeping parents, like an unfortunate buck, with a flat piece of lead in my head, and a brief epitaph on my breast, "Killed on Wednesday morning." No, I won't (*starting up, and walking about*). I won't submit to it; I'll accept the challenge, but first I'll write an anonymous letter to the local authorities, giving them information of this intended duel, and desiring them to place me under immediate restraint. That's feasible; on further consideration, it's capital. My character will be saved—I shall be bound over—he'll be bound over—I shall resume my journey—reach the house—marry the girl—pocket the fortune, and laugh at him. No time to be lost; it shall be done forthwith. (*Goes to table, and writes.*) There; the challenge accepted, with a bold defiance, that'll look very brave when it comes to be printed. Now for the other. (*Writes.*) "To the Mayor—Sir—A strange Gentleman at the St. James's Arms, whose name is unknown to the writer of this communication, is bent upon committing a rash and sanguinary act, at an early hour to-morrow morning. As you value human life, secure the amiable youth, without delay. Think, I implore you, sir, think what would be the feelings of those to whom he is nearest and dearest, if any mischance befal the interesting young man. Do not neglect this solemn

warning; the number of his room is seventeen."
There—(*folding it up*).   Now if I can find any one
who will deliver it secretly.—

TOM SPARKS, *with a pair of boots in his hand,*
peeps in at the C. D.

TOM.

Are these here your'n ?

STRANGE GENTLEMAN.

No.

TOM.

Oh! (*going back*).

STRANGE GENTLEMAN.

Hallo! stop, are you the Boots?

TOM (*still at the door*).

I'm the head o' that branch o' the establishment.
There's another man under me, as brushes the dirt
off, and puts the blacking on.   The fancy work's
my department; I do the polishing, nothing else.

STRANGE GENTLEMAN.

You are the upper Boots, then?

TOM.

Yes, I'm the reg'lar ; t'other one's only the
deputy; top boots and half boots, I calls us.

STRANGE GENTLEMAN.

You're a sharp fellow.

I.   8

TOM.

Ah! I'd better cut then (*going*).

STRANGE GENTLEMAN.

Don't hurry, Boots—don't hurry; I want you.
(*Rises, and comes forward, R. H.*)

TOM (*coming forward, L. H.*).

Well!

STRANGE GENTLEMAN.

Can—can—you be secret, Boots?

TOM.

That depends entirely on accompanying circumstances;—see the point?

STRANGE GENTLEMAN.

I think I comprehend your meaning, Boots.
You insinuate that you could be secret (*putting his
hand in his pocket*) if you had—five shillings for
instance—isn't that it, Boots?

TOM.

That's the line o' argument I should take up;
but that an't exactly my meaning.

STRANGE GENTLEMAN.

No!

TOM.

No. A secret's a thing as is always a rising to
one's lips. It requires an astonishing weight to
keep one on 'em down.

STRANGE GENTLEMAN.

Ah!

TOM.

Yes; I don't think I could keep one snug—
reg'lar snug, you know—

STRANGE GENTLEMAN.

Yes, regularly snug, of course.

TOM.

—If it had a less weight a-top on it, than ten
shillins.

STRANGE GENTLEMAN.

You don't think three half-crowns would do it?

TOM.

It might, I won't say it wouldn't, but I couldn't
warrant it.

STRANGE GENTLEMAN.

You could the other!

TOM.

Yes.

STRANGE GENTLEMAN.

Then there it is. (*Gives him four half-crowns*
You see these letters?

TOM.

Yes, I can manage that without my spectacles.

STRANGE GENTLEMAN.

Well; that's to be left at the Royal Hotel. This,

8 *

this, is an anonymous one; and I want it to be delivered at the Mayor's house, without his knowing from whom it came, or seeing who delivered it.

TOM (*taking the letters*).

I say—you're a rum 'un, you are.

STRANGE GENTLEMAN.

Think so! Ha, ha! so are you.

TOM.

Ay, but you're a rummer one than me.

STRANGE GENTLEMAN.

No, no, that's your modesty.

TOM.

No it an't. I say, how vell you did them last hay-stacks. How do you contrive that ere now, if it's a fair question. Is it done with a pipe, or do you use them Lucifer boxes?

STRANGE GENTLEMAN.

Pipe—Lucifer boxes—hay-stacks! Why, what do you mean?

TOM (*looking cautiously round*).

I know your name, old 'un.

STRANGE GENTLEMAN.

You know my name! (*Aside.*) Now how the devil has he got hold of that, I wonder!

TOM.

Yes, I know it. It begins with a " S."

STRANGE GENTLEMAN.

Begins with an S!

TOM.

And ends with a " G " (*winking*). We've all heard talk of *Swing* down here.

STRANGE GENTLEMAN.

Heard talk of Swing! Here's a situation! Damme, d'ye think I'm a walking carbois of vitriol, and burn everything I touch?—Will you go upon the errand you're paid for?

TOM.

Oh, I'm going—I'm going. It's nothing to me, you know; I don't care. I'll only just give these boots to the deputy, to take them to whoever they belong to, and then I'll pitch this here letter in at the Mayor's office-window, in no time.

STRANGE GENTLEMAN.

Will you be off?

TOM.

Oh, I'm going, I'm going. Close, you knows, close!

[*Exit* TOM, C. DOOR.

STRANGE GENTLEMAN.

In five minutes more the letter will be delivered;

in another half hour, if the Mayor does his duty,
I shall be in custody, and secure from the vengeance of this infuriated monster. I wonder whether
they 'll take me away ? Egad! I may as well be
provided with a clean shirt and a night-cap in case.
Let 's see, she said the next room was my bed-
room, and as I have accepted the challenge, I may
venture so far now. (*Shouldering the portmanteau.*)
What a capital notion it is; there 'll be all the
correspondence in large letters, in the county paper,
and my name figuring away in roman capitals,
with a long story, how I was such a desperate
dragon, and so bent upon fighting, that it took four
constables to carry me to the Mayor, and one boy
to carry my hat. It 's a capital plan—must be done
—the only way I have of escaping unpursued from
this place, unless I could put myself in the General Post, and direct myself to a friend in town.
And then it 's a chance whether they 'd take me in,
being so much over weight.

[*Exit* STRANGE GENTLEMAN, *with portmanteau,*
L. H.

MRS. NOAKES, *peeping in* C. DOOR, *then entering.*

MRS. NOAKES.

This is the room, ladies, but the gentleman has
stepped out somewhere, he won't be long, I dare
say. Pray come in, Miss.

Enter MARY *and* FANNY WILSON, C. DOOR.

MARY (C.).

This is the Strange Gentleman's apartment, is it?

MRS. NOAKES (R.).

Yes, Miss; shall I see if I can find him, ladies, and tell him you are here?

MARY.

No; we should prefer waiting till he returns, if you please.

MRS. NOAKES.

Very well, ma'am. He'll be back directly, I dare say; for it's very near his dinner time.

[*Exit* MRS. NOAKES, C. DOOR.

MARY.

Come, Fanny, dear; don't give way to these feelings of depression. Take pattern by me—I feel the absurdity of our situation acutely; but you see that I keep up, nevertheless.

FANNY.

It is easy for you to do so. *Your* situation is neither so embarrassing, nor so painful a one as mine.

MARY.

Well, my dear, it *may* not be, certainly; but the circumstances which render it less so are, I own,

somewhat incomprehensible to me.   My hare-
brained, mad-cap swain, John Johnson, implores
me to leave my guardian's house, and accompany
him on an expedition to Gretna Green.   I with
immense reluctance, and after considerable pressing—

FANNY.

Yield a very willing consent.

MARY.

Well, we won't quarrel about terms; at all
events I *do* consent.   He bears me off, and when
we get exactly half-way, discovers that his money
is all gone, and that we must stop at this Inn,
until he can procure a remittance from London,
by post.   I think, my dear, you'll own that *this* is
rather an embarrassing position.

FANNY.

Compare it with mine.   Taking advantage of
your flight, I send express to *my* admirer, Charles
Tomkins, to say that I have accompanied you;
first, because I should have been miserable if left
behind with a peevish old man alone; secondly,
because I thought it proper that your sister should
accompany you——

MARY.

And, thirdly, because you knew that he would
immediately comply with this indirect assent to

his entreaties of three months' duration, and follow
you without delay, on the same errand.   Eh, my
dear?

FANNY.

It by no means follows that such was my intention, or that I knew he would pursue such a
course, but supposing he *has* done so ; supposing
this Strange Gentleman should be himself——

MARY.

Supposing !—Why, you know it is.   You told
him not to disclose his name, on any account ;
and the *Strange Gentleman* is not a very common
travelling name, I should imagine ; besides the
hasty note, in which he said he should join you
here.

FANNY.

Well, granted that it is he.   In what a situation
am I placed.   You tell me, for the first time,
that *my* violent intended must on no account be
beheld by *your* violent intended, just now, because
of some old quarrel between them, of long standing, which has never been adjusted to this day.
What an appearance this will have!   How am I
to explain it, or relate your present situation ?   I
should sink into the earth with shame and confusion.

MARY.

Leave it to me.   It arises from my heedlessness.

I will take it all upon myself, and see him alone. But tell me, my dear—as you got up this love affair with so much secrecy and expedition during the four months you spent at Aunt Martha's, I have never yet seen Mr. Tomkins, you know. Is he so very handsome ?

FANNY.

See him, and judge for yourself.

MARY.

Well, I will; and you may retire, till I have paved the way for your appearance. But just assist me first, dear, in making a little noise to attract his attention, if he really be in the next room, or I may wait here all day.

DUET.

At end of which

[*Exit* FANNY, C. DOOR. MARY *retires up* R. H.

Enter STRANGE GENTLEMAN, L. H.

STRANGE GENTLEMAN.

There ; now with a clean shirt in one pocket, and a night-cap in the other, I'm ready to be carried magnanimously to my dungeon in the cause of love.

MARY (*aside*).

He says, he's ready to be carried magnanimously

to a dungeon in the cause of love.   I thought it
was Mr. Tomkins!   Hem! (*coming down* L. H.)

STRANGE GENTLEMAN (*seeing her*).

Hallo!   Who's this!   Not a disguised peace
officer in petticoats.   Beg your pardon, ma'am.
(*Advancing towards her.*)   What—did—you—

MARY.

Oh, Sir; I feel the delicacy of my situation.

STRANGE GENTLEMAN (*aside*).

Feels the delicacy of her situation; Lord bless
us, what's the matter!   Permit me to offer you a
seat, ma'am, if you're in a delicate situation.   (*He
places chairs ; they sit.*)

MARY.

You are very good, Sir.   You are surprised to
see me here, Sir?

STRANGE GENTLEMAN.

No, no, at least not very; rather, perhaps—
rather.   (*Aside.*)   Never was more astonished in
all my life!

MARY (*aside*).

His politeness, and the extraordinary tale I have
to tell him, overpower me.   I must summon up
courage.   Hem!

STRANGE GENTLEMAN.

Hem!

MARY.

Sir!

STRANGE GENTLEMAN.

Ma'am!

MARY.

You have arrived at this house in pursuit of a young lady, if I mistake not?

STRANGE GENTLEMAN.

You are quite right, ma'am. (*Aside.*) Mysterious female!

MARY.

If you *are* the gentleman I'm in search of, you wrote a hasty note a short time since, stating that you would be found here this afternoon.

STRANGE GENTLEMAN (*drawing back his chair*).

I—I—wrote a note, ma'am!

MARY.

You need keep nothing secret from me, Sir. I know all.

STRANGE GENTLEMAN (*aside*).

That villain, Boots, has betrayed me! Know all, ma'am?

MARY.

Every thing.

STRANGE GENTLEMAN (*aside*).

It must be so. She's a constable's wife.

MARY.

You *are* the writer of that letter, Sir ? I think I am not mistaken.

STRANGE GENTLEMAN.

You are not, ma'am; I confess I did write it. What was I to do, ma'am? Consider the situation in which I was placed.

MARY.

In your situation, you had, as it appears to me, only one course to pursue.

STRANGE GENTLEMAN.

You mean the course I adopted ?

MARY.

Undoubtedly.

STRANGE GENTLEMAN.

I am very happy to hear you say so, though of course I should like it to be kept a secret.

MARY.

Oh, of course.

STRANGE GENTLEMAN (*drawing his chair close to her, and speaking very softly*).

Will you allow me to ask you, whether the constables are down stairs ?

MARY (*surprised*).

The constables !

STRANGE GENTLEMAN.

Because if I am to be apprehended, I should like to have it over. I am quite ready, if it must be done.

MARY.

No legal interference has been attempted. There is nothing to prevent your continuing your journey to-night.

STRANGE GENTLEMAN.

But will not the other party follow?

MARY (*looking down*).

The other party, I am compelled to inform you, is detained here by—by want of funds.

STRANGE GENTLEMAN (*starting up*).

Detained here by want of funds! Hurrah! Hurrah! I have caged him at last. I'm revenged for all his blustering and bullying. This is a glorious triumph, ha, ha, ha! I have nailed him —nailed him to the spot!

MARY.

(*Rising indignantly.*) This exulting over a fallen foe, Sir, is mean and pitiful. In my presence, too, it is an additional insult.

STRANGE GENTLEMAN.

Insult! I wouldn't insult you for the world, after the joyful intelligence you have brought me.

—I could hug you in my arms!—One kiss, my little constable's deputy. (*Seizing her.*)

MARY (*struggling with him.*)

Help! help!

Enter JOHN JOHNSON. C. DOOR.

JOHN.

What the devil do I see! (*Seizes* STRANGE GENTLEMAN *by the collar*).

MARY. L. H.

John, and Mr. Tomkins, met together! They 'll kill each other.—Here, help! help!

[*Exit* MARY, *running.* C. DOOR.

JOHN (*shaking him*).

What do you mean by that, scoundrel?

STRANGE GENTLEMAN.

Come, none of your nonsense—there 's no harm done.

JOHN.

No harm done.—How dare you offer to salute that lady?

STRANGE GENTLEMAN.

What did you send her here for?

JOHN.

I send her here!

STRANGE GENTLEMAN.

Yes, *you*; you gave her instructions, I suppose. (*Aside.*) Her husband, the constable, evidently.

JOHN.

That lady, Sir, is attached to me.

STRANGE GENTLEMAN.

Well, I know she is; and a very useful little person she must be, to be attached to any body,— it's a pity she can't be legally sworn in.

JOHN.

Legally sworn in! Sir, that is an insolent reflection upon the temporary embarrassment which prevents our taking the marriage vows. How dare you to insinuate——

STRANGE GENTLEMAN.

Pooh! pooh!—don't talk about daring to insinuate; it doesn't become a man in your station of life——

JOHN.

My station of life!

STRANGE GENTLEMAN.

But as you have managed this matter very quietly, and say you're in temporary embarrassment—here—here's five shillings for you. (*Offers it.*)

JOHN.

Five shillings! (*raises his cane.*)

STRANGE GENTLEMAN (*flourishing a chair*).

Keep off, sir!

Enter MARY, TOM SPARKS, *and* Two *Waiters.*

MARY.

Separate them, or there'll be murder!

TOM *clasps* STRANGE GENTLEMAN *round the waist—the Waiters seize* JOHN JOHNSON.

TOM.

Come, none o' that 'ere, Mr. S. We don't let private rooms for such games as these.—If you want to try it on wery partickler, we don't mind making a ring for you in the yard, but you mustn't do it here.

JOHN.

Let me get at him.   Let me go; waiters—Mary, don't hold me.   I insist on your letting me go.

STRANGE GENTLEMAN.

Hold him fast.—Call yourself a *peace* officer, you prize-fighter!

JOHN (*struggling*).

Let me go, I say!

STRANGE GENTLEMAN.

Hold him fast !   Hold him fast!

[TOM *takes* STRANGE GENTLEMAN *off* R. H. *Waiters take* JOHN *off* L. H., MARY *following.*

SCENE II.—*Another Room in the Inn.*

Enter JULIA DOBBS *and* OVERTON.   L. H.

JULIA.

You seem surprised, Overton.

OVERTON.

Surprised, Miss Dobbs! Well I may be, when, after seeing nothing of you for three years and more, you come down here without any previous notice, for the express purpose of running away— positively running away, with a young man. I am astonished, Miss Dobbs!

JULIA.

You would have had better reason to be astonished if I had come down here with any notion of positively running away with an old one, Overton.

OVERTON.

Old or young, it would matter little to me, if you had not conceived the preposterous idea of entangling me—*me*, an attorney, and mayor of the town, in so ridiculous a scheme.—Miss Dobbs, I can't do it.—I really cannot consent to mix myself up with such an affair.

JULIA.

Very well, Overton, very well. You recollect

that in the lifetime of that poor old dear, Mr. Woolley, who——

OVERTON.

——Who would have married you, if he hadn't died; and who, as it was, left you his property, free from all incumbrances, the incumbrance of himself, as a husband, not being among the least.

JULIA.

Well, you may recollect, that in the poor old dear's life-time, sundry advances of money were made to you, at my persuasion, which still remain unpaid. Oblige me by forwarding them to my agent in the course of the week, and I free you from any inter-ference in this little matter. (*Crosses to* L. H. *and is going.*)

OVERTON.

Stay, Miss Dobbs, stay. As you say, we *are* old acquaintances, and there certainly *were* some small sums of money, which—which——

JULIA.

Which certainly *are* still outstanding.

OVERTON.

Just so, just so ; and which, perhaps, you would be likely to forget, if you had a husband—eh, Miss Dobbs, eh?

JULIA.

I have little doubt that I should. If I gained

9 *

one through your assistance, indeed—I can safely say I should forget all about them.

OVERTON.

My dear Miss Dobbs, we perfectly understand each other.—Pray proceed.

JULIA.

Well—dear Lord Peter——

OVERTON.

That's the young man you 're going to run away with, I presume?

JULIA.

That's the young *nobleman* who's going to run away with me, Mr. Overton.

OVERTON.

Yes, just so.—I beg your pardon—pray go on.

JULIA.

Dear Lord Peter is young and wild, and the fact is, his friends do not consider him very sagacious or strong-minded. To prevent their interference, our marriage is to be a secret one. In fact, he is stopping now at a friend's hunting seat in the neighbourhood ; he is to join me here ; and we are to be married at Gretna.

OVERTON.

Just so.—A matter, as it seems to me, which you can conclude without my interference.

JULIA.

Wait an instant. To avoid suspicion, and prevent our being recognised and followed, I settled with him that you should give out in this house that he was a lunatic, and that I—his aunt—was going to convey him in a chaise, to-night, to a private asylum at Berwick. I have ordered the chaise at half-past one in the morning. You can see him, and make our final arrangements. It will avert all suspicion, if I have no communication with him, till we start. You can say to the people of the house that the sight of me makes him furious.

OVERTON.

Where shall I find him ?—Is he here ?

JULIA.

You know best.

OVERTON.

I!

JULIA.

I desired him, immediately on his arrival, to write you some mysterious nonsense, acquainting you with the number of his room.

OVERTON (*producing a letter*).

Dear me! he has arrived, Miss Dobbs.

JULIA.

No!

OVERTON.

Yes—see here—a most mysterious and extraordinary composition, which was thrown in at my
office window this morning, and which I could make
neither head nor tail of.   Is that his handwriting?
(*giving her the letter.*)

JULIA (*taking letter*).

I never saw it more than once, but I know he
writes very large and straggling.—(*Looks at letter.*)
Ha, ha, ha!   This is capital, isn't it?

OVERTON.

Excellent!—Ha, ha, ha!—So mysterious!

JULIA.

Ha, ha, ha!—So very good.—" Rash act."

OVERTON.

Yes.   Ha, ha!

JULIA.

" Interesting young man."

OVERTON.

Yes.—Very good.

JULIA.

" Amiable youth!"

OVERTON.

Capital!   .

JULIA.

" Solemn warning!"

OVERTON.

Yes.—That's best of all.   (*They both laugh.*)

JULIA.

Number seventeen, he says. See him at once, that's a good creature. (*Returning the letter.*)

OVERTON (*taking letter*).

I will. (*He crosses to* L. H. *and rings a bell.*)

Enter WAITER. L. H.

Who is there in number seventeen, waiter?

WAITER.

Number seventeen, sir? — Oh!—the strange gentleman, sir.

OVERTON.

Show me the room.

[*Exit* WAITER. L. H.

(*Looking at* JULIA, *and pointing to the letter.*) "The Strange Gentleman."—Ha, ha, ha! Very good—very good indeed.—Excellent notion! (*They both laugh.*)

[*Exeunt severally.*

SCENE III.—*Same as the first.—A small table, with wine, dessert, and lights on it,* R. H. *of* C. DOOR ; *two chairs.*

STRANGE GENTLEMAN *discovered seated at table.*

STRANGE GENTLEMAN.

" The other party is detained here, by want of

funds." Ha, ha, ha! I can finish my wine at my leisure, order my gig when I please, and drive on to Brown's in perfect security. I'll drink the other party's good health, and long may he be detained here. (*Fills a glass.*) Ha, ha, ha! The other party; and long may he—(*A knock at* c. DOOR.) Hallo! I hope *this* isn't the other party. Talk of the—(*A knock at* c. DOOR.) Well— (*setting down his glass*)—this is the most extraordinary private room that was ever invented. I am continually disturbed by unaccountable knockings. (*A gentle tap at* c. DOOR.) There's another; that was a gentle rap—a persuasive tap— like a friend's fore-finger on one's coat-sleeve. It *can't* be Tinkles with the gruel.—Come in.

OVERTON *peeping in at* c. DOOR.

OVERTON.

Are you alone, my Lord?

STRANGE GENTLEMAN (*amazed*).

Eh!

OVERTON.

Are you alone, my Lord?

STRANGE GENTLEMAN.

My Lord!

OVERTON (*stepping in, and closing the door*).

You are right, sir, we cannot be too cautious, for we do not know who may be within hearing. You are very right, sir.

STRANGE GENTLEMAN (*rising from table, and coming forward* R. H.).

It strikes me, sir, that you are very wrong.

OVERTON.

Very good, very good; I like this caution; it shows me you are wide awake.

STRANGE GENTLEMAN.

Wide awake!—damme, I begin to think I am fast asleep, and have been for the last two hours.

OVERTON (*whispering*).

I—am—the mayor.

STRANGE GENTLEMAN (*in the same tone*).

Oh!

OVERTON.

This is your letter? (*Shows it;* STRANGE GENTLEMAN *nods assent solemnly.*) It will be necessary for you to leave here to-night, at half-past one o'clock, in a postchaise and four ; and the higher you bribe the postboys to drive at their utmost speed, the better.

STRANGE GENTLEMAN.

You don't say so ?

OVERTON.

I do indeed. You are not safe from pursuit here.

STRANGE GENTLEMAN.

Bless my soul, can such dreadful things happen in a civilized community, Mr. Mayor?

OVERTON.

It certainly does at first sight appear rather a hard case that people cannot marry whom they please, without being hunted down in this way.

STRANGE GENTLEMAN.

To be sure. To be hunted down, and killed as if one was game, you know.

OVERTON.

Certainly ; and you *an't* game, you know.

STRANGE GENTLEMAN.

Of course not. But can't you prevent it ? can't you save me by the interposition of your power ?

OVERTON.

My power can do nothing in such a case.

STRANGE GENTLEMAN.

Can't it though ?

OVERTON.

Nothing whatever.

STRANGE GENTLEMAN.

I never heard of such dreadful revenge, never!

Mr. Mayor, I am a victim, I am the unhappy victim of parental obstinacy.

OVERTON.

Oh, no ; don't say that. You may escape yet.

STRANGE GENTLEMAN (grasping his hand).

Do you think I may? Do you think I may, Mr. Mayor?

OVERTON.

Certainly! certainly! I have little doubt of it, if you manage properly.

STRANGE GENTLEMAN.

I thought I was managing properly. I understood the other party was detained here, by want of funds.

OVERTON.

Want of funds!—There's no want of funds in that quarter, I can tell you.

STRANGE GENTLEMAN.

An't there, though?

OVERTON.

Bless you, no. Three thousand a year!—But who told you there was a want of funds?

STRANGE GENTLEMAN.

Why, she did.

OVERTON.

She! you have seen her then? She told me you had not.

STRANGE GENTLEMAN.

Nonsense ; don't believe her. She was in this very room half an hour ago.

OVERTON.

Then I must have misunderstood her, and you must have misunderstood her too.—But to return to business. Don't you think it would keep up appearances if I had you put under some restraint ?

STRANGE GENTLEMAN.

I think it would. I am very much obliged to you. (*Aside.*) This regard for my character in an utter stranger, and in a Mayor too, is quite affecting.

OVERTON.

I 'll send somebody up, to mount guard over you.

STRANGE GENTLEMAN.

Thank'ee, my dear friend, thank'ee.

OVERTON.

And if you make a little resistance, when we take you up-stairs to your bed-room, or away in the chaise, it will be keeping up the character, you know.

STRANGE GENTLEMAN.

To be sure.—So it will.—I 'll do it.

OVERTON.

Very well, then. I shall see your Lordship

again by and bye.—For the present, my Lord, good evening. (*Going.*)

STRANGE GENTLEMAN.

Lord!—Lordship!—Mr. Mayor!

OVERTON.

Eh?—Oh!—I see. (*Comes forward.*) Practising the lunatic, my Lord. Ah, very good—very vacant look indeed.—Admirable, my Lord, admirable!—I say, my Lord—(*pointing to letter—*) "*Amiable youth!*"—"Interesting young man."—"Strange Gentleman."—Eh? Ha, ha, ha! Knowing trick indeed, my Lord, very!

[*Exit* OVERTON.   C. D.

STRANGE GENTLEMAN.

That mayor is either in the very last stage of mystified intoxication, or in the most hopeless state of incurable insanity.—I have no doubt of it. A little touched here (*tapping his forehead*). Never mind, he is sufficiently sane to understand my business at all events. (*Goes to table and takes a glass.*) Poor fellow!— I'll drink his health, and speedy recovery. (*A knock at* C. DOOR.) It is a most extraordinary thing, now, that every time I propose a toast to myself, some confounded fellow raps at that door, as if he were receiving it with the utmost enthusiasm. Private room!—I might as well be sitting behind the little shutter of a

Two-penny Post Office, where all the letters put in were to be post-paid. (*A knock at* c. DOOR.) Perhaps it's the guard! I shall feel a great deal safer if it is. Come in.

(*He has brought a chair forward, and sits* L. H.)

> *Enter* TOM SPARKS, c. DOOR, *very slowly, with an enormous stick. He closes the door, and, after looking at the* STRANGE GENTLEMAN *very steadily, brings a chair down* L. H., *and sits opposite him.*

STRANGE GENTLEMAN.

Are you sent by the mayor of this place, to mount guard over me?

TOM.

Yes, yes.—It's all right.

STRANGE GENTLEMAN. (*Aside.*)

It's all right—I'm safe. (*To* TOM, *with affected indignation.*) Now mind, I have been insulted by receiving this challenge, and I want to fight the man who gave it me. I protest against being kept here. I denounce this treatment as an outrage.

TOM.

Ay, ay. Any thing you please—poor creature; don't put yourself in a passion. It'll only make you worse. (*Whistles.*)

STRANGE GENTLEMAN.

This is most extraordinary behaviour.—I don't

understand it.—What d'ye mean by behaving in this manner ? (*Rising.*)

TOM. (*Aside.*)

He's a getting wiolent. I must frighten him with a steady look.—I say, young fellow, do you see this here eye ? (*Staring at him, and pointing at his own eye.*)

STRANGE GENTLEMAN. (*Aside.*)

Do I see his eye!—What can he mean by glaring upon me, with that large round optic!—Ha! a terrible light flashes upon me.—He thought I was "Swing" this morning. It was an insane delusion. —That eye is an insane eye.—He's a madman!

TOM.

Madman! Damme, I think he is a madman with a wengeance.

STRANGE GENTLEMAN.

He acknowledges it. He is sensible of his misfortune!—Go away—leave the room instantly, and tell them to send somebody else.—Go away !

TOM.

Oh, you unhappy lunatic !

STRANGE GENTLEMAN.

What a dreadful situation !—I shall be attacked, strangled, smothered, and mangled, by a madman ! Where's the bell ?

TOM (*advancing and brandishing his stick*).

Leave that 'ere bell alone—leave that 'ere bell alone—and come here!

STRANGE GENTLEMAN.

Certainly, Mr. Boots, certainly.—He's going to strangle me. (*Going towards table.*) Let me pour you out a glass of wine, Mr. Boots—pray do! (*Aside.*) If he said "Yes," I'd throw the decanter at his temple.

TOM.

None o' your nonsense.—Sit down there. (*Forces him into a chair.* L. H.) I'll sit here. (*Opposite him.* R. H.) Look me full in the face, and I won't hurt you. Move hand, foot, or eye, and you'll never want to move either of 'em again.

STRANGE GENTLEMAN.

I'm paralysed with terror.

TOM.

Ha! (*raising his stick in a threatening attitude.*)

STRANGE GENTLEMAN.

I'm dumb, Mr. Boots—dumb, sir.

> [*They sit gazing intently on each other;* TOM *with the stick raised, as the Act Drop slowly descends.*

END OF ACT FIRST.

ACT II.

SCENE I.—*The same as* SCENE III., ACT I.

TOM SPARKS discovered in the same attitude watching the STRANGE GENTLEMAN, *who has fallen asleep with his head over the back of his Chair.*

TOM.

He's asleep; poor unhappy wretch! How very mad he looks with his mouth wide open and his eyes shut! (STRANGE GENTLEMAN *snores*.) Ah! there's a wacant snore ; no meaning in it at all. I cou'd ha' told he was out of his senses from the very tone of it. (*He snores again.*) That's a wery insane snore. I should say he was melancholly mad from the sound of it.

Enter, through C. DOOR, OVERTON, MRS. NOAKES, *a Chamber-maid, and Two Waiters ;* MRS. NOAKES *with a warming-pan, the Maid with a light.* STRANGE GENTLEMAN *starts up, greatly exhausted.*

I. 10

TOM (*starting up in* C.).

Hallo!—Hallo! keep quiet, young fellow. Keep quiet!

STRANGE GENTLEMAN.   L. H.

Out of the way, you savage maniac. Mr. Mayor (*crossing to him*, R. H.), the person you sent to keep guard over me is a madman, sir. What do you mean by shutting me up with a madman?—what do you mean, sir, I ask?

OVERTON. R. H. C. (*Aside to* STRANGE GENTLEMAN.)

Bravo! bravo! very good indeed—excellent!

STRANGE GENTLEMAN.

Excellent, sir!—It's horrible!—The bare recollection of what I have endured, makes me shudder, down to my very toe-nails.

MRS. NOAKES.   R. H.

Poor dear!—Mad people always think other people mad.

STRANGE GENTLEMAN.

Poor dear! Ma'am! What the devil do you mean by "Poor dear?" How dare you have a madman here, ma'am, to assault and terrify the visitors to your establishment?

MRS. NOAKES.

Ah! terrify indeed! I'll never have another, to please anybody, you may depend upon that, Mr.

Overton. (*To* STRANGE GENTLEMAN.) There, there.—Don't exert yourself, there's a dear.

STRANGE GENTLEMAN. C.

Exert myself!—Damme! it's a mercy I have any life left to exert myself with. It's a special miracle, ma'am, that my existence has not long ago fallen a sacrifice to that sanguinary monster in the leather smalls.

OVERTON. R. C. (*Aside to* STRANGE GENTLEMAN.)

I never saw any passion more real in my life. Keep it up, it's an admirable joke.

STRANGE GENTLEMAN.

Joke!—joke!—Peril a precious life, and call it a joke,—you, a man with a sleek head and a broadbrimmed hat, who ought to know better, calling it a joke.—Are you mad too, sir,—are you mad? (*Confronting* OVERTON.)

TOM. L. H. (*Very loud.*)

Keep your hands off. Would you murder the wery mayor, himself, you mis-rable being?

STRANGE GENTLEMAN.

Mr. Mayor, I call upon you to issue your warrant for the instant confinement of that one-eyed Orson in some place of security.

OVERTON (*aside, advancing a little*).

He reminds me that he had better be removed to his bed-room. He is right.—Waiters, carry the

gentleman up-stairs.— Boots, you will continue to
watch him in his bed-room.

STRANGE GENTLEMAN.

He continue!—What, am I to be boxed up again
with this infuriated animal, and killed off, when he
has done playing with me?—I won't go—I won't
go—help there, help!

(*The Waiters cross from* R. H. *to behind him.*)

(*Enter* JOHN JOHNSON *hastily.* C. DOOR.)

JOHN (*coming forward* L. H.).

What on earth is the meaning of this dreadful
outcry, which disturbs the whole house?

MRS. NOAKES.

Don't be alarmed, sir, I beg.—They're only
going to carry an unfortunate gentleman, as is out
of his senses, to his bed-room.

STRANGE GENTLEMAN. C. ,(*To* JOHN.)

Constable—constable—do your duty—appre-
hend these persons—every one of them. Do you
hear, officer, do you hear?—(*The Waiters seize
him by the arms.*)—Here—here—you see this.
You've seen the assault committed. Take them
into custody—off with them.

MRS. NOAKES.

Poor creature!—He thinks you are a constable,
sir,

JOHN.

Unfortunate man! It is the second time to-day that he has been the victim of this strange delusion.

STRANGE GENTLEMAN (*breaking from Waiters and going to* JOHN). L. H.

Unfortunate man!—What, do *you* think I am mad?

JOHN.

Poor fellow! His hopeless condition is pitiable indeed. (*Goes up.*)

STRANGE GENTLEMAN (*returning to* C.).

They 're all mad!—Every one of 'em!

MRS. NOAKES.

Come now, come to bed—there's a dear young man, do.

STRANGE GENTLEMAN.

Who are you, you shameless old ghost, standing there before company, with a large warming-pan, and asking me to come to bed?—Are *you* mad?

MRS. NOAKES.

Oh! he's getting shocking now. Take him away.—Take him away.

OVERTON.

Ah, you had better remove him to his bed-room at once.

(*The Waiters take him up by the feet and shoulders.*)

STRANGE GENTLEMAN.

Mind, if I survive this, I 'll bring an action of false imprisonment against every one of you. Mark my words—especially against that villanous old mayor.—Mind, I 'll do it!

(*They bear him off, struggling and talking—the others crowding round, and assisting.*)

OVERTON (*following*).

How well he does it !   [*Exeunt* L. H. 1st E.

Enter a Waiter, showing in CHARLES TOMKINS *in a travelling coat.* C. DOOR.

WAITER.   L. H.

This room is disengaged now, sir. There *was* a gentleman in it, but he has just left it.

CHARLES.

Very well, this will do. I may want a bed here to-night, perhaps, waiter.

WAITER.

Yes, sir.—Shall I take your card to the bar, sir?

CHARLES.

My card !—No, never mind.

WAITER.

No name, sir?

CHARLES.

No—it doesn't matter.

WAITER (*aside, as going out*).
Another Strange Gentleman!

[*Exit* WAITER. C. DOOR.

CHARLES.

Ah !—(*Takes off coat.*)—The sun and dust on this long ride have been almost suffocating. I wonder whether Fanny has arrived ? If she has —the sooner we start forward on our journey further North the better. Let me see ; she would be accompanied by her sister, she said in her note —and they would both be on the look-out for me. Then the best thing I can do is to ask no questions, for the present at all events, and to be on the look-out for them. (*Looking towards* C. DOOR.) Why here she comes, walking slowly down the long passage, straight towards this room—she can't have seen me yet.—Poor girl, how melancholy she looks! I'll keep in the back ground for an instant, and give her a joyful surprise. (*He goes up* R. H.)

Enter FANNY. C. DOOR.

FANNY. L. H.

Was ever unhappy girl placed in so dreadful a situation!—Friendless, and almost alone, in a strange place—my dear, dear Charles a victim to an attack of mental derangement, and I unable to avow my interest in him, or express my anxious sympathy and solicitude for his sufferings! I cannot bear this dreadful torture of agonising suspense. I must and will see him, let the cost be what it may. (*She is going* L. H.)

CHARLES (*coming forward* R. H.).

Hist! Fanny!

FANNY (*starting, and repressing a scream*).

Ch—Charles—here in this room!

CHARLES.

Bodily present, my dear, in this very room. My darling Fanny, let me strain you to my bosom. (*Advancing.*)

FANNY (*shrinking back*).

N—n—no, dearest Charles, no, not now.— (*Aside.*)—How flushed he is!

CHARLES.

No!—Fanny, this cold reception is a very different one to what I looked forward to meeting with, from you.

FANNY (*advancing, and offering the tip of her finger*).

N—n—no—not cold, Charles ; not cold. I do not mean it to be so, indeed.—How is your head, now, dear ?

CHARLES.

How is my head! After days and weeks of suspense and anxiety, when half our dangerous journey is gained, and I meet you here, to bear you whither you can be made mine for life, you greet me with the tip of your longest finger, and inquire after my head.—Fanny, what can you mean?

CENTER: FANNY.

You—you have startled me rather, Charles.—I thought you had gone to bed.

CENTER: CHARLES.

Gone to bed!—Why 1 have but this moment arrived.

CENTER: FANNY (*aside*).

Poor, poor Charles!

CENTER: CHARLES.

Miss Wilson, what am I to—

CENTER: FANNY.

No, no; pray, pray, do not suffer yourself to be excited—

CENTER: CHARLES.

Suffer myself to be excited!—Can I possibly avoid it? can I do aught but wonder at this extraordinary and sudden change in your whole demeanour?—Excited! But five minutes since, I arrived here, brimful of the hope and expectation which had buoyed up my spirits during my long journey. 1 find you cold, reserved, and embarrassed —everything but what 1 expected to find you— and then you tell me not to be excited.

FANNY (*aside*).

He is wandering again.   The fever is evidently upon him.

CHARLES.

This altered manner and ill-disguised confusion all convince me of what you would fain conceal. Miss Wilson, you repent of your former determination, and love another!

FANNY.

Poor fellow!

CHARLES.

Poor fellow!—What, am I pitied?

FANNY.

Oh, Charles, do not give way to this.   Consider how much depends upon your being composed.

CHARLES.

I see how much depends upon my being composed, ma'am — well, very well. — A husband depends upon it, ma'am.   Your new lover is in this house, and if he overhears my reproaches he will become suspicious of the woman who has jilted *another*, and may jilt *him*.   That's it, madam—a great deal depends, as you say, upon my being composed.—A great deal, ma'am.

FANNY.

Alas! these are indeed the ravings of frenzy!

CHARLES.

Upon my word, ma'am, you must form a very modest estimate of your own power, if you imagine that disappointment has impaired my senses. Ha, ha, ha!—I am delighted. I am delighted to have escaped you, ma'am. I am glad, ma'am—damn'd glad! (*Kicks a chair over.*)

FANNY (*aside*).

I must call for assistance. He grows more incoherent and furious every instant.

CHARLES.

I leave you, ma'am.—I am unwilling to interrupt the tender *tête-à-tête* with the other gentleman, to which you are, no doubt, anxiously looking forward. —To you I have no more to say. To *him* I must beg to offer a few rather unexpected congratulations on his approaching marriage.

[*Exit* CHARLES *hastily*. C. DOOR.

FANNY.

Alas! it is but too true. His senses have entirely left him.

[*Exit* L. H.

Scene Second and Last. —*A Gallery in the Inn, leading to the Bed-rooms. Four Doors in the Flat, and one at each of the upper Entrances, numbered from 20 to 25, beginning at the* R. H. *A pair of boots at the door of* 23.

Enter Chamber-maid *with two lights; and* Charles Tomkins. R. H. 1*st* E.

MAID.

This is your room, sir, No. 21. (*Opening the door.*)

CHARLES.

Very well. Call me at seven in the morning.

MAID.

Yes, sir. (*Gives him a light, and*

[*Exit* Chamber-maid. R. H. 1*st* E.

CHARLES.

And at nine, if I can previously obtain a few words of explanation with this unknown rival, I will just return to the place from whence I came, in the same coach that brought me down here. I wonder who he is and where he sleeps. (*Looking round.*) I have a lurking suspicion of those boots (*pointing to No.* 23). They are an ill-looking, underhanded sort of pair, and an undefinable instinct tells me that they have clothed the feet of the

rascal I am in search of.   Besides myself, the
owner of those ugly articles is the only person who
has yet come up to bed.   I will keep my eyes open
for half an hour or so ; and my ears to.

[*Exit* CHARLES *into No.* 21.

Enter R. H. 1*st* E. MRS. NOAKES *with two lights,*
followed by MARY *and* FANNY.

MRS. NOAKES.

Take care of the last step, ladies.   This way,
ma'am, if you please.   No. 20 is your room,
ladies: nice large double-bedded room, with coals
and a rushlight.

FANNY.   R. H.   (*Aside to* MARY.)

I must ask which is his room.   I cannot rest
unless I know he has at length sunk into the slumber
he so much needs.   (*Crosses to* MRS. NOAKES,
who is L. H.)   Which is the room in which the
Strange Gentleman sleeps ?

MRS. NOAKES.

No. 23, ma'am.   There's his boots outside the
door.   Don't be frightened of him, ladies.   He's
very quiet now, and our Boots is a watching him.

FANNY.

Oh, no—we are not afraid of him.   (*Aside.*)
Poor Charles!

MRS. NOAKES (*going to door No.* 20, *which is 3rd* E. R. H.).

This way, if you please; you'll find every thing very comfortable, and there's a bell-rope at the head of the bed, if you want anything in the morning. Good night, ladies.

As MARY *and* FANNY *pass* MRS. NOAKES, FANNY *takes a light*

[*Exeunt* FANNY *and* MARY *into No.* 20.

MRS. NOAKES (*tapping at No.* 23).

Tom—Tom—

Enter TOM *from No.* 23.

TOM (*coming forward,* L. H.).

Is that you, missis?

MRS. NOAKES.   R. H.

Yes.—How's the Strange Gentleman, Tom?

TOM.

He vas wery boisterous half an hour ago, but I punched his head a little, and now he's uncommon comfortable. He's fallen asleep, but his snores is still wery incoherent.

MRS. NOAKES.

Mind you take care of him, Tom. They'll take him away in half an hour's time. It's very nearly one o'clock now.

TOM.

I 'll pay ev'ry possible attention to him. If he offers to call out, I shall whop him again.

[*Exit* TOM *into No.* 23.

MRS. NOAKES (*looking off* R. H.).

This way, ma'am, if you please. Up these stairs.

Enter JULIA DOBBS *with a light.* R. H. 1*st* E.

JULIA.

Which did you say was the room in which I could arrange my dress for travelling?

MRS. NOAKES.

No. 22, ma'am ; the next room to your nephew's. Poor dear—he 's fallen asleep, ma'am, and I dare say you 'll be able to take him away very quietly by and bye.

JULIA (*aside*).

Not so quietly as you imagine, if he plays his part half as well as Overton reports he does. (*To* MRS. NOAKES.) Thank you.—For the present, good night.

[*Exit* JULIA *into No.* 22.

MRS. NOAKES.

Wish you good night, ma'am. There.—Now I think I may go down-stairs again, and see if Mr. Overton wants any more negus. Why who 's this?

(*Looking off* R. H.) Oh, I forgot—No. 24 an't
a-bed yet.—It's him.

(*Enter* JOHN JOHNSON *with a light*, R. H. 1*st* E.)

MRS. NOAKES.

No. 24, sir, if you please.

JOHN.

Yes, yes, I know. The same room I slept in
last night. (*Crossing* L. H.)

MRS. NOAKES.

Yes, sir.—Wish you good night, sir.

[*Exit* MRS. NOAKES. R. II 1*st* E.

JOHN.

Good night, ma'am. The same room I slept in
last night, indeed, and the same room I may sleep
in to-morrow night, and the next night, and the
night after that, and just as many more nights as I
can get credit here, unless this remittance arrives.
I could raise the money to prosecute my journey
without difficulty were I on the spot; but my confounded thoughtless liberality to the post-boys has
left me absolutely penniless. Well, we shall see
what to-morrow brings forth. (*He goes into No.*
24, *but immediately returns and places his boots
outside his room door, leaving it ajar.*)

[*Exit* JOHN *into No.* 24.

CHARLES *peeping from No. 21, and putting out his boots.*

CHARLES.

There's another pair of boots. Now I wonder which of these two fellows is the man. I can't help thinking it's No. 23.—Hallo ! (*He goes in and closes his door.*)

The door of No. 20 opens; FANNY comes out with a light in a night shade. No. 23 opens. She retires into No. 20.

Enter TOM SPARKS, with a stable lantern from No. 23.

TOM (*closing the door gently*).
Fast asleep still. I may as vell go my rounds, and glean for the deputy. (*Pulls out a piece of chalk from his pocket, and takes up boots from No. 23.*) Twenty-three. It's difficult to tell what a fellow is ven he han't got his senses, but I think this here twenty-three's a timorious faint-hearted genus. (*Examines the boots.*) You want new soleing, No. 23. (*Goes to No. 24, takes up boots and looks at them.*) Hallo ! here's a bust: and there's been a piece put on in the corner.—I must let my missis know. The bill's always doubtful ven there's any mending. (*Goes to No. 21, takes up boots.*) French calf Vellingtons. —All's right here. These here French calves always comes it strong—light vines, and all that

'ere. (*Looking round.*) Werry happy to see there an't no high-lows—they never drinks nothing but gin and vater. Them and the cloth boots is the vurst customers an inn has.—The cloth boots is always obstemious, only drinks sherry vine and vater, and never eats no suppers. (*He chalks the No. of the room on each pair of boots as he takes them up.*) Lucky for you, my French calves, that you an't done with the patent polish, or you 'd ha' been witrioled in no time. I don't like to put oil o' witriol on a well-made pair of boots ; but ven they 're rubbed vith that 'ere polish, it must be done, or the profession 's ruined.

[*Exit* TOM *with boots,* R. H. 1*st* E.

Enter FANNY *from No. 20, with light as before.*

FANNY.

I tremble at the idea of going into his room, but surely at a moment like this, when he is left to be attended by rude and uninterested strangers, the strict rules of propriety which regulate our ordinary proceedings may be dispensed with. I will but satisfy myself that he sleeps, and has those comforts which his melancholy situation demands, and return immediately. (*Goes to No. 23, and knocks.*)

CHARLES TOMKINS *peeping from No* 21.

CHARLES.

I 'll swear I heard a knock.—A woman! Fanny

Wilson—and at that door at this hour of the night!

(FANNY *comes forward.*)

Why what an ass I must have been ever to have loved that girl.—It *is* No. 23, though.—I 'll throttle him presently.   The next room-door open—I 'll watch there.   (*He crosses to No. 24, and goes in.*)

FANNY *returns to No.* 23, *and knocks—the door opens and the* STRANGE GENTLEMAN *appears, night-cap on his head and a light in his hand. —*FANNY *screams and runs back into No.* 20.

STRANGE GENTLEMAN (*coming forward.*)

Well, of all the wonderful and extraordinary houses that ever did exist, this particular tenement is the most extraordinary.   I 've got rid of the madman at last—and it 's almost time for that vile old mayor to remove me.   But where ?—I 'm lost, bewildered, confused, and actually begin to think I am mad.   Half these things I 've seen to-day must be visions of fancy—they never could have really happened.   No, no, I 'm clearly mad !—I 've not the least doubt of it now.   I 've caught it from that horrid Boots.   He has inoculated the whole establishment.   We 're all mad together.—(*Looking off* R. H.)   Lights coming up stairs !—Some more lunatics.

[*Exit* STRANGE GENTLEMAN *in No.* 23.

11 *

Enter R. H. 1*st* E. OVERTON *with a cloak*, MRS.
NOAKES, TOM SPARKS *with lantern, and*
Three Waiters with lights. The Waiters
range up R. H. *side.* TOM *is in* R. H. *corner*
and MRS. NOAKES *next to him.*

OVERTON.

Remain there till I call for your assistance
(*Goes up to No.* 23 *and knocks.*)

Enter STRANGE GENTLEMAN *from No.* 23.

Now, the chaise is ready.—Muffle yourself up in
this cloak. (*Puts it on the* STRANGE GENTLEMAN.
—*They come forward.*)

STRANGE GENTLEMAN.   L. H.

Yes.

OVERTON.   C.

Make a little noise when we take you away, you
know.

STRANGE GENTLEMAN.

Yes—yes.—I say, what a queer room this is of
mine.   Somebody has been tapping at the wall for
the last half hour, like a whole forest of wood-
peckers.

OVERTON.

Don't you know who that was ?

STRANGE GENTLEMAN.

No.

OVERTON.

The other party.

STRANGE GENTLEMAN (*alarmed*).

The other party!

OVERTON.

To be sure.—The other party is going with you.

STRANGE GENTLEMAN.

Going with me!—In the same chaise!

OVERTON.

Of course.—Hush! (*Goes to No.* 22. *Knocks.*)

Enter JULIA DOBBS *from No.* 22, *wrapped up in a large cloak.*

Look here! (*Bringing her forward.* JULIA *is next to* MRS. NOAKES.)

STRANGE GENTLEMAN (*starting into* L. H. *corner*).

I won't go—I won't go. This is a plot—a conspiracy. I won't go, I tell you. I shall be assassinated.—I shall be murdered!

FANNY *and* MARY *appear at No.* 20, JOHNSON *and* TOMKINS *at* 24.

JOHN (*at the door*).

I told you he was mad.

CHARLES (*at the door*).

I see—I see—poor fellow!

JULIA (*crossing to* STRANGE GENTLEMAN *and taking his arm*).

Come, dear, come.

MRS. NOAKES.

Yes, do go, there's a good soul.   Go with your affectionate aunt.

STRANGE GENTLEMAN (*breaking from her*).

My affectionate aunt!

JULIA *returns to her former position.*

TOM.

He don't deserve no affection.   I niver see such an un-fectionate fellow to his relations.

STRANGE GENTLEMAN.   L. H.

Take that wretch away, and   smother him between two feather beds.   Take him away, and make a sandwich of him directly.

JULIA (*to* OVERTON, *who is in* C.).

What voice was that?—It was not Lord Peter's. (*Throwing off her cloak.*)

OVERTON.

Nonsense — nonsense. — Look   at him.   (*Pulls cloak off* STRANGE GENTLEMAN.)

STRANGE GENTLEMAN . (*turning round*).

A woman!

JULIA.

A stranger!

OVERTON.

A stranger!   What, an't he your husband that is to—your mad nephew, I mean?

JULIA.

No!

ALL.

No!

STRANGE GENTLEMAN.

No!—no, I 'll be damned if I am. I an't any-body's nephew.—My aunt 's dead, and I never had an uncle.

MRS. NOAKES.

And an't he mad, ma'am?

JULIA.

No.

STRANGE GENTLEMAN.

Oh, I 'm *not* mad.—I was mistaken just now.

OVERTON.

And isn't he going away with you?

JULIA.

No.

MARY (*coming forward* R. H., *next to* MRS. NOAKES).

And isn't his name Tomkins?

STRANGE GENTLEMAN (*very loud*).

No!

(*All these questions and answers should be very rapid.* JOHNSON *and* TOMKINS *advance to the ladies, and they all retire up.*)

MRS. NOAKES.

What *is* his name? (*Producing a letter.*) It

an't Mr. Walker Trott, is it? (*She advances a little towards him.*)

STRANGE GENTLEMAN.

Something so remarkably like it, ma'am, that, with your permission, I'll open that epistle. (*Taking letter.*)

All go up, but JULIA *and* STRANGE GENTLEMAN.

(*Opening letter.*) Tinkle's hand. (*Reads.*) " The challenge was a *ruse*. By this time I shall have been united at Gretna Green to the charming Emily Brown."—Then, through a horror of duels, I have lost a wife !

JULIA (R. H. *with her handkerchief to her eyes*).

And through Lord Peter's negligence, I have lost a husband!

STRANGE GENTLEMAN.

Eh! (*Regards her a moment, then beckons* OVERTON, *who comes forward*, L. H.) I say, didn't you say something about three thousand a year this morning ?

OVERTON.

I did.

STRANGE GENTLEMAN.

You alluded to that party ? (*Nodding towards* JULIA.)

OVERTON.

I did.

STRANGE GENTLEMAN.

Hem! (*Puts* OVERTON *back.*) Permit me, ma'am (*going to her*), to sympathize most respectfully with your deep distress.

JULIA.

Oh, sir! your kindness penetrates to my very heart.

STRANGE GENTLEMAN (*aside*).

Penetrates to her heart!—It's taking the right direction.—If I understand your sorrowing murmur, ma'am, you contemplated taking a destined husband away with you, in the chaise at the door?

JULIA.

Oh! sir,—spare my feelings—I did.—The horses were ordered and paid for ; and everything was ready. (*Weeps.*)

STRANGE GENTLEMAN (*aside*).

She weeps.——Expensive thing, posting, ma'am.

JULIA.

Very, sir.

STRANGE GENTLEMAN.

Eighteen-pence a mile, ma'am, not including the boys.

JULIA.

Yes, sir.

STRANGE GENTLEMAN.

You've lost a husband, ma'am—*I* have lost a wife.—Marriages are made above—I'm quite certain ours is booked.—Pity to have all this expense for nothing—let 's go together.

JULIA (*drying her eyes*).

The suddenness of this proposal, sir—

STRANGE GENTLEMAN.

Requires a sudden answer, ma'am.—You don't say no—you mean yes. Permit me to—(*kisses her*).—All right! Old one, (*to* OVERTON, *who comes down* L. H.) I've done it.—Mrs. Noakes, (*she comes down* R. H.) don't countermand the chaise.—We 're off directly.

CHARLES (*who with* FANNY *comes down* L. H. C.).

So are we.

JOHN (*who with* MARY *comes down* R. H. C.).

So are we, thanks to a negotiated loan, and an explanation as hasty as the quarrel that gave rise to it.

STRANGE GENTLEMAN.

Three post-chaises and four, on to Gretna, directly.

[*Exeunt* WAITERS. R. H. 1*st* E.

I say—we 'll stop here as we come back?

JOHN *and* CHARLES.

Certainly.

STRANGE GENTLEMAN.

But before I go, as I fear I have given a great deal of trouble here to-night—permit me to inquire whether you will view my mistakes and perils with an indulgent eye, and consent to receive " *The Strange Gentleman* " again to-morrow.

JOHN. JULIA. STRANGE GENTLEMAN.

MARY. FANNY.

MRS. NOAKES. CHARLES.

TOM. OVERTON.

R. H. L. H.

CURTAIN.

THE END.

SECOND ACT, THIRTY MINUTES.

THE
VILLAGE COQUETTES.

[*The Village Coquettes: A Comic Opera. In Two Acts. By Charles Dickens. The Music by John Hullah. London: Richard Bentley, New Burlington Street,* 1836.]

DEDICATION.

To J. P. HARLEY, ESQ.

MY DEAR SIR,

My dramatic bantlings are no sooner born, than you father them. You have made my " Strange Gentleman " exclusively your own; you have adopted Martin Stokes with equal readiness; and you still profess your willingness to do the same kind office for all future scions of the same stock.

I dedicate to you the first play I ever published; and you made for me the first play I ever produced:—the balance is in your favour, and I am afraid it will remain so.

That you may long contribute to the amusement of the public, and long be spared to shed a lustre, by the honour and integrity of your private life, on the profession which for many years you have done so much to uphold, is the sincere and earnest wish of, my dear Sir,

Yours most faithfully,

CHARLES DICKENS.

December 15th, 1836.

PREFACE.

"Either the Honourable Gentleman is in the right, or he is not," is a phrase in very common use within the walls of Parliament. This drama may have a plot, or it may not; and the songs may be poetry, or they may not; and the whole affair, from beginning to end, may be great nonsense, or it may not, just as the honourable gentleman or lady who reads it may happen to think. So, retaining his own private and particular opinion upon the subject, (an opinion which he formed upwards of a year ago, when he wrote the piece,) the Author leaves every such gentleman or lady, to form his or hers, as he or she may think proper, without saying one word to influence or conciliate them.

All he wishes to say is this ;—that he hopes Mr. Braham, and all the performers who assisted in the representation of this opera, will accept his warmest thanks for the interest they evinced in it,

I.   12

from its very first rehearsal, and for their zealous efforts in his behalf—·efforts which have crowned it with a degree of success far exceeding his most sanguine anticipations; and of which no form of words could speak his acknowledgment.

It is needless to add that the *libretto* of an opera must be, to a certain extent, a mere vehicle for the music; and that it is scarcely fair or reasonable to judge it by those strict rules of criticism which would be justly applicable to a five-act tragedy, or a finished comedy.

DRAMATIS PERSONÆ.

SQUIRE NORTON, ...	MR. BRAHAM.
THE HON. SPARKINS FLAM (*his friend*),	MR. FORESTER.
OLD BENSON (*a small farmer*), . .	MR. STRICKLAND.
MR. MARTIN STOKES (*a very small farmer with a very large circle of particular friends*)	MR. HARLEY.
GEORGE EDMUNDS (*betrothed to Lucy*),	MR. BENNETT.
YOUNG BENSON, ...	MR. J. PARRY.
JOHN MADDOX (*attached to Rose*), .	MR. GARDNER.
LUCY BENSON, ...	MISS RAINFORTH.
ROSE (*her cousin*), ...	MISS J. SMITH.

Time occupied in Representation—Two hours and a half.

Period—The Autumn of 1729.

Scene—An English Village.

The Passages marked with inverted commas were omitted in the representation.

12 *

THE VILLAGE COQUETTES.

ACT I.

SCENE I.—*A Rick-yard, with a cart laden with corn-sheaves. JOHN MADDOX, and labourers, unloading it. Implements of husbandry, &c. lie scattered about. A gate on one side. JOHN MADDOX is in the cart, and dismounts at the conclusion of the Chorus.*

ROUND.

Hail to the merry Autumn days, when yellow corn-
    fields shine,
Far brighter than the costly cup that holds the
    monarch's wine!
Hail to the merry harvest time, the gayest of the
    year,
The time of rich and bounteous crops, rejoicing,
    and good cheer!
'Tis pleasant on a fine Spring morn to see the
    buds expand,
'Tis pleasant in the Summer time to view the
    teeming land ;

'Tis pleasant on a Winter's night to crouch
  around the blaze,—
But what are joys like these, my boys, to Autumn's
  merry days!
Then hail to merry Autumn days, when yellow
  corn-fields shine,
Far brighter than the costly cup that holds the
  monarch's wine!
And hail to merry harvest time, the gayest of the
  year,
The time of rich and bounteous crops, rejoicing,
  and good cheer!

JOHN.

Well done, my lads; a good day's work, and a
warm one. Here, Tom, (*to* VILLAGER,) run into
the house, and ask Miss Rose to send out some beer
for the men, and a jug for Master Maddox; and
d'ye hear, Tom, tell Miss Rose it's a fine evening,
and that if she'll step out herself, it'll do her good,
and do me good into the bargain. (*Exit* VILLAGER.)
That's right, my lads, stow these sheaves away,
before the sun goes down. Let's begin fresh in
the morning, without any leavings of to-day. By
this time to-morrow the last load will have been
carried, and then for our Harvest-Home!

VILLAGERS.

Hurrah! Hurrah!
    (*First four lines of Round repeated.*)

Enter MARTIN STOKES.

MARTIN.

Very good! very good, indeed!—always sing while you work—capital custom! I always do when I work, and I never work at all when I can help it;—another capital custom. John, old fellow, how are you?—give us your hand,—hearty squeeze,—good shake,—capital custom number three. Fine dry weather for the harvest, John. Talking of that, I'm dry too: you always give away plenty of beer, here;—capital custom number four. Trouble you for the loan of that can, John.

JOHN (*taking it from the cart*).

Here's the can, but as to there being anything good in it it's as dry as the weather, and as empty as you. Hoo! hoo! (*laughing boisterously, is suddenly checked by a look from* MARTIN).

MARTIN.

Hallo, John, hallo! I have often told you before, Mr. Maddox, that I don't consider you in a situation of life which entitles you to make jokes, far less to laugh at 'em. If you must make a joke, do it solemnly, and respectfully. If *I* laugh, that's quite enough, and it must be far more gratifying to your feelings than any contortions of that enormous mouth of yours.

JOHN.

Well, perhaps, as you say, I oughtn't to make jokes till I arrive, like you, at the dignity of a small piece of ground and a cottage; but I must laugh at a joke, sometimes.

MARTIN.

Must, must you !—Rather presuming fellow, this Maddox. (*Aside.*)

JOHN.

Why, when you make one of them rum jokes of yours,—'cod, I must laugh then!

MARTIN.

Oh! ah! you may laugh then, John ; always laugh at my jokes,—capital custom number five; no harm in that, because you can't help it, you know.—Knowing fellow, though. (*Aside.*)

JOHN.

Remember that joke about the old cow, as you made five years ago?—'cod, that was a joke! Hoo! hoo ! hoo!—I never shall forget that joke. I never see a cow, to this day, without laughing.

MARTIN.

Ha! ha! ha ! very good, very good !—Devilish clever fellow this! (*Aside.*) Well, Jack, you behave yourself well, all the evening, and perhaps I may make that joke again before the day's out.

JOHN.

Thank 'ee, that's very kind.

MARTIN.

Don't mention it, don't mention it; but I say, John, I called to speak to you about more important matters.—Something wrong here, an't there?

(*Mysteriously.*)

JOHN.

Wrong! you're always fancying something wrong.

MARTIN.

Fancying,—come, I like that. I say, why don't you keep your harvest-home at home, to-morrow night? Why are we all to go up to the Squire's, as if we couldn't be merry in Benson's barn. And why is the Squire always coming down here, looking after some people, and cutting out other people?—an't that wrong? Where's George Edmunds—old Benson's so fond of, and that Lucy *was* fond of too, once upon a time,—eh? An't that wrong? Where's your sweetheart, Rose?—An't her walkings, and gigglings, and whisperings, and simperings, with the Squire's friend, Mr. Sparkins Flam, the talk of the whole place? Nothing wrong there,—eh? (*Maddox goes up.*) Had him there; I knew there was something wrong. I'll keep a sharp eye upon these doings, for I don't like these new-fangled customs. It was

all very well in the old time, to see the Squire's
father come riding among the people on his bay
cob, nodding to the common folks, shaking hands
with me, and all that sort of thing; but when you
change the old country-gentleman into a dashing
fop from London, and the steady old steward into
Mr. Sparkins Flam, the case is very different. We
shall see,—but if I might tell Miss Lucy Benson a
bit of my mind, I should say, " Stick to an independent young fellow, like George Edmunds, and
depend upon it you will be happier than you would
with all the show and glitter of a squire's lady."
And I should say to Rose, very solemn,
" Rose—"

(*Rose enters unperceived, with beer.*)
" Rose—"

ROSE (*starting*).

Lord bless us!—What a hollow voice!—Why,
it's Mr. Stokes!—What on earth is the matter
with him ?

MARTIN (*not seeing her*).

Rose,—if you would be happy and contented, if
you would escape destruction, shield yourself from
dangerous peril, and save yourself from horrid
ruin!—

ROSE.

What dreadful words!—

MARTIN.

You will at once, and without delay, bestow your hand on John Maddox; or if you would aspire to a higher rank in life, and a loftier station in society, you will cultivate the affections of Mr. Stokes,—Mr. Martin Stokes,—a young gentleman of great mental attractions, and very considerable personal charms;—leaving the false and fatal Flam to the ignominious fate which——

ROSE.

Why, Mr. Stokes.——

MARTIN.

Ignominious fate which——

ROSE.

Dear, he must be in a fit!   Mr. Stokes!

MARTIN.

Eh?—Ah! Miss Rose,—It's you, is it?

ROSE.

Me! Yes, and here have I been waiting all this time, while you were talking nonsense to yourself. Here, I have brought you some beer.

MARTIN.

Oh! Miss Rose, if you go on in this way, you'll bring us to our bier, instead of bringing our beer to us. (*Looking round.*)   You may laugh, if you want to, very much, John.

JOHN.

Hoo! hoo! hoo!

ROSE.

Be quiet, oaf! And pray, sir, (*to* MARTIN) to what may your most humorous observation refer?

MARTIN.

Why, my dear Miss Rose, you know my way,—always friendly,—always thinking of the welfare of those I like best, and very seldom receiving any gratitude in return.

ROSE.

I know you very seldom deserve any.

MARTIN.

Ah! that's exactly my meaning; that's the way, you see. The moment I begin to throw out a hint to one of my dear friends, out comes some unkind and rude remark. But I bear it all for their sakes. I won't allow you to raise my ill nature,—you shan't stop me. I was going to say,—don't you think—now *don't* you think—that you—don't be angry—make rather—don't colour up,—*rather* too free with Mr. Sparkins Flam?

ROSE.

I make free with Mr. Sparkins Flam! Why you odious, insolent creature!

MARTIN.

Ah, of course—always the way—I told you so—I knew you'd say that.

ROSE.

And you, John, you mean-spirited scarecrow;
will you stand there, and see me insulted by an
officious, impertinent—

MARTIN.

Go on, go on! (*A gun fired.*) Hallo! (*Looking
off.*) Here they are, the Squire and Mr. Sparkins
Flam.

ROSE (*hastily adjusting her dress*).

My goodness! Mr. Spar——run, John, run,
there's a dear!

JOHN (*not moving*).

Very dear, I dare say.

ROSE.

Run, and tell my uncle and Lucy, that Mr.
Spar—— I mean that the Squire's coming.

JOHN.

I wouldn't ha' gone any how; but nobody need
go now, for here they are. Now, I'm extinguished
for the rest of the day.

(*Enter through the gate* SQUIRE NORTON *and* MR.
SPARKINS FLAM, *dressed for sporting, with
guns, &c. and two gamekeepers. On the other
side, old* BENSON *and* LUCY. MARTIN, *during
the whole scene, thrusts himself in the* SQUIRE'S
way, to be taken notice of.)

SQUIRE (*to gamekeeper, and putting down his gun*).

Take the birds into the house. Benson, we have
had a good day's sport, but a tiring one; and as
the load is heavy for my fellows, you'll let our
game remain where it is. I could not offer it to a
better friend.

BENSON.

Your honour's very good, but—

SQUIRE.

Nay, you make a merit of receiving the smallest
favour.

BENSON.

Not a merit of receiving, nor a boast of refusing
it; but a man in humble station should be cautious
how he receives favours from those above him,
which he never asks, and can never return. I have
had too many such favours forced upon me by your
honour, lately, and would rather not increase the
number.

SQUIRE.

But such a trifle—

BENSON.

A trifle from an equal, but a condescension from
a superior. Let your men carry your birds up to
the Hall, sir, or, if they are tired, mine shall do it
for them, and welcome. (*Retires up.*)

FLAM (*aside*).

Swine and independence! Leather breeches and liberty!

SQUIRE.

At least I may be permitted to leave a few brace, as a present to the ladies. Lucy, I hope, will not object. (*Crosses to her.*)

LUCY.

I feel much flattered by your honour's politeness —and—and—and—

ROSE.

My cousin means to say, sir, that we 're very much obliged to your honour and Mr. Flam for your politeness, and that we are very willing to accept of anything, your honour.

FLAM (*aside*).

Condescending little savage!

SQUIRE.

You have spoken well, both for yourself and your cousin. Flam, this is Rose—the pretty little Rose, you know.

FLAM.

Know! can I ever forget the charming Rose —the beautiful—the—the—(*aside*) the Cabbage Rose!

SQUIRE (*aside*).

Keep that girl engaged, while I talk to the other one,

ROSE.

Oh, Mr. Flam!

FLAM.

Oh, Miss Rose!   (*He salutes her.*)

BENSON.

Your honour will not object to taste our ale, after your day's sport.   The afternoon is fresh and cool, and 'twill be pleasant here in the air.   Here, Ben, Thomas, bring mugs here—quick—quick—and a seat for his honour.

(*Exeunt* BENSON, MADDOX, &c.)

SQUIRE.

It will be delightful—won't it, Flam?

FLAM.

Inexpressibly charming!   (*Aside.*) An amateur tea-garden.   (*He retires a little up with* ROSE—*she coquetting.*)

SQUIRE (*to* LUCY).

And in such society, how much the pleasure will be enhanced!

LUCY.

Your honour knows I ought not to listen to you —George Edmunds would—

SQUIRE.

Edmunds!   a rustic!—you cannot love that Edmunds, Lucy.   Forget him—remember your own worth.

LUCY.

I wish I could, sir. My heart will tell me though, weak and silly as I am, that I cannot better show the consciousness of my own worth, than by remaining true to my first and early love. Your Honour rouses my foolish pride; but real true love is not to be forgotten easily.

Song.—LUCY.

Love is not a feeling to pass away,
Like the balmy breath of a summer day;
It is not—it cannot be—laid aside;
It is not a thing to forget or hide.
It clings to the heart, ah, woe is me!
As the ivy clings to the old oak tree.

Love is not a passion of earthly mould,
As a thirst for honour, or fame, or gold:
For when all these wishes have died away,
The deep strong love of a brighter day,
Though nourish'd in secret, consumes the more,
As the slow rust eats to the iron's core.

Re-enter OLD BENSON, JOHN MADDOX, *and* VILLAGERS, *with jugs, seats, &c.;* SQUIRE NORTON *seats himself next* LUCY, *and* ROSE *contrives to sit next* MR. SPARKINS FLAM, *which* MARTIN *and* MADDOX *in vain endeavour to prevent.*

I.   .   13

SQUIRE.

Flam, you know these honest people? all tenants of my own.

FLAM.

Oh, yes, I know 'em—pleasant fellows! This—this is—what's his name?

BENSON.

Martin, sir,—Martin Stokes.

MARTIN (*starting forward*).

A—a—*Mr.* Stokes, at your service, sir,—how do you do, sir? (*shaking* FLAM *by the hand, while speaking*). I hope you are quite well, sir; I am delighted to see you looking so well, sir. I hope your majestic father, and your fashionable mother, are in the enjoyment of good health, sir. I should have spoken to you before, sir, only you have been so very much engaged, that I couldn't succeed in catching your honourable eye ;—very happy to see you, sir.

FLAM.

Ah. Pleasant fellow, this Martin !—agreeable manners,—no reserve about him.

MARTIN.

Sir, you do me a great deal of honour. Mr. Norton, sir, I have the honour of drinking your remarkably good health,—I admire you, sir.

SQUIRE (*laughing*).

Sir, I feel highly gratified, I 'm sure.

MARTIN (*aside*).

He 's gratified!—I flatter myself I have produced a slight impression here.   (*Drinks.*)

FLAM (*turns round, sees* MADDOX).

Ah, Ox!

JOHN.

Ox! Who do you call Ox? Maddox is my
name.

FLAM.

Oh, mad Ox! true; I forgot the lunacy:—your
health, mad Ox.

SQUIRE (*rising, and coming forward*).

Come, Flam, another glass.   Here, friends, is
success to our Harvest Home!

MARTIN.

Hear, hear! a most appropriate toast, most elo-
quently given,—a charming sentiment, delightfully
expressed.   Gentlemen (*to* VILLAGERS), allow me
to have the pleasure of proposing Mr. Norton, if
you please.   Take your time from me.   (*He gives
the time, and they all cheer.*)   Mr. Norton, sir, I beg
to call upon you for a song.

13 *

Song.—SQUIRE NORTON.

That very wise head, old Æsop, said,
  The bow should be sometimes loose ;
Keep it tight for ever, the string you sever :—
  Let's turn his old moral to use.
The world forget, and let us yet,
  The glass our spirits buoying,
Revel to-night in those moments bright
  Which make life worth enjoying.
The cares of the day, old moralists say,
  Are quite enough to perplex one ;
Then drive to-day's sorrow away till tomorrow,
  And then put it off till the next one.
        Chorus.—The cares of the day, &c.

Some plodding old crones, the heartless drones !
  Appeal to my cool reflection,
And ask me whether such nights can ever
  Charm sober recollection.
Yes, yes ! I cry, I'll grieve and die,
  When those I love forsake me ;
But while friends so dear surround me here,
  Let Care, if he can, o'ertake me.
        Chorus.—The cares of the day, &c.

During the Chorus, SQUIRE NORTON *and* FLAM
*resume their guns, and go up the stage, followed
by the various characters. The Chorus concludes as the Scene closes.*

SCENE II.—*An open spot near the village, with stile and pathway leading to the church, which is seen in the distance.* GEORGE EDMUNDS *enters, with a stick in his hand.*

EDMUNDS.

How thickly the fallen leaves lie scattered at the feet of that old row of elm-trees! When I first met Lucy on this spot, it was a fine spring day, and those same leaves were trembling in the sunshine, as green and bright as if their beauty would last for ever. What a contrast they present now, and how true an emblem of my own lost happiness!

Song.—GEORGE EDMUNDS.

Autumn leaves, autumn leaves, lie strewn around
    me here;
Autumn leaves, autumn leaves, how sad, how cold,
    how drear!
    How like the hopes of childhood's day,
      Thick clustering on the bough!
    How like those hopes is their decay,—
      How faded are they now!
Autumn leaves, autumn leaves, lie strewn around
    me here;
Autumn leaves, autumn leaves, how sad, how cold,
    how drear!

Wither'd leaves, wither'd leaves, that fly before
the gale;
Wither'd leaves, wither'd leaves, ye tell a mournful
tale,
Of love once true, and friends once kind,
And happy moments fled:
Dispersed by every breath of wind,
Forgotten, changed, or dead!
Autumn leaves, autumn leaves, lie strewn around
me here;
Autumn leaves, autumn leaves, how sad, how cold,
how drear!

An hour past the old time, and still no Lucy!
'Tis useless lingering here: I 'll wait no longer. A
female crossing the meadow!—'Tis Rose, the bearer
of a letter or a message perhaps.

Enter ROSE. (*She avoids him.*)

EDMUNDS.

No! Then I will see Lucy at once, without a
moment's delay. (*Going.*)

ROSE.

No, no, you can't. (*Aside.*) There 'll certainly
be bloodshed! I am quite certain Mr. Flam will
kill him. He offered me, with the most insinuating
speeches, to cut John's throat at a moment's notice:
and when the Squire complimented him on being a

good shot, he said he should like to "bag" the whole male population of the village. (*To him.*) You can't see her.

EDMUNDS.

Not see her, and she at home! Were you instructed to say this, Rose?

ROSE.

I say it, because I know you can't see her. She is not well; and—and——

EDMUNDS.

And Mr. Norton is there, you would say.

ROSE.

Mr. Norton!

EDMUNDS.

Yes, Mr. Norton. Was he not there last evening? Was he not there the evening before? Is he not there at this moment?

Enter JOHN MADDOX.

JOHN.

There at this moment?—of course he is.

ROSE (*aside*).

John here!

JOHN.

Of course he is; of course he was there last night; and of course he was there the evening before. He's always there, and so is his bosom friend and confidential demon, Mr. Sparkins Flam. Oh! George, we're injured men, both of us.

EDMUNDS.

Heartless girl! (*Retires up.*)

JOHN (*to* ROSE).

Faithless person!

ROSE.

Don't call me a person.

JOHN.

You *are* a person, perjured, treacherous, and deceiving! Oh! George, if you had seen what I have seen to-day. Soft whisperings and loving smiles, gentle looks and encouraging sighs,—such looks and sighs as used once upon a time to be bestowed on us, George! If you had seen the Squire making up to Lucy, and Rose making up to Flam:—but I am very glad you did not see it, George, very. It would have broken your heart, as it has broken mine! Oh, Rose! could you break my heart?

ROSE.

I could break your head with the greatest pleasure, you mischief-making booby; and if you don't make haste to wherever you're going, somebody that I know of will certainly do so, very quickly.

JOHN.

Will he, will he ?—your friend, Mr. Flam, I suppose! Let him—that's all: let him! (*Retires up.*)

ROSE.

Oh! I'll let him ; you needn't be afraid of my interfering. Dear, dear, I wish Mr. Flam would come, for I will own, notwithstanding what graver people may say, that I enjoy a little flirtation as much as any one.

Song.—ROSE.

Some folks who have grown old and sour,
Say love does nothing but annoy.
The fact is, they have had their hour,
So envy what they can't enjoy.
I like the glance—I like the sigh—
That does of ardent passion tell!
If some folks were as young as I,
I 'm sure they 'd like it quite as well.

Old maiden aunts so hate the men,
So well know how wives are harried,
It makes them sad—not jealous—when
They see their poor dear nieces married.
All men are fair and false, they know,
And with deep sighs they assail 'em,
It 's so long since they tried men, though,
I rather think their memories fail 'em.

—Here comes Mr. Flam. You'd better go, John. I know you'll be murdered.

JOHN.

Here I shall stop; let him touch me, and he shall feel the weight of my indignation.

Enter FLAM.

FLAM.

Ah, my charmer! Punctual to my time, you see, my sweet little Damask Rose!

JOHN (*coming down*).

A great deal more like a monthly one,—constantly changing, and gone the moment you wear it.

ROSE.

Impertinent creature!

FLAM.

Who is this poetical cauliflower?

JOHN.

Don't pretend not to know me. You know who I am, well enough.

FLAM.

As I live, it's the Ox!—retire, Ox, to your pasture, and don't rudely disturb the cooing of the doves. Go and graze, Ox!

JOHN.

Suppose I choose to remain here, what then?

FLAM.

Why then you must be driven off, mad Ox.
(*To Rose.*)   Who is that other grasshopper ?

ROSE.

Hush, hush ! for Heaven's sake don't let him
hear you!   It 's young Edmunds.

FLAM.

Young Edmunds ?   And who the devil is young
Edmunds ?   For beyond the natural inference that
young Edmunds is the son of old Edmunds, curse
me if the fame of young Edmunds has ever
reached my ears.

ROSE (*in a low tone*).

It 's Lucy's former lover, whom she has given
up for the Squire.

FLAM.

The rejected cultivator ?

ROSE.

The same.

FLAM.

Ah ! I guessed as much from his earthy appearance.   But, my darling Rose, I must speak with
you,—I must—(*putting his arm round her waist,
sees* JOHN.)   Good-bye, Ox !

JOHN.

Good-bye !

FLAM.

Pleasant walk to you, Ox!

JOHN (*not moving*).

Thankee;—same to you!

FLAM.

That other clodpole must not stay here either.

ROSE.

Yes, yes! he neither sees nor hears us. Pray
let him remain.

FLAM (*to* JOHN).

You understand, Ox, that it is my wish that you
forthwith retire and graze,—or in other words, that
you at once, and without delay, betake yourself to
the farm, or the devil, or any other place where
you are in your element, and won't be in the way.

JOHN.

Oh yes, I understand that.

FLAM.

Very well ; then the sooner you create a scarcity
of such animals in this market, the better. Now,
my dear Rose (*puts his arm round her waist
again*). Are you gone, Ox ?

JOHN.

No.

FLAM.

Are you going?

JOHN.

By no means.

FLAM.

This insolence is not to be borne.

ROSE.

Oh, pray don't hurt him,—pray don't. Go away, you stupid creature, if you don't want to be ruined.

JOHN.

That's just the very advice I would give you, Rose; do *you* go away, if you don't want to be ruined. As for me, this is a public place, and here I'll remain just as long as I think proper.

FLAM (*quitting* ROSE, *and advancing towards him*).
You will?

JOHN.

I will.

ROSE.

Oh, dear, dear! I knew he'd be murdered all along. I was quite certain of it.

JOHN.

Don't frown and scowl at me,—it won't do,—it only makes me smile; and when you talk of insolence and put my blood up, I tell you at once, that I am not to be bullied.

FLAM.

Bullied?

JOHN.

Ay, bullied was the word,—bullied by a coward, if you like that better.

FLAM.

Coward! (*seizes his gun by the barrel, and aims a blow at him, with the butt-end; EDMUNDS rushes forward, and strikes it up with his stick.*)

EDMUNDS.

Hold your hand, sir,—hold your hand, or I'll fell you to the ground. Maddox, leave this place directly: take the opposite path, and I'll follow you. (*Exit MADDOX.*) As for you, sir, who by the way of vindicating yourself from the charge of cowardice, raise your gun against an unarmed man, tell your protector, the Squire, from me, that he and his companions might content themselves with turning the heads of our farmers' daughters, and endeavouring to corrupt their hearts, without wantonly insulting the men they have most injured. Let this be a lesson to you, sir,—although you were armed, you would have had the worst of a scuffle, and you may not have the benefit of a third person's interference at so critical a moment, another time;—remember this warning, sir, and benefit by it. (*Exit.*)

FLAM (*aside*).

If Norton does not take a dear revenge for this

insult, I have lost my influence with him. Bully! coward! They shall rue it.

ROSE (*with her apron to her eyes*).

Oh, Mr. Flam! I can't bear to think that you should have suffered all this, on my account.

FLAM (*aside*).

On her account!—a little vanity! (*To her.*) Suffered! Why, my dear, it was the drollest and most humorous affair that ever happened. Here stand I,—the Honourable Sparkins Flam,—on this second day of September, one thousand seven hundred and twenty-nine ; and positively and solemnly declare that all the coffee-houses, play-houses, faro-tables, brag-tables, assemblies, drums and routs of a whole season put together, could not furnish such a splendid piece of exquisite drollery. The idea is admirable. My affecting to quarrel with a ploughman, and submitting to be lectured by another caterpillar, whom 1 suffer to burst into a butterfly importance!

ROSE.

Then you were not really quarrelling ?

FLAM.

Bless you, no ! I was only acting.

ROSE.

Lor' ! how well you do act, to be sure.

FLAM.

Come, let us retire into the house, or after this
joke we shall be the gaze of all the animated
potatoes that are planted in this hole of a village.
Why do you hesitate, Damask ?

ROSE.

Why, I have just been thinking that if you go to
all these coffee-houses, and play-houses, and fairs,
and brags, and keep playing drums, and routing
people about, you 'll forget me, when you go back
to London.

FLAM (*aside*).

More than probable. (*To her.*) Never fear; you
will be generally known as Rose the lovely, and I
shall be universally denominated Flam the constant.

Duet.—ROSE *and* SPARKINS FLAM.

FLAM.

'Tis true I 'm caress'd by the witty,
　　The envy of all the fine beaux,
The pet of the court and the city,
　　But still I 'm the lover of Rose.

ROSE.

Country sweethearts, oh, how I despise!
　　And oh ! how delighted I am
To think that I shine in the eyes
　　Of the elegant—sweet—Mr. Flam.

FLAM.

Allow me (*offers to kiss her*).

ROSE.

Pray don't be so bold, sir. (*Kisses her.*)

FLAM.

What sweets on that honey'd lip hang!

ROSE.

Your presumption, I know, I should scold, sir,
But I really *can't* scold Mr. Flam.

Both.

Then let us be happy together,
  Content with the world as it goes,
An unchangeable couple for ever,
  Mr. Flam and his beautiful Rose.

]*Exeunt.*)

SCENE III.—*The Farmer's Kitchen. A table and chairs.*

Enter OLD BENSON *and* MARTIN.

BENSON.

Well, Stokes. Now you have the opportunity you have desired, and we are alone, I am ready to listen to the information which you wished to communicate to my private ear.

I.   14

MARTIN.

Exactly;—you said information, I think ?

BENSON.

You said information, or I have forgotten.

MARTIN.

Just so, exactly ; I said information. I *did* say information, why should I deny it ?

BENSON.

I see no necessity for your doing so, certainly. Pray go on.

MARTIN.

Why, you see, my dear Mr. Benson, the fact is —won't you be seated ? Pray sit down (*brings forward two chairs ;—they sit*). There, now,—let me see,—where was I ?

BENSON.

You were going to begin, I think.

MARTIN.

Oh,—ah !—so I was ;—I hadn't begun, had I?

BENSON.

No, no! Pray begin again, if you had.

MARTIN.

Well, then, what I have got to say is not so much information, as a kind of advice, or suggestion, or hint, or something of that kind; and it relates to—eh ?—(*looking very mysterious*).

BENSON.

What?

MARTIN.

Yes (*nodding*). Don't you think there's something wrong there?

BENSON.

Where ?

MARTIN.

In that quarter.

BENSON.

In what quarter ?   Speak more plainly, sir.

MARTIN.

You know what a friendly feeling I entertain to your family.   You know what a very particular friend of mine you are.   You know how anxious I always am to prevent anything going wrong.

BENSON.

Well ! (*abruptly*).

MARTIN.

Yes, I see you're very sensible of it, but I'll take it for granted: you needn't bounce and fizz about, in that way, because it makes one nervous. Don't you think, now, *don't* you think, that ill-natured people may say;—don't be angry, you know, because if I wasn't a very particular friend of the family, I wouldn't mention the subject on any account ;—don't you think that ill-natured

14 *

people may say there's something wrong in the
frequency of the Squire's visits here ?

BENSON (*starting up furiously*).

What!

MARTIN (*aside*).

Here he goes again!

BENSON.

Who dares suspect my child?

MARTIN.

Ah, to be sure, that's exactly what I say.   Who
dares?   Damme, I should like to see 'em!

BENSON.

Is it you ?

MARTIN.

I ! Bless you, no, not for the world! I !—Come,
that's a good one.   I only say what other people
say, you know; that's all.

BENSON.

And what are these tales, that idle busy fools
prate of with delight, among themselves, caring
not whose ears they reach, so long as they are kept
from the old man, whose blindness—the blindness
of a fond and doting father—is subject for their
rude and brutal jeering.   What are they ?

MARTIN.

Dear me, Mr. Benson, you keep me in a state of
perpetual excitement.

BENSON.

Tell me, without equivocation, what do they say?

MARTIN.

Why, they say they think it—not exactly wrong, perhaps; don't fly out, now—but among those remarkable coincidences which do occur sometimes, that whenever you go out of your house, the Squire and his friend should come into it ; that Miss Lucy and Miss Rose, in the long walks they take every day, should be met and walked home with by the same gentlemen; that long after you have gone to bed at night, the Squire and Mr. Sparkins Flam should still be seen hovering about the lane and meadow ; and that one of the lattice windows should be always open, at that hour.

BENSON.

This is all ?

MARTIN.

Ye—yes,—yes, that's all.

BENSON.

Nothing beside ?

MARTIN.

Eh?

BENSON.

Nothing beside ?

MARTIN.

Why, there *is* something else, but I know you'll begin to bounce about again, if I tell it you.

BENSON.

No, no! let me hear it all.

MARTIN.

Why, then, they do say that the Squire has been heard to boast that he had practised on Lucy's mind—that when he bid her, she would leave her father and her home, and follow him over the world.

BENSON.

They lie! Her breast is pure and innocent! Her soul is free from guilt; her mind from blemish. They lie! I'll not believe it. Are they mad? Do they think that I stand tamely by, and look upon my child's disgrace? Heaven! do they know of what a father's heart is made?

MARTIN.

My dear Mr. Benson, if you——

BENSON.

This coarse and brutal boast shall be disowned. (*Going;* MARTIN *stops him.*)

MARTIN.

My dear Mr. Benson, you know it may not have been made after all,—my dear sir,——

BENSON (*struggling*).

Unhand me, Martin! Made or not made, it has gone abroad, fixing an infamous notoriety on me and mine. I 'll hear its truth or falsehood from himself. (*Breaks from him and exit.*)

MARTIN, *solus*.

There 'll be something decidedly wrong here presently. Hallo! here 's another very particular friend in a fume.

Enter YOUNG BENSON *hastily*.

MARTIN.

Ah! my dear fellow, how——

YOUNG BENSON.

Where is Lucy?

MARTIN.

I don't know, unless she has walked out with the Squire.

YOUNG BENSON.

The Squire!

MARTIN.

To be sure; she very often walks out with the Squire. Very pleasant recreation walking out with the Squire;—capital custom, an't it?

YOUNG BENSON.

Where 's my father?

MARTIN.

Why, upon my word, I am unable to satisfy your

curiosity in that particular either. All I know of him is that he whisked out of this room in a rather boisterous and turbulent manner for an individual at his time of life, some few seconds before you whisked in. But what's the matter?— you seem excited. Nothing wrong, is there?

YOUNG BENSON (*aside*).

This treatment of Edmunds, and Lucy's altered behaviour to him, confirm my worst fears. Where is Mr. Norton?

MARTIN (*calling off*).

Ah! to be sure,—where is Mr. Norton?

Enter SQUIRE.

SQUIRE.

Mr. Norton is here. Who wishes to see him?

MARTIN.

To be sure, sir. Mr. Norton is here : who wishes to see him?

YOUNG BENSON.

I do.

MARTIN.

I don't. Old fellow, good-bye! Mr. Norton, good evening! (*Aside.*) There'll be something wrong here, in a minute. (*Exit.*)

SQUIRE.

Well, young man?

YOUNG BENSON.

If you contemplate treachery here, Mr. Norton, look to yourself. My father is an old man ; the chief prop of his declining years is his child,—my sister. For your actions here, sir, you shall render a dear account to me.

SQUIRE.

To *you*, peasant !

YOUNG BENSON.

To me, sir. One other scene like that enacted by your creature, at your command, to-night, may terminate more seriously to him. For your behaviour here you are responsible to me.

SQUIRE.

Indeed ! Anything more, sir ?

YOUNG BENSON.

Simply this :—after injuring the old man beyond reparation, and embittering the last moments of his life, you may possibly attempt to shield yourself under the paltry excuse, that, as a gentleman, you cannot descend to take the consequences from my hand. You *shall* take them from me, sir, if I strike you to the earth first.

[*Exit.*

SQUIRE.

Fiery and valorous, indeed ! As the suspicions

of the family are aroused, no time is to be lost: the girl must be carried off to-night, if possible. With Flam's assistance and management, she may be speedily removed from within the reach of these rustic sparks. In my cooler moments, the reflection of the misery I may inflict upon the old man makes my conduct appear base and dishonourable, even to myself. Pshaw! hundreds have done the same thing before me, who have been lauded and blazoned forth as men of honour. Honour in such cases,—an idle tale!—a by-word! Honour! There is much to be gleaned from old tales; and the legend of the child and the old man speaks but too truly.

Song.—SQUIRE NORTON.

The child and the old man sat alone
    In the quiet peaceful shade
Of the old green boughs, that had richly grown
    In the deep thick forest glade.
It was a soft and pleasant sound,
    That rustling of the oak;
And the gentle breeze play'd lightly round,
    As thus the fair boy spoke:—

" Dear father, what can honour be,
    Of which I hear men rave?
Field, cell and cloister, land and sea,
    The tempest and the grave:—

It lives in all, 'tis sought in each,
   'Tis never heard or seen:
Now tell me, father, I beseech,
   What can this honour mean?"

"It is a name,—a name, my child,—
   It lived in other days,
When men were rude, their passions wild,
   Their sport, thick battle-frays.
When in armour bright, the warrior bold,
   Knelt to his lady's eyes:
Beneath the abbey-pavement old
   That warrior's dust now lies.

"The iron hearts of that old day
   Have moulder'd in the grave;
And chivalry has pass'd away,
   With knights so true and brave,
The honour, which to them was life,
   Throbs in no bosom now;
It only gilds the gambler's strife,
   Or decks the worthless vow." *

Enter LUCY.

SQUIRE.

Lucy, dear Lucy.

---

* In John Hullah's music to this song, the last two lines
are printed as follows:
   "The name adorns the gambler's strife,
      Or gilds the worthless vow."—ED.

LUCY.

Let me entreat you not to stay here, sir! you will be exposed to nothing but insult and attack. Edmunds and my brother have both returned, irritated at something that has passed with my cousin Rose:—for my sake,—for my sake, Mr. Norton, spare me the pain of witnessing what will ensue, if they find you here. You little know what I have borne already.

SQUIRE.

For your sake, Lucy, I would do much; but why should I leave you to encounter the passion and ill-will, from which you would have me fly?

LUCY.

Oh, I can bear it, sir; I deserve it but too well.

SQUIRE.

Deserve it !—you do yourself an injustice, Lucy. No; rather let me remove you from a house where you will suffer nothing but persecution, and confer upon you a title which the proudest lady in the land might wear. Here— here, on my knees (*he bends on his knee, and seizes her hand*).

Enter FLAM.

" SQUIRE (*rising*).

" Flam here !

" FLAM (*aside*).

" Upon my word !—I thought we had been
" getting on pretty well in the open air, but
" they 're beating us hollow here, under cover.

" SQUIRE.

" Lucy, but one word, and I understand your
" decision.

" LUCY.

" I—I cannot subdue the feelings of uneasiness
" and distrust which the great difference between
" your Honour's rank and mine awakens in my
" mind.

" SQUIRE.

" Difference ! Hundreds of such cases happen
" every day.

" LUCY.

" Indeed!

" SQUIRE.

" Oh, 'tis a matter of general notoriety,—isn't
" it, Flam ?

" FLAM.

" No doubt of it. (*Aside.*) Don't exactly know
" yet what they are talking about, though.

" SQUIRE.

" A relation of my own, a man of exalted rank,
" courted a girl far his inferior in station, but only
" beneath him in that respect. In all others she

" was on a footing of equality with himself, if not
" far above him.

" LUCY.

" And were they married ?

" FLAM (*aside*).

" Rather an important circumstance in the case.
" I *do* remember that.

" SQUIRE.

" They were,—after a time, when the resentment
" of his friends, occasioned by his forming such an
" attachment, had subsided, and he was able to
" acknowledge her, without involving the ruin of
" both.

" LUCY.

" They were married privately at first, then ?

" FLAM (*aside*).

" I must put in a word here. Oh, yes, it was
" all comfortably arranged to everybody's satisfac-
" tion,—wasn't it, Norton ?

" SQUIRE.

" Certainly. And a happy couple they were,
" weren't they, Flam ?

" FLAM.

" Happiest of the happy. As happy as (*aside*)—
" a separation could make them.

" SQUIRE.

" Hundreds of great people have formed similar
" attachments,—haven't they, Flam ?

" FLAM.

" Undoubtedly. There was the Right Honourable
" Augustus Frederick Charles Thomson Camharado,
" and the German Baron Hyfenstyfenlooberhausen,
" and they were both married—(*aside*) to somebody
" else, first. Not to mention Damask and I, who
" are models of constancy. By-the-by, I have lost
" sight of her, and I am interrupting you. (*Aside*
" *to* SQUIRE, *as he goes out.*) I came to tell you that
" she is ripe for an elopement, if you urge her
" strongly. Edmunds has been reproaching her to
" my knowledge. She 'll consent while her passion
" lasts. (*Exit.*)"

SQUIRE.

Lucy, I wait your answer. One word from you,
and a few hours will place you far beyond the reach
of those who would fetter your choice and control
your inclinations. You hesitate. Come, decide.
The Squire's lady, or the wife of Edmunds!

Duet.—LUCY *and* SQUIRE NORTON.

SQUIRE.

In rich and lofty station shine,
  Before his jealous eyes:
In golden splendour, lady mine,
  This peasant youth despise.

LUCY (*apart*: *the* SQUIRE *regarding her attentively*).

Oh ! It would be revenge indeed
With scorn his glance to meet.
I, I, his humble pleading heed !
I 'd spurn him from my feet.

SQUIRE.

With love and rage her bosom 's torn,
And rash the choice will be ;

LUCY.

With love and rage my bosom's torn,
And rash the choice will be.

SQUIRE.

From hence she quickly must be borne,
Her home, her home, she 'll flee.

LUCY.

Oh ! long shall I have cause to mourn
My home, my home, for thee !

Enter OLD BENSON.

BENSON.

What do I see !   The Squire and Lucy.

SQUIRE.

Listen.   A chaise and four fleet horses, under
the direction of a trusty friend of mine, will be in
waiting on the high road, at the corner of the Elm-
Tree avenue, to-night, at ten o'clock.   They shall

bear you whither we can be safe, and in secret, by
the first light of morning.

LUCY.

His cruel harshness ;—it would be revenge,
indeed. But my father—my poor old father !

SQUIRE.

Your father is prejudiced in Edmunds' favour;
'and so long as he thinks there is any chance of
your being his, he will oppose your holding communication with me. Situated as you are now, you
only stand in the way of his wealth and advance-
ment. Once fly with me, and in four and twenty
hours you will be his pride, his boast, his support.

OLD BENSON *coming forward.*

BENSON.

It is a lie, a base lie!—(LUCY *shrieks and throws
herself at his feet*). My pride! my boast! She
would be my disgrace, my shame : an outcast from
her father's roof, and from the world. Support!—
support *me* with the gold coined in her infamy and
guilt! Heaven help me! Have I cherished her
for this !

LUCY (*clinging to him*).

Father !—dear, dear father !

SQUIRE.

Hear me speak, Benson. Be calm.

BENSON.

Calm !—Do you know that from infancy I have

I. ·   15

almost worshipped her, fancying that I saw in her young mind the virtues of a mother, to whom the anguish of this one hour would have been worse than death!   Calm!—Do you know that I have a heart and soul within me; or do you believe that because I am of lower station, I am a being of a different order from yourself, and that Nature has denied me thought and feeling !   Calm !   Man, do you know that I am this girl's father ?

SQUIRE.

Benson, if you will not hear me, at least do not, by hastily exposing this matter, deprive me of the inclination of making you some reparation.

BENSON.

Reparation!   You need be thankful, sir, for the grasp she has upon my arm.   Money!   If she were dying for want, and the smallest coin from you could restore her to life and health, sooner than she should take it from your hand, I would cast her from a sick bed to perish on the road-side.

SQUIRE.

Benson, a word.

BENSON.

Do not, I caution you ; do not talk to me, sir. I am an old man, but I do not know what passion may make me do.

SQUIRE.

These are high words, Benson. A farmer !

BENSON.

Yes, sir ; a farmer,—one of the men on whom you, and such as you, depend for the money they squander in profligacy and idleness. A farmer, sir ! I care not for your long pedigree of ancestors, —my forefathers made them all. Here, neighbours, friends ! (ROSE, MADDOX, STOKES, VILLAGERS, &c., *crowd on the stage.*) Hear this, hear this ! your landlord, a high-born gentleman, entering the houses of your humble farmers, and tempting their daughters to destruction !

Enter YOUNG BENSON *and* GEORGE EDMUNDS.

YOUNG BENSON.

What 's that I hear ? (*rushing towards the* SQUIRE, STOKES *interposes*).

MARTIN.

Hallo, hallo! Take hold of the other one, John. (MADDOX *and he remove them to opposite sides of the stage.*) Hold him tight, John, hold him tight. Stand still, there 's a good fellow. Keep back, Squire. Knew there 'd be something wrong,— ready to come in at the nick of time,—capital custom.

FLAM *enters and stands next the* SQUIRE.

SQUIRE.

Exposed, baited ! Benson, are you mad ?

15 *

Within the last few hours my friend here has been attacked and insulted on the very land you hold, by a person in your employ and young Edmunds there. I, too, have been threatened and insulted in the presence of my tenantry and workmen. Take care you do not drive me to extremities. Remember—the lease of this farm for seventy years, which your father took of mine, expires tomorrow ; and that I have the power to refuse its renewal. Again I ask you, are you mad?

BENSON.

Quit my house, villain!

SQUIRE.   •

Villain! quit *my* house, then. This farm is mine: and you and yours shall depart from under its roof, before the sun has set tomorrow. (BENSON *sinks into a chair in centre, and covers his face with his hands.*)

Sestette and Chorus.

LUCY—ROSE—EDMUNDS—SQUIRE NORTON—FLAM —YOUNG BENSON—*and Chorus.*

YOUNG BENSON.

Turn him from the farm! From his home will you cast
    The old man who has till'd it for years?
Every tree, every flower, is link'd with the past,
    And a friend of his childhood appears.

Turn *him* from the farm! O'er its grassy hill-side,
  A gay boy he once loved to range ;
His boyhood has fled, and its dear friends are dead,
  But these meadows have never known change.

EDMUNDS.

Oppressor, hear me.

LUCY.

On my knees I implore.

SQUIRE.

I command it, and you will obey.

ROSE.

Rise, dear Lucy, rise ; you shall not kneel before
  The tyrant who drives us away.

SQUIRE.

Your sorrows are useless, your prayers are in vain;
  I command it, and you will begone.
I 'll hear no more.

EDMUNDS.

No, they shall not beg again,
  Of a man whom I view with deep scorn.

FLAM.

Do not yield.

YOUNG BENSON—SQUIRE—LUCY—ROSE.

Leave the farm!

EDMUNDS.

Your power I despise.

SQUIRE.

And your threats, boy, I disregard, too.

FLAM.

Do not yield.

YOUNG BENSON—SQUIRE—LUCY—ROSE.

Leave the farm!

ROSE.

If he leaves it, he dies.

EDMUNDS.

This base act, proud man, you shall rue.

YOUNG BENSON.

Turn him from the farm! From his home will you
cast
The old man who has till'd it for years?
Every tree, every flower, is link'd with the past,
And a friend of his childhood appears!

SQUIRE.

Yes, yes, leave the farm! From his home I will
cast
The old man who has till'd it for years;
Though each tree and flower is link'd with the past,
And a friend of his childhood appears.

Chorus.

He has turn'd from his farm, from his home he
has cast
The old man who has till'd it for years;
Though each tree and flower is link'd with the past,
And a friend of his childhood appears.

END OF THE FIRST ACT.

ACT II.

SCENE I.—*An Apartment in the Hall. A breakfast-table, with urn and tea - service. A Livery Servant arranging it.* FLAM, *in a morning gown and slippers, reclining on the sofa.*

FLAM.

Is the Squire out of bed yet ?

SERVANT.

Yes, sir, he will be down directly.

FLAM.

Any letters from London ?

SERVANT.

One for your honour, that the man brought over from the market-town, this morning.

FLAM.

Give it me, blockhead! (*Servant gives it, and exit.*) Never like the look of a great official-folded letter, with a large seal, "it's always an unpleasant one. " Talk of discovering a man's character from his

" handwriting!—I 'll back myself against any odds
" to form a very close guess at the contents of a
" letter from the form into which it is folded. This,
" now, I should say, is a decidedly hostile fold."
Let us see—' King's Bench Walk—September 1st,
1729. Sir, I am instructed by my client, Mr.
Edward Montague, to apply to you—(the old story
—for the immediate payment, I suppose— what's
this?)—to apply to you for the instant restitution of the sum of two hundred and fifty pounds,
his son lost to you at play ; and to acquaint you,
that unless it is immediately forwarded to my
office, as above, the circumstances of the transac-
tion will be made known; and the unfair and
fraudulent means by which you deprived the young
man of his money, publicly advertised.—I am, Sir,
your obedient Servant, John Ellis.'   The devil!
" who would believe now, that such a trifling cir-
" cumstance as the mere insinuation of a small
" piece of gold into the corner of two dice would
" influence a man's destiny!"   What's to be done?
If, by some dextrous stroke, I could manage to curry
favour with Norton, and procure some handsome
present in return for services rendered,—for, 'work
and labour done and performed,' as my obedient
servant, John Ellis, would say, I might keep my
head above water yet.   I have it!   He shall have
a joyful surprise.   I 'll carry this girl off for him,

and he shall know nothing of the enterprise until it is completed, or at least till she is fairly off. I have been well rewarded for similar services before, and may securely calculate on his gratitude in the present instance.   He is here.   (*Puts up the letter.*)

Enter SQUIRE NORTON.

SQUIRE (*seating himself at table*).

Has any application for permission to remain on the farm been made from Benson, this morning, Flam?

FLAM.

None.

SQUIRE.

I am very sorry for it, although I admire the old man's independent spirit.   I am very sorry for it. Wrong as I know I have been, I would rather that the first concession came from him.

FLAM.

Concession!

SQUIRE.

The more I reflect upon the occurrences of yesterday, Flam, the more I regret that, under the influence of momentary passion and excitement, I should have used so uncalled-for a threat against my father's oldest tenant.   It is an act of baseness to which I look back with abhorrence.

FLAM (*aside*).

What weathercock morality is this !

SQUIRE.

It was unnecessary violence.

FLAM.

Unnecessary!   Oh, certainly ; no doubt you could have attained your object without it, and can still.   There is no occasion to punish the old man.

SQUIRE.

Nor will I.   He shall not leave the farm, if I myself implore, and beg him to remain.

Enter SERVANT.

SERVANT.

Two young women to speak with your honour.

Enter LUCY *and* ROSE.

SQUIRE.

Lucy !

FLAM (*aside*).

She must be carried off to-night, or she certainly will save me the trouble, and I shall lose the money.

LUCY.

Your honour may be well surprised to see me here, after the events of yesterday.   It has cost me no trifling struggle to take this step, but I hope my better feelings have at length prevailed, and con-

quered my pride and weakness.   I wish to speak
to your honour, with nobody by.

FLAM (aside).

Nobody by !   I rather suspect I 'm not particularly wanted here.   (<i>To them.</i>) Pray allow us to
retire for a few moments.   Rose, my dear.

ROSE.

Well !

FLAM.

Come along.

LUCY.

Rose will remain here.   I brought her for that
purpose.

FLAM.

Bless me ! that 's very odd.   As you please, of
course, but I really think you 'll find her very
much in the way.   (<i>Aside.</i>) Acting propriety ! So
much the better for my purpose; a little coyness
will enhance the value of the prize. (<i>Exit</i> FLAM.)

LUCY.

Mr. Norton, I come here to throw myself upon
your honourable feelings, as a man and as a gentleman.   Oh, sir ! now that my eyes are opened to
the misery into which I have plunged myself, by
my own ingratitude and treachery, do not—do not
add to it the reflection that I have driven my father
in his old age from the house where he was born,
and in which he hoped to have died.

SQUIRE.

Be calm, Lucy; your father shall continue to hold the farm ; the lease shall be renewed.

LUCY.

I have more to say to your Honour still, and what I have to add may even induce your Honour to retract the promise you have just now made me.

SQUIRE.

Lucy ! what can you mean ?

LUCY.

Oh, sir ! call me coquette, faithless, treacherous, deceitful, what you will ; I deserve it all ;—but believe me, I speak the truth when I make the humiliating avowal.   A weak, despicable vanity induced me to listen with a ready ear to your Honour's addresses, and to cast away the best and noblest heart that ever woman won.

SQUIRE.

Lucy, 'twas but last night you told me that your love for Edmunds had vanished into air; that you hated and despised him.

LUCY.

I know it, sir, too well.   He laid bare my own guilt, and showed me the ruin which impended over me.   He spoke the truth.   Your Honour more than confirmed him.

SQUIRE (*after a pause*).

Even the avowal you have just made, unexpected as it is, shall not disturb my resolution. Your father shall not leave the farm.

Quartett—LUCY—ROSE—SQUIRE NORTON, *and afterwards* YOUNG BENSON.

SQUIRE.

Hear me, when I swear that the farm is your own
   Through all changes Fortune may make ;
The base charge of falsehood I never have known;
   This promise I never will break.

ROSE *and* LUCY.

Hear him, when he swears that the farm is our own
   Through all changes Fortune may make ;
The base charge of falsehood he never has known;
   This promise he never will break.

Enter YOUNG BENSON.

YOUNG BENSON.

My sister here ! Lucy ! begone, I command.

SQUIRE.

To your home I restore you again.

YOUNG BENSON.

No boon I 'll accept from that treacherous hand
   As the price of my sister's fair fame.

SQUIRE.

To your home !

YOUNG BENSON (*to* LUCY).

Hence away!

LUCY.

Brother dear, I obey.

SQUIRE.

I restore.

YOUNG BENSON.

Hence away!

YOUNG BENSON, ROSE, *and* LUCY.

Let us leave.

LUCY.

He swears it, dear brother.

SQUIRE.

I swear it.

YOUNG BENSON.

Away!

SQUIRE.

I swear it.

YOUNG BENSON.

You swear to deceive.

SQUIRE.

Hear me, when I swear that the farm is your own
Through all changes Fortune may make.

LUCY *and* ROSE.

Hear him, when he swears that the farm is our own
Through all changes Fortune may make.

YOUNG BENSON.

Hear him swear, hear him swear, that the farm is
  our own
Through all changes Fortune may make.

SQUIRE.

The base charge of falsehood I never have known,
This promise I never will break.

LUCY *and* ROSE.

The base charge of falsehood he never has known,
This promise he never will break.

YOUNG BENSON.

The base charge of falsehood he often has known,
This promise he surely will break.

(Exeunt omnes.)

Re-enter FLAM, *in a walking-dress.*

FLAM.

The coast is clear at last.   What on earth the
conversation can have been, at which Rose *was*
wanted, and I was not, I confess my inability to
comprehend; but away with speculation, and now
to business.—

(Rings.

Enter SERVANT.

Pen and ink.

SERVANT.

Yes, sir.   (*Exit* SERVANT.)

FLAM (*solus*).

Nearly all the tenantry will be assembled here at the ball to-night; and if the father of this rustic dulcinea is reinstated in his farm, he and his people will no doubt be among the number. It will be easy enough to entice the girl into the garden, through the window opening on the lawn; a chaise can be waiting in the quiet lane at the side, and some trusty fellow can slip a hasty note into Norton's hands informing him of the flight, and naming the place at which he can join us. (*Re-enter* SERVANT *with pen, ink, taper, and two sheets of note-paper; he places them on the table and exit.*) I may as well reply to my friend Mr. John Ellis's obliging favour now, too, by promising that the money shall be forwarded in the course of three days' post. (*Takes the letter from his pocket, and lays it on the table.*) Lie you there. First, for Norton's note.—"Dear Norton,—Knowing your wishes— seized the girl—no blame attach to you. Join us as soon as people have dispersed in search of her in all directions but the right one,—fifteen miles off." (*Folds it ready for an envelope and lays it by the side of the other letter.*) Now for John Ellis. Why, what does the rascal mean by bringing but two sheets of paper? No matter: that affair will keep cool till to-morrow, when I have less business on my hands, and more money in my pockets, I hope. (*Crumples the letter he has just written, hastily up, thrusts it into his pocket, and folds the wrong one in the envelope.   As he is sealing it*

Enter MARTIN, *very cautiously.*)

MARTIN (*peeping*).

There he is, hatching some mysterious and diabolical plot.   If I can only get to the bottom of these dreadful designs, I shall immortalise myself. What a lucky dog I am, to be such a successful gleaner of news, and such a confidential person into the bargain, as to be the first to hear that he wanted some trustworthy person.   All comes of talking to everybody I meet, and drawing out everything they hear.   Capital custom!   He don't see me. Hem! (*Coughs very loud, and when* FLAM *looks round, nods familiarly.*)   How are you again?

FLAM.

How am I again!   Who the devil are you?— and what do you want here?

MARTIN.

Hush!

FLAM.

Eh?

MARTIN.

Hush!   I'm the man.

FLAM.

The man!

I.   .   16

MARTIN.

Yes, the man that you asked the ostler at the George to recommend you; the trustworthy man that knows all the by-roads well, and can keep a secret; the man that you wanted to lend you a hand in a job, that——

FLAM.

Hush, hush!

MARTIN.

Oh! you're beginning to hush now, are you?

FLAM.

Haven't I seen your face before?

MARTIN.

To be sure you have. You recollect admiring my manners at Benson's yesterday. You must remember Mr. Martin Stokes. You *can't* have forgotten him—not possible!

FLAM (*aside*).

A friend of Benson!—a dangerous rencontre. Another moment, and our conversation might have taken an awkward turn. (*To him.*) So you are Stokes, eh? Benson's friend Stokes?

MARTIN.

To be sure. Ha, ha! I knew you couldn't have forgotten me. Pleasant Stokes they call me, clever Stokes sometimes;—but that's flattery.

FLAM.

No, surely.

MARTIN.

Yes, 'pon my life! it is. Can't bear flattery,—don't like it at all.

FLAM.

Well, Mr. Stokes——

MARTIN (*aside*).

Now for the secret.

FLAM.

I am very sorry you have had the trouble of coming up here, Mr. Stokes, because I have changed my plan, and shall not require your valuable services. (*Goes up to the table.*)

MARTIN (*aside*).

Something wrong here: try him again. You're sure you don't want me?

FLAM.

Quite.

MARTIN.

That's unlucky, because, as I have quarrelled with Benson——

FLAM.

Quarrelled with Benson!

MARTIN.

What! didn't you know that?

16 *

FLAM.

Never heard of it. Now I think of it, Mr.
Stokes, I *shall* want your assistance. Pray, sit
down, Mr. Stokes.

MARTIN.

With pleasure. (*They sit.*) I say, I *thought* you
wanted me.

FLAM.

Ah! you 're a sharp fellow.

MARTIN.

You don't mean that ?

FLAM.

I do, indeed.

MARTIN (*aside*).

You would, if you knew all.

FLAM (*aside*).

Conceited hound!

MARTIN (*aside*).

Poor devil !

FLAM.

Mr. Stokes, I needn't impress upon a gentleman
of your intelligence, the necessity of secrecy in
this matter.

MARTIN.

Of course not: see all—say nothing. Capital
custom :—(*aside*) not mine though. Go on.

FLAM.

You wouldn't mind playing Benson a trick,—
just a harmless trick.

" MARTIN.

" Certainly not.   Go on.

" FLAM.

" I 'll trust you.

" MARTIN.

" So you may.   Go on."

FLAM.

A chaise and four will be waiting to-night, at ten
o'clock precisely, at the little gate that opens from
the garden into the lane.

" MARTIN.

" No: will it though?   Go on."

FLAM.

" Don't interrupt me, Stokes."   Into that chaise
you must assist me in forcing as quickly as possible
and without noise——

" MARTIN.

" Yes.   Go on.

" FLAM.

" Whom do you think?   ˋ

" MARTIN.

" Don't know."

FLAM.

Can't you guess whom?

MARTIN.

No.

FLAM.

Try.

MARTIN.

Eh! what !—Miss——

FLAM.

Hush, hush! You understand me, I see. Not another word; not another syllable.

MARTIN.

But do you really mean to run away with——

FLAM (*stopping his mouth*).

You understand me;—that's quite sufficient.

MARTIN (*aside*).

He's going to run away with Rose. Why, if I hadn't found this out, John Maddox,—one of my most particular friends,—would have gone stark, staring, raving mad with grief. (*To him.*) But what will become of Miss Lucy, when she has lost Rose?

FLAM.

No matter. We cannot take them both, without the certainty of an immediate discovery. "Meet "me at the corner of the avenue, before the ball "commences, and I will communicate any further "instructions I may have to give you. Meanwhile" take this (*gives him money*) as an earnest of what you shall receive when the girl is secured. Remember, silence and secrecy.

MARTIN.

Silence and secrecy, (*Exit* FLAM)—confidence and two guineas. I am perfectly bewildered with this tremendous secret. What shall I do? Where shall I go?—To my particular friend, old Benson, or young Benson, or George Edmunds? or—no; I'll go and paralyse my particular friend, John Maddox. Not a moment is to be lost. I am all in a flutter. Run away with Rose! I suppose he'll run away with Lucy next. *I* shouldn't wonder. Run away with Rose! I never did— (*Exit hastily*).

SCENE II.—*An open spot in the Village.*

Enter SQUIRE NORTON.

SQUIRE.

My mind is made up. This girl has opened her whole heart to me; and it would be worse than villainy to pursue her further. I will seek out Benson and Edmunds, and endeavour to repair the mischief my folly has occasioned. I have sought happiness in the dissipation of crowded cities, in vain. A country life offers health and cheerfulness; and a country life shall henceforth be mine, in all seasons.

Song.—SQUIRE NORTON.

There 's a charm in Spring, when every thing
    Is bursting from the ground ;
When pleasant showers bring forth the flowers,
    And all is life around.

In summer day, the fragrant hay
    Most sweetly scents the breeze;
And all is still, save murmuring rill,
    Or sound of humming bees.

Old Autumn come, with trusty gun
    In quest of birds we roam:
Unerring aim, we mark the game,
    And proudly bear it home.

A winter's night has its delight,
    Well warm'd to bed we go;
A winter's day, we 're blithe and gay,
    Snipe-shooting in the snow.

A country life without the strife
    And noisy din of town,
Is all I need, I take no heed
    Of splendour or renown.

And when I die, oh, let me lie
    Where trees above me wave;
Let wild plants bloom, around my tomb,
    My quiet country grave!   (*Exit.*)

SCENE III.—*The Rick-yard. Same as Act I.,
Scene I.*

EDMUNDS *and* MADDOX *meeting.*

JOHN.

Ah, George! Why this is kind to come down
to the old farm to-day, and take one peep at us,
before we leave it for ever. I suppose it's fancy,
now, George, but to my thinking I never saw the
hedges look so fresh, the fields so rich, or the old
house so pretty and comfortable, as they do this
morning. It's fancy that, George,—an't it?

EDMUNDS.

It's a place you may well be fond of, and
attached to, for it's the prettiest spot in all the
country round.

JOHN.

Ah! you always enter into my feelings; and
speaking of that, I want to ask your advice about
Rose. I meant to come up to you to-day, on
purpose. Do you think she is fond of me, George?

EDMUNDS (*smiling*).

What do *you* think? She has not shown any
desperate warmth of affection, of late, has she?

JOHN.

No—no, she certainly has not, but she used to
once, and the girl has got a good heart after all;

and she came crying to me, this morning, in the little paddock, and somehow or other, my heart melted towards her; and—and—there's something very pleasant about her manner,—isn't there, George?

EDMUNDS.

No doubt of it, as other people besides ourselves would appear to think.

JOHN.

You mean Mr. Flam? (*Edmunds nods assent.*) Ah! it's a bad business, altogether; but still there are some excuses to be made for a young country girl, who has never seen a town gentleman before, and can't be expected to know as well as you and I, George, what the real worth of one is. However that may be, Rose came into the little paddock this morning, as I was standing there, looking at the young colts, and thinking of all our misfortunes; and first of all she walked by me, and then she stopped at a little distance, and then she walked back, and stopped again; and I heard her sobbing as if her heart would burst: and then she came a little nearer, and at last she laid her hand upon my arm, and looked up in my face: and the tears started into my eyes, George, and I couldn't bear it any longer, for I thought of the many pleasant days we had been happy together, and it hurt me to think that she should ever have done anything to make her afraid of me, or me unkind to her.

EDMUNDS.

You 're a good fellow, John, an excellent fellow. Take her ; I believe her to have an excellent disposition, though it is a little disguised by girlish levity sometimes;—you may safely take her,—if she had far less good feeling than she actually possesses, she could never abuse your kind and affectionate nature.

JOHN.

Is that your advice? Give me your hand, George (*they shake hands*), I will take her. You shall dance at our wedding, and I don't quite despair yet of dancing at yours, at the same time.

EDMUNDS.

At mine! Where is the old man? I came here to offer him the little cottage in the village, which belongs to me. There is no tenant in it now: it has a pretty garden, of which I know he is fond, and it may serve his turn till he has had time to look about him.

JOHN.

He is somewhere about the farm; walk with me across the yard, and perhaps we may meet him— this way.　　　　　　　　　　　　　 [*Exeunt.*

Enter YOUNG BENSON.

YOUNG BENSON.

The worst portion of the poor old man's hard trial is past. I have lingered with him in every field on the land, and wandered through every room in the old house. I can neither blame his grief, nor console him in his affliction, for the farm has been the happy scene of my birth and boyhood; and I feel, in looking on it, for the last time, as if I were leaving the dearest friends of my youth, for ever.

Song.—YOUNG BENSON.

My fair home is no longer mine ;
  From its roof-tree I 'm driven away,
Alas! who will tend the old vine,
  Which I planted in infancy's day !
The garden, the beautiful flowers,
  The oak with its branches on high,
Dear friends of my happiest hours,
  Among ye, I long hoped to die.
The briar, the moss, and the bramble,
  Along the green paths will run wild:
The paths where I once used to ramble,
  An innocent, light-hearted child.

At the conclusion of the song enter to the symphony OLD BENSON, *with* LUCY *and* ROSE.

YOUNG BENSON (*advancing to meet him*).

Come, father, come !

OLD BENSON.

I am ready, boy. We have but to walk a few steps, and the pang of leaving is over. Come, Rose, bring on that unhappy girl ; come!

As they are going, enter the SQUIRE, *who meets them.*

SQUIRE.

I am in time.

BENSON (*to* YOUNG BENSON, *who is advancing*).

Harry, stand back. Mr. Norton, if by this visit you intend to mock the misery you have inflicted here, it is a heartless insult that might have been spared.

SQUIRE.

You do me an injustice, Benson. I come here, —not to insult your grief, but to entreat, implore you, to remain. The lease of this farm shall be renewed ;—I beseech you to remain here.

BENSON.

It is not the quitting even the home of my infancy, which most men love, that bows my spirit down to-day. Here, in this old house, for near two hundred years, my ancestors have lived and died, and left their names behind them free from spot or blemish. I am the first to cross its threshold with the brand of infamy upon me. Would to God I had been borne from its porch a senseless corpse many weary years ago, so that I had been spared this hard calamity! You have moved an old man's weakness, but not with your revenge, sir. You implore me to remain here. I spurn your offer. *Here!* A father yielding to the destroyer of his child's good name and honour! Say no more, sir. Let me pass.

Enter, behind, STOKES *and* EDMUNDS.

SQUIRE.

Benson, you are guilty of the foulest injustice, not to me, but to your daughter. After her fearless confession to me this morning of her love for Edmunds, and her abhorrence of my professions, I honour her too much to injure her or you.

LUCY.

Dear father, it is true indeed. The noble behaviour of his Honour to me, this morning, I can never forget, or be too grateful for.

BENSON.

Thank God! thank God! I can look upon her once again. My child! my own child! (*He embraces her with great emotion.*) I have done your Honour wrong, and I hope you'll forgive me. (*They shake hands.*)

MARTIN (*running forward*).

So have I! so have I! I have done his Honour wrong, and I hope he'll forgive me too. You don't leave the farm, then? Hurrah! (*A man carrying a pail, some harness, &c., crosses the stage.*) Hallo, young fellow! go back, go back! don't take another thing away, and bring back all you have carried off; they are going to stop in the farm. Hallo! you fellows! (*Calling off.*) Leave the barn alone, and put everything in its place. They are going to stop in the farm. (*Exit bawling.*)

BENSON (*seeing* EDMUNDS).

What! George here, and turning away from his old friend, too, without a look of congratulation or a shake of the hand, just at the time, when of all others, he had the best right to expect it! For shame, George, for shame!

EDMUNDS.

My errand here is rendered useless. By accident, and not intentionally, I partly overheard just now the nature of the avowal made by your daughter to Mr. Norton this morning.

BENSON.

You believe it, George. You cannot doubt its truth.

EDMUNDS.

I *do* believe it. But I have been hurt, slighted,

set aside for another. My honest love has been despised; my affection has been remembered, only to be tried almost beyond endurance. Lucy, all this from *you* I freely forgive. Be what you have been once, and what you may so well become again. Be the high-souled woman; not the light and thoughtless trifler that disgraces the name. Let me see you this, and you are mine again. Let me see you what you have been of late, and I never can be yours!

BENSON.

Lead her in, Rose. Come, dear, come! (*The* BENSONS *and* ROSE *lead her slowly away.*)

EDMUNDS.

Mr. Norton, if this altered conduct be sincere, it deserves a much better return than my poor thanks can ever be to you. If it be feigned, to save some purposes of your own, the consequences will be upon your head.

SQUIRE.

And I shall be prepared to meet them.

Duet.—SQUIRE NORTON *and* EDMUNDS.

SQUIRE.

Listen, though I do not fear you,
Listen to me, ere we part.

EDMUNDS.

List to *you!* Yes, I will hear you.

SQUIRE.

Yours alone is Lucy's heart,
I swear it, by that Heaven above me.

EDMUNDS.

What ! can I believe my ears !
Could I hope that she still loves me !

SQUIRE.

Banish all these doubts and fears,
If a love were e'er worth gaining,
If love were ever fond and true,
No disguise or passion feigning,
Such is her young love for you.

Listen, though I do not fear you,
Listen to me ere we part.

EDMUNDS.

List to you! yes, I will hear you,
Mine alone is her young heart.

[*Exeunt severally.*

SCENE IV.—*The avenue leading to the Hall,
by moonlight. The house in the distance,
gaily illuminated.*

Enter FLAM *and* MARTIN.

FLAM.

You have got the letter I gave you for the
Squire ?

All right.   Here it is.

The moment you see me leave the room, slip it into the Squire's hand; you can easily do so, without being recognised, in the confusion of the dance, and then follow me.   You perfectly understand your instructions ?

Oh, yes,—I understand them well enough.

There's nothing more, then, that you want to know ?

No, nothing,—oh, yes there is.   I want to know whether—whether——

Well, go on.

Whether you could conveniently manage to let me have another couple of guineas, before you go away in the chaise.   Payment beforehand,—capital custom.   And if you don't, perhaps I may not get them at all, you know : (*aside*) seeing that I don't intend to go at all, I think it's very likely.

You're a remarkably pleasant fellow, Stokes,

in general conversation, — very, — but when you descend into particularities, you become excessively prosy. On some points, — money-matters for instance, — you have a very grasping imagination, and seem disposed to dilate upon them at too great a length. You must cure yourself of this habit, — you must indeed. Good-bye, Stokes ; you shall have the two guineas doubled when the journey is completed. Remember, — ten o'clock.

[*Exit* FLAM.

MARTIN.

I shan't forget ten o'clock, depend upon it. Now to burst upon my particular friend, Mr. John Maddox, with the awful disclosure. He must pass this way on his road to the Hall. Here they come, —don't see him though. (*Groups of male and female villagers in cloaks, &c. cross the stage on their way to the Hall.*)

MARTIN.

How are you, Tom ? How do, Will?

VILLAGERS.

How do, Mas'r Stokes?

MARTIN (*shaking hands with them*).

How do, Susan? Mind, Cary, you 're my first partner. Always kiss your first partner, — capital custom. (*Kisses her.*) Good-bye! See you up at the Hall.

17 *

VILLAGERS.

Ay, ay, Mas'r Stokes.   [*Exeunt Villagers.*

MARTIN.

Not among them. (*More villagers cross.*) Nor
them. Here he comes :—Rose with him too,—innocent little victim, little thinking of the atrocious
designs that are going on against her!

Enter MADDOX *and* ROSE, *arm-in-arm.*

JOHN.

Ha, ha, ha! that was a good 'un,—wasn't it ?
Ah! Martin, I wish I 'd seen you a minute ago. I
made such a joke! How you would ha' laughed!

MARTIN (*mysteriously beckoning* MADDOX *away
from* ROSE, *and whispering*).

I want to speak to you.

JOHN (*whispering*).

What about ?

ROSE.

Lor! don't stand whispering there, John. If
you have anything to say, Mr. Stokes, say it before
me.

JOHN (*taking her arm*).

Ah! say it before her! Don't mind her, Martin;
she's to be my wife, you know, and we 're to
be on the mutual-confidence principle; a'n't we,—
Rose ?

ROSE.

To be sure.   Why don't you speak, Mr. Stokes?
I suppose it's the old story,—something wrong.

MARTIN.

Something wrong!   I rather think there is; and
you little know what it is, or you wouldn't look
so merry.   What I have got to say—don't be
frightened, Miss Rose,—relates to—don't alarm
yourself, Master Maddox.

JOHN.

I a'n't alarming myself; you're alarming me.
Go on!

ROSE.

Go on!—can't you ?

MARTIN.

Relates to Mr. Flam.

JOHN (*dropping* ROSE's *arm*).

Mr. Flam !

MARTIN.

Hush !—and Miss Rose.

ROSE.

Me!   Me and Mr. Flam !

MARTIN.

Mr. Flam intends at ten o'clock, this very night,
—don't be frightened, Miss,—by force, in secret,
and in a chaise and four, too,—to carry off, against
her will, and elope with, Miss Rose.

ROSE.

Me! Oh! (*Screams, and falls into the arms of Maddox.*)

JOHN.

Rub her hands, Martin, she's going off in a fit.

MARTIN.

Never mind; she'd better go off in a fit than a chaise.

ROSE (*recovering*).

Oh, John! don't let me go.

JOHN.

Let you go!—not if I set the whole Hall on fire.

ROSE.

Hold me fast, John.

JOHN.

I'll hold you fast enough, depend upon it.

ROSE.

Come on the other side of me, Mr. Stokes: take my arm; hold me tight, Mr. Stokes.

MARTIN.

Don't be frightened, I'll take care of you. (*Takes her arm.*)

ROSE.

Oh! Mr. Stokes.

MARTIN.

Oh, indeed! Nothing wrong,—eh?

ROSE.

Oh! Mr. Stokes,—pray forgive my having doubted that there was——Oh! what a dreadful thing! What is to be done with me?

MARTIN.

Upon my word, I don't know. I think we had better shut her up in some place under ground,— hadn't we, John?—or, stay,—suppose we borrow the keys of the family vault, and lock her up there, for an hour or two.

JOHN.

Capital!

ROSE.

Lor! ·surely you may find out some more agreeable place than that, John.

MARTIN.

I have it.—I'm to carry her off.

BOTH.

You!

MARTIN.

Me,—don't be afraid of me:—all my management. You dance with her all the evening, and I'll keep close to you. If anybody tries to get her away, you knock him down,—and I'll help you.

JOHN.

That's the plan;—come along.

ROSE.

Oh, I am so frightened! Hold me fast, Mr. Stokes,—Don't let me go, John!

[Exeunt, talking.

Enter LUCY.

LUCY.

Light-hearted revellers! how I envy them! How painful is my situation,—obliged with a sad heart to attend a festivity, from which the only person I would care to meet will, I know, be absent. "But I will not complain. He shall see "that I can become worthy of him, once again. I "have lingered here so long, watching the soft "shades of evening as they closed around me, that "I cannot bear the thought of exchanging this "beautiful scene for the noise and glare of a "crowded room."

Song.—LUCY.

How beautiful at even-tide
To see the twilight shadows pale,
    Steal o'er the landscape, far and wide,
O'er stream and meadow, mound and dale.
    How soft is Nature's calm repose
When evening skies their cool dews weep:
    The gentlest wind more gently blows,
As if to soothe her in her sleep!

The gay morn breaks,
Mists roll away,
All Nature awakes
To glorious day.
In my breast alone
Dark shadows remain;
The peace it has known
It can never regain.

SCENE THE LAST.—*A spacious ball-room, brilliantly illuminated. A window at the end, through which is seen a moonlit landscape. A large concourse of country people, discovered.—The* SQUIRE,— FLAM,— *the* BENSONS,— LUCY, — ROSE,—MARTIN, *and* MADDOX.

SQUIRE.

Welcome, friends, welcome all!   Come, choose your partners, and begin the dance.

FLAM (*to Lucy*).

Your hand, for the dance?

LUCY.

Pray excuse me, sir; I am not well.   My head is oppressed and giddy.   I would rather sit by the window which looks into the garden, and feel the cool evening air.   (*She goes up.   He follows her.*)

JOHN (*aside*).

Stand by me, Martin. He's gone to order the chaise, perhaps.

ROSE.

Oh! pray don't let me be taken away, Mr. Stokes.

MARTIN.

Don't be frightened,—don't be frightened. Mr. Flam is gone. I'll give the Squire the note in a minute.

SQUIRE.

Now,—begin the dance.

A Country Dance.

(MARTIN *and* MADDOX, *in their endeavours to keep close to* ROSE, *occasion great confusion. As the* SQUIRE *is looking at some particular couple in the dance,* MARTIN *steals behind him, thrusts the letter in his hands, and resumes his place. The* SQUIRE *looks round as if to discover the person who has delivered it; but being unsuccessful, puts it up, and retires among the crowd of dancers. Suddenly a violent scream is heard, and the dance abruptly ceases. Great confusion.* MARTIN *and* MADDOX *hold* ROSE *firmly.*)

SQUIRE.

What has happened? Whence did that scream proceed?

SEVERAL VOICES.

From the garden!—from the garden!

EDMUNDS (*without*).

Raise him, and bring him here. Lucy,—dear
Lucy!

BENSON.

Lucy! My child! (*Runs up the stage, and
exit into garden.*)

MARTIN.

His child! Damme! they can't get this one,
so they're going to run away with the other.
Here's some mistake here. Let me go, Rose.
Come along, John. Make way there,—make way!

(*As they run towards the window,* EDMUNDS *appears at it, without a hat, and his dress disordered,
with* LUCY *in his arms. He delivers her to her
father and* ROSE.)

ROSE.

Lucy,—dear Lucy,—look up!

BENSON.

Is she hurt, George?—is the poor child injured?

EDMUNDS.

No, it is nothing but terror; she will be better
instantly. See! she is recovering now. (*Lucy
gradually recovers, as* FLAM, *his clothes torn, and
face disfigured, is led in by* MADDOX *and* MARTIN.)

BENSON.

Mr. Norton, this is an act of perjury and baseness, of which another instant would have witnessed
the completion.

SQUIRE (*to* FLAM).

Rascal! this is your deed.

FLAM (*aside to* NORTON).

That's right, Norton, keep it up.

SQUIRE.

Do not address me with your odious familiarity,
scoundrel!

FLAM.

You don't really mean to give me up?

SQUIRE.

I renounce you from this instant.

FLAM.

You do?—then take the consequences.

SQUIRE.

Benson,—Edmunds,—friends,—I declare to you
most solemnly that I had neither hand nor part in
this disgraceful outrage. It has been perpetrated
without my knowledge, wholly by that scoundrel.

FLAM.

'Tis false; it was done with his consent.
He has in his pocket, at this moment, a letter from
me, acquainting him with my intention.

ALL.

A letter!

SQUIRE.

A letter *was* put into my hands five minutes
since; but it acquainted me, not with this fellow's
intention, but with his real dishonourable and disgraceful character, to which I had hitherto been
a stranger. (*To* FLAM.) Do you know that handwriting, sir? (*showing him the letter*).

FLAM.

Ellis's letter! (*searching his pockets, and producing
the other*). I must,—ass that I was!—I did—
enclose the wrong one.

SQUIRE.

You will quit my house this instant; its roof
shall not shelter you another night. Take that
with you, sir, and begone. (*Throws him a purse.*)

FLAM (*taking it up*).

Ah! I suppose you think this munificent, now
—eh? I could have made twice as much of you
in London, Norton, I could indeed, to say nothing
of my exhibiting myself for a whole week to these
clods of earth, which would have been cheap,
dirt-cheap, at double the money. Bye-bye, Norton!
Farewell, grubs! [*Exit.*

SQUIRE.

Edmunds, you have rescued your future wife

from brutal violence; you will not leave her exposed to similar attempts in future?

EDMUNDS.

.Even if I would, I feel, now that I have pre- served her, that I could not.

SQUIRE.

Then take her, and with her the old farm, which from henceforth is your own. *You* will not turn the old man out, I suppose?

EDMUNDS (*shaking* BENSON *by the hand*).

I don't think we are very likely to quarrel on that score ; and most gratefully do we acknow- ledge your Honour's kindness. Maddox !

JOHN.

Hallo!

EDMUNDS.

I shall not want that cottage and garden we were speaking of, this morning, now. Let me imitate a good example, and bestow it on *your* wife, as *her* marriage portion.

ROSE.

Oh, delightful! Say certainly, John, — can't ycu?

JOHN.

Thank'ee, George, thank'ee! I say, Martin, I have arrived at the dignity of a cottage and a piece of ground, at last.

MARTIN.

Yes, you may henceforth consider yourself on a level with me.

SQUIRE.

Resume the dance.

MARTIN.

I beg your pardon. One word. (*Whispers the* SQUIRE.)

SQUIRE.

I hope not. Recollect, you have been mistaken before, to-day. You had better inquire.

MARTIN.

I will. (*To the audience.*) My very particular friend, if he will allow me to call him so,——

SQUIRE.

Oh, certainly.

MARTIN.

My very particular friend, Mr. Norton, wishes me to ask my other particular friends here, whether there's — anything wrong? We are delighted to hear your approving opinion in the old way. You *can't* do better. It's a capital custom.

Dance and Finale.—Chorus.

Join the dance, with step as light
As every heart should be to-night;
Music, shake the lofty dome,
In honour of our Harvest Home.

Join the dance, and banish care,
All are young, and gay, and fair;
Even age has youthful grown,
In honour of our Harvest Home.

Join the dance, bright faces beam,
Sweet lips smile, and dark eyes gleam ;
All these charms have hither come,
In honour of our Harvest Home.

Join the dance, with step as light,
As every heart should be to-night ;
Music, shake the lofty dome,
In honour of our Harvest Home.

Quintet.

Lucy—Rose—Edmunds—The Squire—Young
Benson.

No light bound
Of stag or timid hare,
O'er the ground
Where startled herds repair,
Do we prize
So high, or hold so dear,
As the eyes
That light our pleasures here.

No cool breeze
That gently plays by night,
O'er calm seas,
Whose waters glisten bright;
No soft moan
That sighs across the lea,
Harvest Home,
Is half so sweet as thee!

Chorus.

Hail to the merry autumn days, when yellow corn-
fields shine,
Far brighter than the costly cup that holds the
monarch's wine!
Hail to the merry harvest time, the gayest of the
year,
The time of rich and bounteous crops, rejoicing,
and good cheer.
Hail! Hail! Hail!

IS SHE HIS WIFE?

OR, SOMETHING SINGULAR!

18 *

[*Is She His Wife? or, Something Singular! A Comic Burletta. In One Act. By "Boz." First performed at the St. James's Theatre, Monday, March 6, 1837.*]

DRAMATIS PERSONÆ.

ALFRED LOVETOWN, ESQ. . . . MR. FORESTER.

MR. PETER LIMBURY . . . . MR. GARDNER.

FELIX TAPKINS, ESQ. (*formerly of the India House, Leadenhall Street, and Prospect Place, Poplar; but now of the Rustic Lodge, near Reading*). . MR. HARLEY.

JOHN (*servant to Lovetown*).

MRS. LOVETOWN . . . . . MISS ALLISON.

MRS. PETER LIMBURY . . . . MADAME SALA.

IS SHE HIS WIFE?

OR, SOMETHING SINGULAR!

SCENE I.—*A Room opening into a Garden. A Table laid for Breakfast; Chairs, etc.* MR. *and* MRS. LOVETOWN, C., *discovered at Breakfast,* R. H. *The former in a dressing-gown and slippers, reading a newspaper. A Screen on one side.*

LOVETOWN (L. H. *of table, yawning*).

Another cup of tea, my dear,—O Lord!

MRS. LOVETOWN (R. H. *of table*).

I wish, Alfred, you would endeavour to assume a more cheerful appearance in your wife's society. If you are perpetually yawning and complaining of *ennui* a few months after marriage, what am I to suppose you 'll become in a few years? It really is very odd of you.

LOVETOWN.

Not at all odd, my dear, not the least in the world; it would be a great deal more odd if I were not.   The fact is, my love, I 'm tired of the country; green fields, and blooming hedges, and feathered songsters, are fine things to talk about and read about and write about; but I candidly confess that I prefer paved streets, area railings and dustman's bells, after all.

MRS. LOVETOWN.

How often have you told me that, blessed with my love, you could live contented and happy in a desert.

LOVETOWN (*reading*).

" Artful impostor ! "

MRS. LOVETOWN.

Have you not over and over again said that fortune and personal attractions were secondary considerations with you ?   That you loved me for those virtues which, while they gave additional lustre to public life, would adorn and sweeten retirement ?

LOVETOWN (*reading*).

" Soothing syrup ! "

MRS. LOVETOWN.

You complain of the tedious sameness of a country life. Was it not you yourself who first proposed our residing permanently in the country? Did you not say that I should then have an ample

sphere in which to exercise those charitable feelings which I have so often evinced, by selling at
those benevolent fancy fairs?

LOVETOWN (*reading*).

" Humane man-traps! "

MRS. LOVETOWN.

He pays no attention to me,—Alfred dear,——

LOVETOWN (*stamping his foot*).

Yes, my life.

MRS. LOVETOWN.

Have you heard what I have just been saying,
dear?

LOVETOWN.

Yes, love.

MRS. LOVETOWN.

And what can you say in reply?

LOVETOWN.

Why, really, my dear, you've said it so often
before in the course of the last six weeks, that I
think it quite unnecessary to say anything more
about it. (*Reads.*) " The learned judge delivered a brief but impressive summary of the
unhappy man's trial."

MRS. LOVETOWN (*aside*).

I could bear anything but this neglect. He
evidently does not care for me.

LOVETOWN (*aside*).

I could put up with anything rather than these constant altercations and little petty quarrels. I repeat, my dear, that I am very dull in this out-of-the-way villa,—confoundedly dull,—horridly dull.

MRS. LOVETOWN.

˜ And *I* repeat that if you took any pleasure in your wife's society, or felt for her as you once professed to feel, you would have no cause to make such a complaint.

LOVETOWN.

If I did not know you to be one of the sweetest creatures in existence, my dear, I should be strongly disposed to say that you were a very close imitation of an aggravating female.

MRS. LOVETOWN.

That's very curious, my dear, for I declare that, if I hadn't known *you* to be such an exquisite, good-tempered, attentive husband, I should have mistaken you for a very great brute.

LOVETOWN.

My dear, you 're offensive.

MRS. LOVETOWN.

My love, you 're intolerable. (*They turn their chairs back to back.*)

MR. FELIX TAPKINS *sings without.*

" The wife around her husband throws
    Her arms to make him stay;
' My dear, it rains, it hails, it blows,
    And you cannot hunt to-day.'
        But a hunting we will go,
And a hunting we will go,—wo—wo—wo!
        And a hunting we will go."

MRS. LOVETOWN.

There's that dear, good-natured creature, Mr.
Tapkins,—do you ever hear *him* complain of the
tediousness of a country life?   Light-hearted creature,—his lively disposition and rich flow of spirits
are wonderful, even to me.   (*Rising.*)

LOVETOWN.

They need not be a matter of astonishment to
anybody, my dear,—he's a bachelor.

MR. FELIX TAPKINS *appears at window*, L. H.

TAPKINS.

Ha, ha! How are you both?—Here's a morning! Bless my heart alive, *what* a morning! I've
been gardening ever since five o'clock, and the
flowers have been actually growing before my very
eyes. The London Pride is sweeping everything
before it, and the stalks are half as high again as
they were yesterday. They're all run up like so

many tailors' bills, after that heavy dew of last
night broke down half my rosebuds with the
weight of its own moisture,—something like a
dew that!—reg'lar *doo*, eh?—come, that's not so
bad for a before-dinner one.

LOVETOWN.

Ah, you happy dog, Felix!

TAPKINS.

Happy! of course I am,—Felix by name, Felix
by nature,—what the deuce should I be unhappy
for, or anybody be unhappy for? What's the use
of it, that's the point.

MRS. LOVETOWN.

Have you finished your improvements yet, Mr.
Tapkins?

TAPKINS.

At Rustic Lodge? (*She nods assent.*) Bless
your heart and soul! you never saw such a place,
—cardboard chimneys, Grecian balconies,—Gothic
parapets, thatched roof.

MRS. LOVETOWN.

Indeed!

TAPKINS.

Lord bless you, yes,—green verandah, with ivy
twining round the pillars.

MRS. LOVETOWN.

How very rural!

TAPKINS.

Rural, my dear Mrs. Lovetown! delightful! The French windows, too! Such an improvement!

MRS. LOVETOWN.

I should think they were!

TAPKINS.

Yes, *I* should think they were. Why, on a fine summer's evening the frogs hop off the grass-plot into the very sitting-room.

MRS. LOVETOWN.

Dear me!

TAPKINS.

Bless you, yes! Something like the country,-- quite a little Eden. Why, when I'm smoking under the verandah, after a shower of rain, the black beetles fall into my brandy and water.

MR. *and* MRS. LOVETOWN.

No! Ha! ha! ha!

TAPKINS.

Yes. And I take 'em out again with the tea-spoon, and lay bets with myself which of them will run away the quickest. Ha! ha! ha! (*They all laugh.*) Then the stable, too. Why, in Rustic Lodge the stables are close to the dining-room window,

LOVETOWN.

No!

TAPKINS.

Yes. The horse can't cough but I hear him. There's compactness. Nothing like the cottage style of architecture for comfort, my boy. By the by, I have left the new horse at your garden-gate this moment.

MRS. LOVETOWN.

The new horse!

TAPKINS.

The new horse! Splendid fellow,—such action! Puts out its feet like a rocking-horse, and carries its tail like a hat-peg. Come and see him.

LOVETOWN (*laughing*).

I can't deny you anything.

TAPKINS.

No, that's what they all say, especially the—eh? (*Nodding and winking.*)

LOVETOWN.

Ha! ha! ha!

MRS. LOVETOWN.

Ha! ha! ha! I'm afraid you're a very bad man, Mr. Tapkins; I'm afraid you're a shocking man, Mr. Tapkins.

TAPKINS.

Think so? No, I don't know,—not worse than other people similarly situated. Bachelors, my dear Mrs. Lovetown, bachelors—eh! old fellow? (*Winking to* LOVETOWN.)

LOVETOWN.

Certainly, certainly.

TAPKINS.

We know—eh? (*They all laugh.*) By the by, talking of bachelors puts me in mind of Rustic Lodge, and talking of Rustic Lodge puts me in mind of what I came here for. You must come and see me this afternoon. Little Peter Limbury and his wife are coming.

MRS. LOVETOWN.

I detest that man.

LOVETOWN.

The wife is supportable, my dear.

TAPKINS.

To be sure, so she is. You'll come, and that's enough. Now come and see the horse.

LOVETOWN.

Give me three minutes to put on my coat and boots, and I'll join you. I won't be three minutes.

[*Exit* LOVETOWN, R. H.

TAPKINS.

Look sharp, look sharp!—Mrs. Lovetown, will you excuse me one moment? (*Crosses to* L.; *calling off.*) Jim,—these fellows never know how to manage horses,—walk him gently up and down,—throw the stirrups over the saddle to show the people that his master's coming, and if anybody asks what that fine animal's pedigree is, and who he belongs to, say he's the property of Mr. Felix Tapkins of Rustic Lodge, near Reading, and that he's the celebrated horse who ought to have won the Newmarket Cup last year, only he didn't.

[*Exit* TAPKINS.

MRS. LOVETOWN.

My mind is made up,—I can bear Alfred's coldness and insensibility no longer, and come what may I will endeavour to remove it. From the knowledge I have of his disposition I am convinced that the only mode of doing so will be by rousing his jealousy and wounding his vanity. This thoughtless creature will be a very good instrument for my scheme. He plumes himself on his gallantry, has no very small share of vanity, and is easily led. I see him crossing the garden. (*She brings a chair hastily forward and sits* R. H.)

Enter FELIX TAPKINS, L. H. *window.*

TAPKINS (*singing*).

" My dear, it rains, it hails, it blows,——"

MRS. LOVETOWN (*tragically*).

Would that I had never beheld him!

TAPKINS (*aside*).

Hallo! She's talking about her husband. I knew by their manner there had been a quarrel, when I came in this morning.

MRS. LOVETOWN.

So fascinating, and yet so insensible to the tenderest of passions as not to see how devotedly I love him.

TAPKINS (*aside*).

I thought so.

MRS. LOVETOWN.

That he should still remain unmarried is to me extraordinary.

TAPKINS.

Um!

MRS. LOVETOWN.

He ought to have married long since.

TAPKINS (*aside*).

Eh! Why, they aren't married!—" ought to have married long since."—I rather think he ought.

I.   19

MRS. LOVETOWN.

And, though I am the wife of another,——

TAPKINS (*aside*).

Wife of another!

MRS. LOVETOWN.

Still, I grieve to say that I cannot be blind to his extraordinary merits.

TAPKINS.

Why, he's run away with somebody else's wife! The villain!—I must let her know I'm in the room, or there's no telling what I may hear next. (*Coughs.*)

MRS. LOVETOWN (*starting up in affected confusion*).

Mr. Tapkins! (*They sit.*) Bring your chair nearer. I fear, Mr. Tapkins, that I have been unconsciously giving utterance to what was passing in my mind. I trust you have not overheard my confession of the weakness of my heart.

TAPKINS.

No—no—not more than a word or two.

MRS. LOVETOWN.

That agitated manner convinces me that you have heard more than you are willing to confess. Then why—why should I seek to conceal from you —that though I esteem my husband, I—I—love —another?

TAPKINS.

I heard you mention that little circumstance.

MRS. LOVETOWN.

Oh!   (*Sighs.*)

TAPKINS (*aside*).

What the deuce is she Oh-ing at?   She looks at me as if I were Lovetown himself.

MRS. LOVETOWN (*putting her hand on his shoulder with a languishing air*).

Does my selection meet with your approbation?

TAPKINS (*slowly*).

It doesn't.

MRS. LOVETOWN.

No!

TAPKINS.

Decidedly not.   (*Aside.*)   I'll cut that Lovetown out, and offer myself.   Hem!   Mrs. Lovetown.

MRS. LOVETOWN.

Yes, Mr. Tapkins.

TAPKINS.

I know an individual——

MRS. LOVETOWN.

Ah! an individual!

TAPKINS.

An individual,—I may, perhaps, venture to say

19 *

an estimable individual,—who for the last three months has been constantly in your society, who never yet had courage to disclose his passion, but who burns to throw himself at your feet. Oh! (*Aside.*) I 'll try an Oh or two now,—Oh! (*Sighs.*) That 's a capital Oh!

MRS. LOVETOWN (aside).

He must have misunderstood me before, for he is evidently speaking of himself.   Is the gentleman you speak of handsome, Mr. Tapkins?

TAPKINS.

He is generally considered remarkably so.

MRS. LOVETOWN.

Is he tall? ·

TAPKINS.

About the height of the Apollo Belvidere.

MRS. LOVETOWN.

Is he stout?

TAPKINS.

Of nearly the same dimensions as the gentleman I have just named.

MRS. LOVETOWN.

His figure is——

TAPKINS.

Quite a model.

MRS. LOVETOWN.

And he is——

TAPKINS.

Myself.   (*Throws himself on his knees and seizes
her hand.*)

Enter LOVETOWN, R. H.

TAPKINS *immediately pretends to be diligently looking
for something on the floor.*

MRS. LOVETOWN.

Pray don't trouble yourself.   I 'll find it.   Dear
me! how could I lose it?

LOVETOWN.

What have you lost, love?   I should almost
imagine that you had lost yourself, and that our
friend Mr. Tapkins here had just found you.

TAPKINS (*aside*).

Ah! you always will have your joke,—funny
dog! funny dog!   Bless my heart and soul, there 's
that immortal horse standing outside all this time!
He 'll catch his death of cold!   Come and see him
at once,—come—come.

LOVETOWN.

No.   I can't see him to-day.   I had forgotten.
I 've letters to write,—business to transact,—I 'm
engaged.

TAPKINS (*to* MRS. LOVETOWN).

Oh! if he 's engaged, you know, we 'd better
not interrupt him.

MRS. LOVETOWN.

Oh! certainly! Not by any means.

TAPKINS (*taking her arm*).

Good-bye, old fellow.

LOVETOWN (*seating himself at table*).

Oh!—good-bye.

TAPKINS (*going*).

Take care of yourself. I'll take care of Mrs. L.

[*Exeunt* TAPKINS *and* MRS. LOVETOWN, C.

LOVETOWN.

What the deuce does that fellow mean by laying such emphasis on Mrs. L. ? What's my wife to him, or he to my wife ? Very extraordinary! I can hardly believe that even if he had the treachery to make any advances, she would encourage such a preposterous intrigue. (*Walks to and fro.*) She spoke in his praise at breakfast-time, though,— and they have gone away together to see that confounded horse. But stop, I must keep a sharp eye upon them this afternoon, without appearing to do so. I would not appear unnecessarily suspicious for the world. Dissembling in such a case, though, is difficult—very difficult.

Enter a SERVANT, L. H.

SERVANT.

Mr. and Mrs. Peter Limbury.

LOVETOWN.

Desire them to walk in.

[*Exit* SERVANT, L. H.

A lucky visit! it furnishes me with a hint. This Mrs. Limbury is a vain, conceited woman, ready to receive the attentions of anybody who feigns admiration for her, partly to gratify herself, and partly to annoy the jealous little husband whom she keeps under such strict control. If I pay particular attention to *her*, I shall lull my wife and that scoundrel Tapkins into a false security, and have better opportunities of observation. They are here.

Enter MR. *and* MRS. LIMBURY, L. H.

LOVETOWN.

My dear Mrs. Limbury.   (*Crosses to* C.)

LIMBURY.

Eh?

LOVETOWN (*not regarding him*).

How charming—how delightful—how divine you look to-day.

LIMBURY (*aside*).

Dear Mrs. Limbury,—charming,—divine and beautiful look to-day! They are smiling at each other,—he squeezes her hand. I see how it is. I always thought he paid her too much attention.

LOVETOWN.

Sit down,—sit down.

LOVETOWN *places the chairs so as to sit between them, which* LIMBURY *in vain endeavours to prevent.*

MRS. LIMBURY.

Peter and I called as we passed in our little pony-chaise, to inquire whether we should have the pleasure of seeing you at Tapkins's this afternoon.

LOVETOWN.

Is it possible you can ask such a question ? Do you think I could stay away ?

MRS. LIMBURY.

Dear Mr. Lovetown ! (*Aside.*) How polite,— he's quite struck with me.

LIMBURY (*aside*).

Wretched miscreant ! a regular assignation before my very face.

LOVETOWN (*to* MRS. LIMBURY).

Do you know I entertained some apprehensions —some dreadful fears—that you might not be there.

LIMBURY.

Fears that we mightn't be there ? Of course we shall be there.

MRS. LIMBURY.

Now don't talk, Peter.

LOVETOWN.

I thought it just possible, you know, that you might not be agreeable——

MRS. LIMBURY.

O, Peter is always agreeable to anything that is agreeable to me.   Aren't you, Peter ?

LIMBURY.

Yes, dearest.   (*Aside.*) Agreeable to anything that's agreeable to her!   O Lor'!

MRS. LIMBURY.

By the by, Mr. Lovetown, how do you like this bonnet ?

LOVETOWN.

O, beautiful !

LIMBURY (*aside*).

I must change the subject.   Do you know, Mr. Lovetown, I have often thought, and it has frequently occurred to me—when——

MRS. LIMBURY.

Now don't talk, Peter.   (*To* LOVETOWN.) The colour is so bright, is it not ?

LOVETOWN.

It might appear so elsewhere, but the brightness of those eyes casts it quite into shade.

MRS. LIMBURY.

I know you are a connoisseur in ladies' dresses; how do you like those shoes ?

LIMBURY (*aside*).

Her shoes!   What will she ask his opinion of next ?

LOVETOWN.

O, like the bonnet, you deprive them of their fair chance of admiration.   That small and elegant foot engrosses all the attention which the shoes might otherwise attract.   That taper ankle, too—

LIMBURY (*aside*).

Her taper ankle !   My bosom swells with the rage of an ogre.   Mr. Lovetown,—I——

MRS. LIMBURY.

Now, pray do not talk so, Limbury.   You 've put Mr. Lovetown out as it is.

LIMBURY (*aside*).

Put him out !   I wish I could put him out, Mrs. Limbury.   I must.

Enter SERVANT, *hastily.*

SERVANT.

I beg your pardon, sir, but the bay pony has got his hind leg over the traces, and he 's kicking the chaise to pieces!

LIMBURY.

Kicking the *new* chaise to pieces!

LOVETOWN.

Kicking the new chaise to pieces! The bay pony! Limbury, my dear fellow, fly to the spot! (*Pushing him out.*)

LIMBURY.

But, Mr. Lovetown, I——

MRS. LIMBURY.

Oh! he'll kick somebody's brains out, if Peter don't go to him.

LIMBURY.

But perhaps he'll kick my brains out if I do go to him.

LOVETOWN.

Never mind, don't lose an instant,—not a moment. (*Pushes him out, both talking together.*)

[*Exit* LIMBURY.

(*Aside.*) Now for it,—here's my wife. Dearest Mrs. Limbury—(*Kneels by her chair, and seizes her hand.*)

Enter MRS. LOVETOWN, C.

MRS. LOVETOWN (*aside*).

Can I believe my eyes? (*Retires behind the screen.*)

MRS. LIMBURY.

Mr. Lovetown!

LOVETOWN.

Nay. Allow me in one hurried interview, which I have sought for in vain for weeks,—for months,—to say how devotedly, how ardently I love you. Suffer me to retain this hand in mine. Give me one ray of hope.

MRS. LIMBURY.

Rise, I entreat you,—we shall be discovered.

LOVETOWN.

Nay, I will not rise till you promise me that you will take an opportunity of detaching yourself from the rest of the company and meeting me alone in Tapkins's grounds this evening. I shall have no eyes, no ears for anyone but yourself.

MRS. LIMBURY.

Well,—well,—I will—I do——

LOVETOWN.

Then I am blest indeed!

MRS. LIMBURY.

I am so agitated. If Peter or Mrs. Lovetown—were to find me thus—I should betray all. I'll teach my husband to be jealous! (*Crosses to* L. H.) Let us walk round the garden.

LOVETOWN.

With pleasure,—take my arm. Divine creature!

(*Aside.*) I'm sure she is behind the screen. I saw her peeping. Come.

[*Exit* LOVETOWN *and* MRS. LIMBURY, L. H.

MRS. LOVETOWN (*coming forward*).

Faithless man! His coldness and neglect are now too well explained. O Alfred! Alfred! how little did I think when I married you, six short months since, that I should be exposed to so much wretchedness! I begin to tremble at my own imprudence, and the situation in which it may place me; but it is now too late to recede. I must be firm. This day will either bring my project to the explanation I so much desire, or convince me of what I too much fear,—my husband's aversion. Can this woman's husband suspect their intimacy? If so, he may be able to prevent this assignation taking place. I will seek him instantly. If I can but meet him at once, he may prevent her going at all.   [*Exit* MRS. LOVETOWN, R. H.

Enter TAPKINS, L. H. *window*.

TAPKINS.

This, certainly, is a most extraordinary affair. Not her partiality for me,—that's natural enough, —but the confession I overheard about her marriage to another. I have been thinking that, after such a discovery, it would be highly improper to allow Limbury and his wife to meet her without warning him of the fact. The best way will be to make him acquainted with the real state of the case. Then he must see the propriety of not bringing his wife to my house to-night. Ah! here he is. I'll make the awful disclosure at once, and petrify him.

Enter LIMBURY, L. H. *window.*

LIMBURY.

That damned little bay pony is as bad as my wife. There's no curbing either of them ; and as soon as I have got the traces of the one all right, I lose all traces of the other.

TAPKINS, R.

Peter!

LIMBURY, L.

Ah! Tapkins!

TAPKINS.

Hush! Hush! (*Looking cautiously round.*) If you have a moment to spare, I've got something of great importance to communicate.

LIMBURY.

Something of great importance, Mr. Tapkins! (*Aside.*) What can he mean ? Can it relate to Mrs. Limbury ? The thought is dreadful. You horrify me !

TAPKINS.

You'll be more horrified presently. What I am about to tell you concerns yourself and your honour very materially; and I beg you to understand that I communicate it—in the strictest confidence.

LIMBURY.

Myself and my honour! I shall dissolve into nothing with horrible anticipations!

TAPKINS (*in a low tone*).

Have you ever observed anything remarkable about Lovetown's manner?

LIMBURY.

Anything remarkable?

TAPKINS.

Ay,—anything very odd, and rather unpleasant?

LIMBURY.

Decidedly! No longer than half an hour ago, —in this very room, I observed something in his manner particularly odd and exceedingly unpleasant.

TAPKINS.

To your feelings as a husband?

LIMBURY.

Yes, my friend, yes, yes;—you know it all, I see!

TAPKINS.

What! Do *you* know it?

LIMBURY.

I'm afraid I do; but go on—go on.

TAPKINS (*aside*).

How the deuce can he know anything about it ?
Well, this oddness arises from the peculiar nature
of his connexion with—— You look very pale.

LIMBURY.

No, no,—go on,—" connexion with— "

TAPKINS.

A certain lady,—you know whom I mean.

LIMBURY.

I do, I do! (*Aside*). Disgrace and confusion !
I 'll kill her with a look ! I 'll wither her with
scornful indignation ! Mrs. Limbury !—viper !

TAPKINS (*whispering with caution*).
They—aren't—married. ·

LIMBURY.

They aren't married ! *Who* aren't ?

TAPKINS.

Those two, to be sure !

LIMBURY.

Those two ! *What* two ?

TAPKINS.

Why, them. And the worst of it is she 's—
she 's married to somebody else.

· LIMBURY.

Well, of course I know that.

TAPKINS.

You know it ?

LIMBURY.

Of course I do. Why, how you talk! Isn't she my wife ?

TAPKINS.

Your wife! Wretched bigamist! Mrs. Lovetown your wife ?

LIMBURY.

Mrs. Lovetown! What! Have you been talking of Mrs. Lovetown all this time? My dear friend! (*Embraces him.*) The revulsion of feeling is almost insupportable. I thought you were talking about Mrs. Limbury.

TAPKINS.

No!

LIMBURY.

Yes. Ha! ha! But I say, what a dreadful fellow this is—another man's wife! Gad, I think he wants to run away with every man's wife he sees. And Mrs. Lovetown, too—horrid !

TAPKINS.

Shocking !

LIMBURY.

I say, I oughtn't to allow Mrs. Limbury to associate with her, ought I ?

I.   20

TAPKINS.

Precisely my idea. You had better induce your wife to stay away from my house to-night.

LIMBURY.

I'm afraid I can't do that.

TAPKINS.

What, has she any particular objection to staying away?

LIMBURY.

She has a very strange inclination to go, and 'tis much the same; however, I'll make the best arrangement I can!

TAPKINS.

Well, so be it. Of course I shall see *you?*

LIMBURY.

Of course.

TAPKINS.

Mind the secret,—close—close—you know, as a Cabinet minister answering a question.

LIMBURY.

You may rely upon me.

[*Exit* LIMBURY, L. II., TAPKINS, R. II.

SCENE II.—*A Conservatory on one side. A Summer-house on the other.*

Enter LOVETOWN *at* L. H.

LOVETOWN.

So far so good. My wife has not dropped the slightest hint of having overheard the conversation between me and Mrs. Limbury ; but she cannot conceal the impression it has made upon her mind, or the jealousy it has evidently excited in her breast. This is just as I wished. I made Mr. Peter Limbury's amiable helpmate promise to meet me here. I know that refuge for destitute reptiles (*pointing to summer-house*) is Tapkins's favourite haunt, and if he has any assignation with my wife, I have no doubt he will lead her to this place. A woman's coming down the walk. Mrs. Limbury, I suppose,—no, my wife, by all that's actionable. I must conceal myself here, even at the risk of a shower of black beetles, or a marching regiment of frogs. (*Goes into conservatory,* L. H.)

Enter MRS. LOVETOWN *from top*, L. H.

MRS. LOVETOWN.

I cannot have been mistaken. I am certain I saw Alfred here ; he must have secreted himself

20 *

somewhere to avoid me. Can his assignation
with Mrs. Limbury have been discovered ? Mr.
Limbury's behaviour to me just now was strange
in the extreme ; and after a variety of incoherent
expressions he begged me to meet him here, on a
subject, as he said, of great delicacy and importance
to myself. Alas! I fear that my husband's
neglect and unkindness are but too well known.
The injured little man approaches. I summon all
my fortitude to bear the disclosure.

Enter MR. LIMBURY *at top*, L. H.

LIMBURY (*aside*).

Now as I could not prevail on Mrs. Limbury to
stay away, the only distressing alternative I have
is to inform Mrs. Lovetown that I know her
history, and to put it to her good feeling whether
she hadn't better go.

LOVETOWN (*peeping*).

Limbury! what the deuce can that little wretch
want here ?

LIMBURY.

I took the liberty, Mrs. Lovetown, of begging
you to meet me in this retired spot, because the
esteem I still entertain for you, and my regard for
your feelings, induce me to prefer a private to a
public disclosure.

LOVETOWN (*peeping*).

" Public disclosure ! " what on earth is he talking about ?   I wish he 'd speak a little louder.

MRS. LOVETOWN.

I am sensible of your kindness, Mr. Limbury, and believe me most grateful for it.   I am fully prepared to hear what you have to say.

LIMBURY.

It is hardly necessary for me, I presume, to say. Mrs. Lovetown, that I have accidentally discovered the whole secret.

MRS. LOVETOWN.

The whole secret, sir ?

LOVETOWN (*peeping*).

Whole secret !   What secret ?

LIMBURY.

The whole secret, ma'am, of this disgraceful—I must call it disgraceful—and most abominable intrigue.

MRS. LOVETOWN (*aside*).

My worst fears are realized,—my husband's neglect is occasioned by his love for another.

LOVETOWN (*peeping*).

Abominable intrigue!   My first suspicions are too well founded.   He reproaches my wife with her infidelity, and she cannot deny it,—that villain Tapkins!

MRS. LOVETOWN (*weeping*).

Cruel—cruel—Alfred !

LIMBURY.

You may well call him cruel, unfortunate woman. His usage of you is indefensible, unmanly, scandalous.

MRS. LOVETOWN.

It is. It is, indeed.

LIMBURY.

It's very painful for me to express myself in such plain terms, Mrs. Lovetown ; but allow me to say, as delicately as possible, that you should not endeavour to appear in society under such unusual and distressing circumstances.

MRS. LOVETOWN.

Not appear in society !   Why should I quit it ?

LOVETOWN (*peeping*).

Shameful woman !

LIMBURY.

Is it possible you can ask such a question ?

MRS. LOVETOWN.

What should I do ?   Where can I go ?

LIMBURY.

Gain permission to return once again to your husband's roof.

MRS. LOVETOWN.

My husband's roof ?

LIMBURY.

Yes, the roof of your husband, your wretched, unfortunate husband !

MRS. LOVETOWN.

Never !

LIMBURY (*aside*).

She's thoroughly hardened, steeped in vice beyond redemption. Mrs. Lovetown, as you reject my well-intentioned advice in this extraordinary manner, I am reduced to the painful necessity of expressing my hope that you will,—now pray don't think me unkind,—that you will never attempt to meet Mrs. Limbury more.

MRS. LOVETOWN.

What ! Can you suppose I am so utterly dead to every sense of feeling and propriety as to meet that person,—the destroyer of my peace and happiness,—the wretch who has ruined my hopes and blighted my prospects for ever ? Ask your own heart, sir,—appeal to your own feelings. *You* are naturally indignant at her conduct. *You* would hold no further communication with her. Can

you suppose, then, *I* would deign to do so ? The
mere supposition is an insult !

[*Exit* MRS. LOVETOWN *hastily at top*, L. H.

LIMBURY.

What can all this mean ? I am lost in a maze
of astonishment, petrified at the boldness with
which she braves it out. Eh ! it's breaking upon
me by degrees. I see it. What did she say ?
" Destroyer of peace and happiness,—person—
ruined hopes and blighted prospects—*her.*" I see
it all. That atrocious Lovetown, that Don Juan
multiplied by twenty, that unprecedented libertine,
has seduced Mrs. Limbury from her allegiance to
her lawful lord and master. He first of all runs
away with the wife of another man, and he is no
sooner tired of her, than he runs away with another
wife of another man. I thirst for his destruction. I—(LOVETOWN *rushes from the conservatory
and embraces* LIMBURY, *who disengages himself.*)
Murderer of domestic happiness ! behold your
victim !

LOVETOWN.

Alas ! you speak but too truly. (*Covering his
face with his hands.*) I am the victim.

LIMBURY.

I speak but too truly !—He avows his own
criminality. I shall throttle him. I know I shall.
I feel it.

Enter MRS. LIMBURY *at back*, L. H.

MRS. LIMBURY (*aside*).

My husband here !   (*Goes into conservatory.*)

Enter TAPKINS *at back*, L. H.

TAPKINS (*aside*).

Not here, and her husband with Limbury.   I 'll reconnoitre.   (*Goes into summer-house*, R. H.)

LIMBURY.

Lovetown, have you the boldness to look an honest man in the face ?

LOVETOWN.

O, spare me !   I feel the situation in which I am placed acutely, deeply.   Feel for me when I say that from that conservatory I overheard the greater part of what passed between you and Mrs. Lovetown.

LIMBURY.

You did ?

LOVETOWN.

Need I say how highly I approve both of the language you used, and the advice you gave her ?

LIMBURY.

What ! you want to get rid of her, do you ?

LOVETOWN.

Can you doubt it ?

TAPKINS (*peeping*).

Hallo ! he wants to get rid of her.   Queer !

LOVETOWN.

Situated as I am, you know, I have no other
resource, after what has passed. I must part from
her.

MRS. LIMBURY (*peeping*).

What can he mean ?

LIMBURY (*aside*).

I should certainly throttle him, were it not that
the coolness with which he refers to the dreadful
event paralyzes me. Mr. Lovetown, look at me !
Sir, consider the feelings of an indignant husband,
sir !

LOVETOWN.

O, I thank you for those words. Those strong
expressions prove the unaffected interest you take
in the matter.

LIMBURY.

Unaffected interest ! I shall go raving mad
with passion and fury! Villain ! Monster ! To
embrace the opportunity afforded him of being on
a footing of friendship.

LOVETOWN.

To take a mean advantage of his being a single
man.

LIMBURY.

To tamper with the sacred engagements of a
married woman.

LOVETOWN.

To place a married man in a disgraceful and humiliating situation.

LIMBURY.

Scoundrel! Do you mock me to my face ?

LOVETOWN.

Mock *you !* What d' ye mean ? Who the devil are you talking about ?

LIMBURY.

Talking about—*you !*

LOVETOWN.

Me !

LIMBURY.

Designing miscreant! Of whom do *you* speak ?

LOVETOWN.

Of whom should I speak but that scoundrel Tapkins ?

TAPKINS (*coming forward*, R.).

Me! What the devil do you mean by that ?

LOVETOWN.

Ha! (*Rushing at him, is held back by* LIMBURY.)

LIMBURY (*to* TAPKINS).

Avoid him. Get out of his sight. He 's raving mad with conscious villainy.

TAPKINS.

What are you all playing at *I spy I* over my two acres of infant hay for ?

LOVETOWN (*to* TAPKINS).

How dare you tamper with the affections of Mrs. Lovetown?

TAPKINS.

O, is that all? Ha! ha! (*Crosses to* C.).

LOVETOWN.

All!

TAPKINS.

Come, come, none of your nonsense.

LOVETOWN.

Nonsense! Designate the best feelings of our nature nonsense!

TAPKINS.

Pooh! pooh! Here, I know all about it.

LOVETOWN (*angrily*).

And so do I, sir! And so do I.

TAPKINS.

Of course you do. And you've managed very well to keep it quiet so long. But you're a deep fellow, by Jove! you're a deep fellow!

LOVETOWN.

Now, mind! I restrain myself sufficiently to ask you once again before I knock you down, by what right dare you tamper with the affections of Mrs. Lovetown?

TAPKINS.

Right! O, if you come to strict right, you know, nobody has a right but her husband.

LOVETOWN.

And who is her husband ?   Who is her husband?

TAPKINS.

Ah! to be sure, that's the question.   Nobody that I know.   I hope—poor fellow——

LOVETOWN.

I'll bear these insults no longer! (*Rushes towards* TAPKINS. LIMBURY *interposes.* LOVE-TOWN *crosses to* R. H.   *A scream is heard from the conservatory—a pause.*)

TAPKINS.

Something singular among the plants! (*He goes into the conservatory and returns with* MRS. LIMBURY.)   A flower that wouldn't come out of its own accord.   I was obliged to force it.   Tolerably full blown now, at all events.

LIMBURY.

My wife! Traitoress! (*Crosses to* L. H.)   Fly from my presence!   Quit my sight!   Return to the conservatory with that demon in a frock-coat!

Enter MRS. LOVETOWN *at top*, L. H. *and comes down* C.

TAPKINS.

Hallo!   Somebody else!

LOVETOWN (*aside*).

My wife here!

MRS. LOVETOWN (*to* LIMBURY).

I owe you some return for the commiseration
you expressed just now for my wretched situation.
The best, the only one I can make you is, to entreat
you to refrain from committing any rash act, however excited you may be, and to control the feelings
of an injured husband.

TAPKINS.

Injured husband! Decidedly singular!

LOVETOWN.

The allusion of that lady I confess my utter
inability to understand. Mr. Limbury, to you an
explanation is due, and I make it more cheerfully,
as my abstaining from doing so might involve the
character of your wife. Stung by the attentions
which I found Mrs. Lovetown had received from a
scoundrel present,——

TAPKINS (*aside*).

That's me.

LOVETOWN.

I—partly to obtain opportunities of watching
her closely, under an assumed mask of levity and
carelessness, and partly in the hope of awaking
once again any dormant feelings of affection that
might still slumber in her breast, affected a passion
for your wife which I never felt, and to which she
never really responded. The second part of my

project, I regret to say, has failed.   The first has succeeded but too well.

LIMBURY.

Can I believe my ears ?   But how came Mrs. Peter Limbury to receive those attentions?

MRS. LIMBURY.

Why, not because I liked them, of course, but to assist Mr. Lovetown in his project, and to teach you the misery of those jealous fears.   Come here, you stupid little jealous, insinuating darling.

[*They retire up* L. H., *she coaxing him.*

TAPKINS (*aside*).

It strikes me very forcibly that I have made a slight mistake here, which is something particularly singular.   [*Turns up* R. H.

MRS. LOVETOWN.

Alfred, hear me !   I am as innocent as yourself. Your fancied neglect and coldness hurt my weak vanity, and roused some foolish feelings of angry pride.   In a moment of irritation I resorted to some such retaliation as you have yourself described. That I did so from motives as guiltless as your own I call Heaven to witness.   That I repent my fault I solemnly assure you.

LOVETOWN.

Is this possible ?

TAPKINS.

Very possible indeed ! Believe your wife's assurance and my corroboration. Here, give and take is all fair, you know. Give me your hand and take your wife's. Here, Mr. and Mrs. L. (*to* LIMBURY.) Double L,—I call them. (*To* LOVE-TOWN.) Small italic and Roman capital. (*To* MR. *and* MRS. LIMBURY, *who come forward.*) Here, it's all arranged. The key to the whole matter is, that I've been mistaken, which is something singular. If I have made another mistake in calculating on *your* kind and lenient reception of our last half-hour's misunderstanding (*to the audience*), I shall have done something more singular still. Do you forbid me committing any more mistakes, or may I announce my intention of doing something singular again ?

THE LAMPLIGHTER:

A FARCE.

1838.

DRAMATIS PERSONÆ.

Mr. Stargazer.

Master Galileo Isaac Newton Flamstead Stargazer
   (*his son*).

Tom Grig (*the Lamplighter*).

Mr. Mooney (*an Astrologer*).

Servant.

Betsy Martin.

Emma Stargazer.

Fanny Brown.

21 *

THE LAMPLIGHTER.

SCENE I.—*The Street, outside of* MR. STARGAZER'S *house. Two street Lamp-posts in front.*

TOM GRIG (*with ladder and lantern, singing as he enters*).

Day has gone down o'er the Baltic's proud bil-ler;
Evening has sigh'd, alas! to the lone wil-ler ;
Night hurries on, night hurries on, earth and ocean
   to kiv-ver ;
Rise, gentle moon, rise, gentle moon, and guide me
   to my——

That ain't a rhyme, that ain't—kiv-ver and lover!
I ain't much of a poet; but if I couldn't make
better verse than that, I'd undertake to be set fire
to, and put up, instead of the lamp, before Alder-
man Waithman's obstacle in Fleet-street. Bil-ler,
wil-ler, kiv-ver—shiver, obviously. That's what
I call poetry. (*Sings.*)

Day has gone down o'er the Baltic's proud bil-ler—

[*During the previous speech he has been occupied in lighting one of the lamps. As he is about to light the other,* MR. STARGAZER *appears at window, with a telescope.*

MR. STARGAZER (*after spying most intently at the clouds*).

Holloa!

TOM (*on ladder*).

Sir, to you! And holloa again, if you come to that.

MR. STARGAZER.

Have you seen the comet?

TOM.

What Comet—the Exeter Comet?

MR. STARGAZER.

What comet? *The* comet—Halley's comet!

TOM.

Nelson's, you mean. I saw it coming out of the yard, not five minutes ago.

MR. STARGAZER.

Could you distinguish anything of a tail?

TOM.

Distinguish a tail? I believe you—four tails!

MR. STARGAZER.

A comet with four tails; and all visible to the naked eye! Nonsense! it couldn't be.

TOM.

You wouldn't say that again if you was down here, old Bantam. (*Clock strikes five.*) You'll tell me next, I suppose, that that isn't five o'clock striking, eh?

MR. STARGAZER.

Five o'clock—five o'clock! Five o'clock P.M. on the thirtieth day of November, one thousand eight hundred and thirty-eight! Stop till I come down—stop! Don't go away on any account—not a foot, not a step.   [*Closes window.*

TOM (*descending, and shouldering his ladder*).

Stop! stop, to a lamplighter, with three hundred and seventy shops and a hundred and twenty private houses waiting to be set a light to! Stop, to a lamplighter!

As he is running off, enter MR. STARGAZER *from his house, hastily.*

MR. STARGAZER (*detaining him*).

Not for your life!—not for your life! The thirtieth day of November, one thousand eight hundred and thirty-eight! Miraculous circumstance! extraordinary fulfilment of a prediction of the planets!

TOM.

What are you talking about?

MR. STARGAZER (*looking about*).

Is there nobody else in sight, up the street or down? No, not a soul! This, then, is the man whose coming was revealed to me by the stars, six months ago!

TOM.

What do you mean?

MR. STARGAZER.

Young man, that I have consulted the Book of Fate with rare and wonderful success,—that coming events have cast their shadows before.

TOM.

Don't talk nonsense to me,—I ain't an event; I'm a lamplighter!

MR. STARGAZER (*aside*).

True!—Strange destiny that one, announced by the planets as of noble birth, should be devoted to so humble an occupation. (*Aloud.*) But you were not *always* a lamplighter?

TOM.

Why, no. I wasn't born with a ladder on my left shoulder, and a light in my other hand. But I took to it very early, though,—I had it from my uncle.

MR. STARGAZER (*aside*).

He had it from his uncle! How plain, and yet how forcible, is his language! He speaks of lamp-lighting, as though it were the whooping-cough or measles! (*To him.*) Ay!

TOM.

Yes, he was the original. You should have known him!—'cod! he was a genius, if ever there was one. Gas was the death of him! When gas lamps was first talked of, my uncle draws himself up, and says, " I 'll not believe it, there 's no sich a thing," he says. " You might as well talk of laying on an everlasting succession of glow-worms!" But when they made the experiment of lighting a piece of Pall Mall——

MR. STARGAZER.

That was when it first came up ?

TOM.

No, no, that was when it was first laid down. Don't mind me ; I can't help a joke, now and then. My uncle was sometimes took that way. When the experiment was made of lighting a piece of Pall Mall, and he had actually witnessed it, with his own eyes, you should have seen my uncle then!

MR. STARGAZER.

So much overcome?

TOM.

Overcome, sir! He fell off his ladder, from weakness, fourteen times that very night; and his last fall was into a wheelbarrow that was going his way, and humanely took him home. "I foresee in this," he says, "the breaking up of our profession; no more polishing of the tin reflectors," he says; "no more fancy-work, in the way of clipping the cottons at two o'clock in the morning; no more going the rounds to trim by daylight, and dribbling down of the *ile* on the hats and bonnets of the ladies and gentlemen, when one feels in good spirits. Any low fellow can light a gas-lamp, and it's all up!" So he petitioned the Government for—what do you call that that they give to people when it's found out that they've never been of any use, and have been paid too much for doing nothing?

MR. STARGAZER.

Compensation?

TOM.

Yes, that's the thing,—compensation. They didn't give him any, though! And then he got very fond of his country all at once, and went about, saying how that the bringing in of gas was a death-blow to his native land, and how that its *ile* and cotton trade was gone for ever, and the whales would go and kill themselves, privately, in spite and vexation at not being caught! After this, he was right-down cracked, and called his 'bacco pipe a gas pipe, and thought his tears was lamp *ile*, and all manner of nonsense. At last, he went and hung himself on a lamp iron, in St. Martin's Lane, that he 'd always been very fond of ; and as he was a remarkably good husband, and had never had any secrets from his wife, he put a note in the twopenny post, as he went along, to tell the widder where the body was.

MR. STARGAZER (*laying his hand upon his arm, and
speaking mysteriously*).

Do you remember your parents ?

TOM.

My mother I do, very well!

MR. STARGAZER.

Was she of noble birth ?

TOM.

Pretty well. She was in the mangling line. Her mother came of a highly respectable family, —such a business, in the sweetstuff and hardbake way !

MR. STARGAZER.

Perhaps your father was——.

TOM.

Why, I hardly know about him. The fact is, there was some little doubt, at the time, who *was* my father. Two or three young gentlemen were paid the pleasing compliment; but their incomes being limited, they were compelled delicately to decline it.

MR. STARGAZER.

Then the prediction is not fulfilled merely in part, but entirely and completely. Listen, young man,—I am acquainted with all the celestial bodies——

TOM.

Are you, though?—I hope they are quite well,— every body.

MR. STARGAZER.

Don't interrupt me. I am versed in the great sciences of astronomy and astrology; in my house there I have every description of apparatus for observing the course and motion of the planets. I'm writing a work about them, which will consist of eighty-four volumes, imperial quarto; and an appendix, nearly twice as long. I read what's going to happen in the stars.

TOM.

Read what's going to happen in the stars! Will any thing particular happen in the stars in the course of next week, now?

MR. STARGAZER.

You don't understand me. I read in the stars what 's going to happen here. Six months ago I derived from this source the knowledge that, precisely as the clock struck five, on the afternoon of this very day, a stranger would present himself before my enraptured sight,—that stranger would be a man of illustrious and high descent,—that stranger would be the destined husband of my young and lovely niece, who is now beneath that roof (*points to his house*);—that stranger is yourself: I receive you with open arms!

TOM.

Me! I, the man of illustrious and high—I, the husband of a young and lovely—Oh! it can't be, you know! the stars have made a mistake—the comet has put 'em out!

MR. STARGAZER.

Impossible! The characters were as plain as pike-staves. The clock struck five; you were here; there was not a soul in sight; a mystery envelopes your birth; you are a man of noble aspect. Does not everything combine to prove the accuracy of my observations?

TOM.

Upon my word, it looks like it! And now I come to think of it, I have very often felt as if I wasn't the small beer I was taken for.   And yet I don't know,—you're quite sure about the noble aspect ?

MR. STARGAZER.

Positively certain.

TOM.

Give me your hand.

MR. STARGAZER.

And my heart, too !   [*They shake hands heartily.*

TOM.

The young lady is tolerably good-looking, is she?

MR. STARGAZER.

Beautiful !   A graceful carriage, an exquisite shape, a sweet voice; a countenance beaming with animation and expression; the eye of a startled fawn.

TOM.

I see ; a sort of game eye.   Does she happen to have any of the—this is quite between you and me, you know,—and I only ask from curiosity,—not because I care about it,—any of the ready?

MR. STARGAZER.

Five thousand pounds! But what of that ? what of that ?   A word in your ear.   I'm in search of the philosopher's stone !   I have very nearly found it—not quite.   It turns everything to gold; that's its property.

TOM.

What a lot of property it must have !

MR. STARGAZER.

When I get it, we 'll keep it in the family.   Not
a word to any one !   What will money be to us ?
We shall never be able to spend it fast enough.

TOM.

Well, you know, we can but try,—I 'll do my
best endeavours.

MR. STARGAZER.

Thank you,—thank you !   But I 'll introduce
you to your future bride at once :—this way, this
way !

TOM.

What, without going my rounds first ?

MR. STARGAZER.

Certainly.   A man in whom the planets take
especial interest, and who is about to have a share
in the philosopher's stone, descend to lamp-
lighting !

TOM.

Perish the base idea ! not by no means !   I 'll
take in my tools though, to prevent any kind
inquiries after me, at your door.   (*As he shoulders
the ladder the sound of violent rain is heard*).
Holloa !

MR. STARGAZER (*putting his hand on his head, in amazement*).

What's that?

TOM.

It's coming down, rather.

MR. STARGAZER.

Rain!

TOM.

Ah! and a soaker, too!

MR. STARGAZER.

It can't be!—it's impossible!—(*Taking a book from his pocket, and turning over the pages hurriedly.*) Look here,—here it is,—here's the weather almanack,—"Set fair,"—I knew it couldn't be! (*with great triumph.*)

TOM (*turning up his collar as the rain increases*).

Don't you think there's a dampness in the atmosphere?

MR. STARGAZER (*looking up*).

It's singular,—it's *like* rain!

TOM.

Uncommonly like.

MR. STARGAZER.

It's a mistake in the elements, somehow. Here it is, "set fair,"—and set fair it ought to be.

" Light clouds floating about." Ah! you see, there are no light clouds;—the weather 's all wrong.

TOM.

Don't you think we had better get under cover ?

MR. STARGAZER (*slowly retreating towards the house*).

I don't acknowledge that it has any right to rain, mind! I protest against this. If Nature goes on in this way, I shall lose all respect for her,—it won't do, you know; it ought to have been two degrees colder, yesterday ; and instead of that, it was warmer. This is not the way to treat scientific men. I protest against it !

[*Exeunt into house, both talking,* TOM *pushing* STARGAZER *on, and the latter continually turning back, to declaim against the weather.*

SCENE II.—*A Room in* STARGAZER'S *house.* BETSY MARTIN, EMMA STARGAZER, FANNY BROWN, *and* GALILEO, *all murmuring together as they enter.*

BETSY.

I say again, young ladies, that it 's shameful! unbearable !

ALL.

Oh! shameful! shameful !

BETSY.

Marry Miss Emma to a great, old, ugly, doting, dreaming As-tron-o-Magician, like Mr. Mooney, who's always winking and blinking through telescopes and that, and can't see a pretty face when it's under his very nose !

GALILEO (*with a melancholy air*).

There never was a pretty face under *his* nose, Betsy, leastways, since I've known him. He's very plain.

BETSY.

Ah ! there's poor young master, too; he hasn't even spirits enough left to laugh at his own jokes. I'm sure I pity him, from the very bottom of my heart.

FANNY *and* EMMA.

Poor fellow !

GALILEO.

Ain't I a legitimate subject for pity ? Ain't it a dreadful thing that I, that am twenty-one come next Lady-day, should be treated like a little boy ? —and all because my father is so busy with the moon's age that he don't care about mine ; and so much occupied in making observations on the sun round which the earth revolves, that he takes no notice of the son that revolves round him ! I wasn't taken out of nankeen frocks and trousers till I became quite unpleasant in 'em.

ALL.

What a shame!

GALILEO.

I wasn't, indeed. And look at me now! Here's a state of things. Is this a suit of clothes for a major,—at least, for a gentleman who is a minor now, but will be a major on the very next Lady-day that comes? Is this a fit——

ALL (*interrupting him*).

Certainly not!

GALILEO (*vehemently*).

I won't stand it—I won't submit to it any longer. I *will* be married.

ALL.

No, no, no! don't be rash.

GALILEO.

I will, I tell you. I'll marry my cousin Fanny. Give me a kiss, Fanny; and Emma and Betsy will look the other way the while. (*Kisses her.*) There!

BETSY.

Sir—sir! here's your father coming!

GALILEO.

Well, then, I'll have another, as an antidote to my father. One more, Fanny.   [*Kisses her.*

MR. STARGAZER (*without*).

This way—this way! You shall behold her immediately.

Enter MR. STARGAZER, TOM *following bashfully,*

MR. STARGAZER.

Where is my——? Oh, here she is! Fanny, my dear, come here. Do you see that gentleman?

[*Aside.*

FANNY.

What gentleman, uncle? Do you mean that elastic person yonder who is bowing with so much perseverance?

MR. STARGAZER.

Hush! yes; that's the interesting stranger.

FANNY.

Why, he is kissing his hand, uncle. What does the creature mean?

MR. STARGAZER.

Ah, the rogue! Just like me, before I married your poor aunt,—all fire and impatience. He means love, my darling, love. I've such a delightful surprise for you. I didn't tell you before, for fear there should be any mistake; but it's all right, it's all right. The stars have settled it all among 'em. He's to be your husband!

FANNY.

My husband, uncle? Goodness gracious, Emma!
[*Converses apart with her.*

MR. STARGAZER (*aside*).

He has made a sensation already. His noble
aspect and distinguished air have produced an
instantaneous impression. Mr. Grig, will you
permit me? (TOM *advances awkwardly.*)—This
is my niece, Mr. Grig,—my niece, Miss Fanny
Brown; my daughter, Emma,—Mr. Thomas Grig,
the favourite of the planets.

TOM.

I hope I see Miss Hemmer in a conwivial state?
(*Aside to* MR. STARGAZER.) I say, I don't know
which is which.

MR. STARGAZER (*aside*).

The young lady nearest here is your affianced
bride. Say something appropriate.

TOM.

Certainly; yes, of course. Let me see. Miss
(*crosses to her*)—I—thank'ee!
[*Kisses her, behind his hat. She screams.*

GALILEO (*bursting from* BETSY, *who has been
restraining him*).

Outrageous insolence!
[BETSY *runs off.*

MR. STARGAZER.

Halloa, sir, halloa!

TOM.

Who is this juvenile salamander, sir?

MR. STARGAZER.

My little boy,—only my little boy; don't mind him. Shake hands with the gentleman, sir, instantly (*to* GALILEO).

TOM.

A very fine boy, indeed! and he does you great credit, sir. How d'ye do, my little man? (*They shake hands*, GALILEO *looking very wrathful, as* TOM *pats him on the head.*) There, that's very right and proper. " 'Tis dogs delight to bark and bite "; not young gentlemen, you know. There, there!

MR. STARGAZER.

Now let me introduce you to that *sanctum sanctorum,*—that hallowed ground,—that philosophical retreat—where I, the *genius loci,*——

TOM.

Eh?

MR. STARGAZER.

The *genius loci*——

TOM (*aside*).

Something to drink, perhaps. Oh, ah! yes, yes!

MR. STARGAZER.

Have made all my greatest and most profound

discoveries! where the telescope has almost grown to my eye with constant application; and the glass retort has been shivered to pieces from the ardour with which my experiments have been pursued. There the illustrious Mooney is, even now, pursuing those researches which will enrich us with precious metal, and make us masters of the world. Come, Mr. Grig.

TOM.

By all means, sir ; and luck to the illustrious Mooney, say I,—not so much on Mooney's account as for our noble selves.

MR. STARGAZER.

Emma !

EMMA.

Yes, papa.

MR. STARGAZER.

The same day that makes your cousin Mrs. Grig, will make you and that immortal man, of whom we have just now spoken, one.

EMMA.

Oh! consider, dear papa,——

MR. STARGAZER.

You are unworthy of him, I know; but he,— kind, generous creature,— consents to overlook your defects, and to take you, for my sake,—devoted man!—Come, Mr. Grig!—Galileo Isaac Newton Flamstead!

GALILEO.

Well?   [*Advancing sulkily.*

MR. STARGAZER.

In name, alas! but not in nature; knowing, even by sight, no other planets than the sun and moon,—here is your weekly pocket-money,—sixpence! Take it all!

TOM.

And don't spend it all at once, my man! Now, sir!

MR. STARGAZER.

Now, Mr. Grig,—go first, sir, I beg!

[*Exeunt* TOM *and* MR. STARGAZER.

GALILEO.

"Come, Mr. Grig!"—"Go first, Mr. Grig!"—"Day that makes your cousin Mrs. Grig!"—I'll secretly stick a penknife into Mr. Grig, if I live to be three hours older!

FANNY (*on one side of him*).

Oh! don't talk in that desperate way,—there's a dear, dear creature!

EMMA (*on the other side*).

No! pray do not;—it makes my blood run cold to hear you.

GALILEO.

Oh! if I was of age!—if I was only of age!—
or we could go to Gretna Green, at threepence a
head, including refreshments and all incidental
expenses. But that could never be! Oh! if I
was only of age!

FANNY.

But what if you were? What could you do,
then?

GALILEO.

Marry you, cousin Fanny; I could marry you
then lawfully, and without anybody's consent.

FANNY.

You forget that, situated as we are, we could
not be married, even if you *were* one-and-twenty;—
we have no money!

EMMA.

Not even enough for the fees!

GALILEO.

Oh! I am sure every Christian clergyman,
under such afflicting circumstances, would marry
us on credit. The wedding-fees might stand over
till the first christening, and then we could settle
the little bill altogether. Oh! why ain't I of age!
—why ain't I of age?

Enter BETSY, *in haste.*

BETSY.

Well! I never could have believed it! There, Miss! I wouldn't have believed it, if I had dreamt it, even with a bit of bride-cake under my pillow! To dare to go and think of marrying a young lady, with five thousand pounds, to a common lamplighter!

ALL.

A lamplighter?

BETSY.

Yes, he's Tom Grig the lamplighter, and nothing more nor less, and old Mr. Stargazer goes and picks him out of the open street, and brings him in for Miss Fanny's husband, because he pretends to have read something about it in the stars. Stuff and nonsense! I don't believe he knows his letters in the stars, and that's the truth; or if he's got as far as words in one syllable, it's quite as much as he has.

FANNY.

Was such an atrocity ever heard of? I, left with no power to marry without his consent, and he almost possessing the power to force my inclinations.

EMMA.

It's actually worse than my being sacrificed to that odious and detestable Mr. Mooney.

BETSY.

Come, Miss, it's not quite so bad as that neither; for Thomas Grig is a young man, and a proper young man enough too, but as to Mr. Mooney,— oh, dear ! no husband is bad enough in my opinion, Miss ; but he is worse than nothing,—a great deal worse.

FANNY.

You seem to speak feelingly about this same Mr. Grig.

BETSY.

Oh, dear no, Miss, not I. I don't mean to say but what Mr. Grig may be very well in his way, Miss ; but Mr. Grig and I have never held any communication together, not even so much as how-dy'e-do. Oh, no indeed, I have been very careful, Miss, as I always am with strangers. I was acquainted with the last lamplighter, Miss, but he's going to be married, and has given up the calling, for the young woman's parents being very respectable, wished her to marry a literary man, and so he has set up as a bill-sticker. Mr. Grig only came upon this beat at five to-night, Miss.

FANNY.

Which is a very sufficient reason why you don't know more of him.

BETSY.

Well, Miss, perhaps it is; and I hope there's no

crime in making friends in this world, if we can, Miss.

FANNY.

Certainly not. So far from it, that I most heartily wish you could make something more than a friend of this Mr. Grig, and so lead him to falsify this prediction.

GALILEO.

Oh ! don't you think you could, Betsy ?

EMMA.

You could not manage at the same time to get any young friend of yours to make something more than a friend of Mr. Mooney, could you, Betsy ?

GALILEO.

But, seriously, don't you think you could manage to give us all a helping hand together, in some way, eh, Betsy ?

FANNY.

Yes, yes, that would be so delightful. I should be grateful to her for ever. Shouldn't you ?

EMMA.

Oh, to the very end of my life !

GALILEO.

And so should I, you know, and lor' ! we should make her so rich, when—when we got rich ourselves, —shouldn't we ?

BOTH.

Oh, that we should, of course.

BETSY.

Let me see. I don't wish to have Mr. Grig to myself, you know. I don't want to be married.

ALL.

No! no! no! Of course she don't.

BETSY.

I haven't the least idea to put Mr. Grig off this match, you know, for anybody's sake, but you young people's. I am going quite *contrairy* to my own feelings, you know.

ALL.

Oh, yes, yes! How kind she is!

BETSY.

Well, I'll go over the matter with the young ladies in Miss Emma's room, and if we can think of anything that seems likely to help us, so much the better; and if we can't, we're none the worst. But Master Galileo musn't come, for he is so horrid jealous of Miss Fanny that I dursn't hardly say anything before him. Why, I declare (*looking off*), there is my gentleman looking about him as if he had lost Mr. Stargazer, and now he turns this way. There—get out of sight. Make haste!

GALILEO.

I may see 'em as far as the bottom stair, mayn't I, Betsy?

BETSY.

Yes, but not a step farther on any consideration. There, get away softly, so that if he passes here, - he may find me alone.

[*They creep gently out,*—GALILEO *returns and peeps in.*

GALILEO.

Hist, Betsy!

BETSY.

Go away, sir.   What have you come back for?

GALILEO (*holding out a large pin*).

I wish you 'd take an opportunity of sticking this a little way into him for patting me on the head just now.

BETSY.

Nonsense, you can't afford to indulge in such expensive amusements as retaliation yet awhile. You must wait till you come into your property, sir.   There.—Get you gone!   [*Exit* GALILEO.

Enter TOM GRIG.

TOM (*aside*).

I never saw such a scientific file in my days. The enterprising gentleman that drowned himself *to see how it felt*, is nothing to him.   There he is, just gone down to the bottom of a dry well in an uncommonly small bucket, to take an extra squint at the stars, they being seen best, I suppose, through the medium of a cold in the head. Halloa! Here is a young female of attractive proportions. I wonder now whether a man of noble aspect would be justified in tickling her.

[*He advances stealthily and tickles her under the arm.*

BETSY (*starting*).

Eh! what! Lor', sir!

TOM.

Don't be alarmed. My intentions are strictly honourable. In other words, I have no intentions whatever.

BETSY.

Then you ought to be more careful, Mr. Grig. That was a liberty, sir.

TOM.

I know it was. The cause of liberty, all over the world,—that's my sentiment! What is your name?

BETSY (*curtseying*).

Betsy Martin, sir.

TOM.

A name famous both in song and story. Would you have the goodness, Miss Martin, to direct me

to that particular apartment wherein the illustrious
Mooney is now pursuing his researches ?

BETSY (*aside*).

A little wholesome fear may not be amiss.   (*To
him, in assumed agitation.*) You are not going into
that room, Mr. Grig?

TOM.

Indeed, I am, and I ought to be there now,
having promised to join that light of science, your
master (a short six, by-the-bye !), outside the door.

BETSY.

That dreadful and mysterious chamber! Another
victim !

TOM.

Victim, Miss Martin !

BETSY.

Oh ! the awful oath of secrecy which binds me
not to disclose the perils of that gloomy, hideous
room.

TOM (*astonished*).

Miss Martin !

BETSY.

Such a fine young man,—so rosy and fresh-
coloured, that he should fall into the clutches of
that cruel and insatiable monster ! I cannot continue to witness such frightful scenes; I must give
warning.

TOM.

If you have anything to unfold, young woman, have the goodness to give *me* warning at once.

BETSY (*affecting to recover herself*).

No, no, Mr. Grig, it 's nothing,—it 's ha ! ha ! ha !—don't mind me, don't mind me, but it certainly is very shocking ;—no,—no,—I don't mean that. I mean funny,—yes. Ha ! ha ! ha !

TOM (*aside, regarding her attentively*).

I suspect a trick here,—some other lover in the case who wants to come over the stars;—but it won't do. I 'll tell you what, young woman (*to her*), if this is a cloak, you had better try it on elsewhere;—in plain English, if you have any object to gain and think to gain it by frightening *me*, it 's all my eye and, and—yourself, Miss Martin.

BETSY.

Well, then, if you will rush upon your fate,—there (*pointing off*)—that 's the door at the end of that long passage and across the gravelled yard. The room is built away from the house on purpose.

TOM.

I 'll make for it at once, and the first object I inspect through that same telescope, which now and then grows to your master's eye, shall be the moon—the moon, which is the emblem of your inconstant and deceitful sex, Miss Martin.

I.   23

Duet.

Air—" *The Young May-moon.*"

TOM.

There comes a new moon twelve times a year.

BETSY.

And when there is none, all is dark and drear.

TOM.

In which I espy—

BETSY.

And so, too, do I—

BOTH.

A resemblance to womankind very clear.

BOTH.

There comes a new moon twelve times in a year;
And when there is none, all is dark and drear.

TOM.

In which I espy—

BETSY.

And so do I—

BOTH.

A resemblance to womankind very clear.

Second Verse.

TOM.

She changes, she's fickle, she drives men mad.

BETSY.

She comes to bring light, and leaves them sad.

TOM.

So restless wild—

BETSY.

But so sweetly wild—

BOTH.

That no better companion could be had.

BOTH.

There comes a new moon twelve times a year ;
And when there is none, all is dark and drear.

TOM.

In which I espy—

BETSY.

And so do I—

BOTH.

A resemblance to womankind very clear.

[*Exeunt.*

SCENE III.—*A large gloomy room; a window with
a telescope directed towards the sky without, a
table covered with books, instruments and
apparatus, which are also scattered about in
other parts of the chamber, a dim lamp, a pair
of globes, &c., a skeleton in a case, and various
uncouth objects displayed against the walls.
Two doors in flat.* MR. MOONEY *discovered,
with a very dirty face, busily engaged in blowing
a fire, upon which is a crucible.*

23 *

Enter MR. STARGAZER, *with a lamp, beckoning to*
TOM GRIG, *who enters with some unwillingness.*

MR. STARGAZER.

This, Mr. Grig, is the *sanctum sanctorum* of
which I have already spoken ; this is at once the
laboratory and observatory.

TOM.

It's not an over-lively place, is it ?

MR. STARGAZER.

It has an air of solemnity which well accords
with the great and mysterious pursuits that are
here in constant prosecution, Mr. Grig.

TOM.

Ah ! I should think it would suit an undertaker
to the life; or perhaps I should rather say to the
death.   What may that cheerful object be now?

[*Pointing to a large phial.*

MR. STARGAZER.

That contains a male infant with three heads,—
we use it in astrology;—it is supposed to be a
charm.

TOM.

I shouldn't have supposed it myself, from his
appearance.   The young gentleman isn't alive,
is he?

MR. STARGAZER.

No, he is preserved in spirits.

[MR. MOONEY *sneezes*.

TOM (*retreating into a corner*).

Halloa! What the —— (MR. MOONEY *looks vacantly round*.) That gentleman, I suppose, is out of spirits?

MR. STARGAZER (*laying his hand upon* TOM'S *arm and looking toward the philosopher*).

Hush! that is the gifted Mooney. Mark well his noble countenance,—intense thought beams from every lineament. That is the great astrologer.

TOM.

He looks as if he had been having a touch at the black art. I say, why don't he say something?

MR. STARGAZER.

He is in a state of abstraction; see he directs his bellows this way, and blows upon the empty air.

TOM.

Perhaps he sees a strange spark in this direction and wonders how he came here. I wish he'd blow me out. (*Aside*.) I don't half like this.

MR. STARGAZER.

You shall see me rouse him.

TOM.

Don't put yourself out of the way on my account;
I can make his acquaintance at any other time.

MR. STARGAZER.

No time like the time present. Nothing
awakens him from these fits of meditation but an
electric shock. We always have a strongly
charged battery on purpose. I'll give him a
shock directly.

> [MR. STARGAZER *goes up and cautiously places*
> *the end of a wire in* MR. MOONEY'S *hand.*
> *He then stoops down beside the table as though*
> *bringing it in contact with the battery.* MR.
> MOONEY *immediately jumps up with a loud*
> *cry and throws away the bellows.*

TOM (*squaring at the philosopher*).

It wasn't me, you know,—none of your nonsense.

MR. STARGAZER (*comes hastily forward*).

Mr. Grig,—Mr. Grig,—not that disrespectful
attitude to one of the greatest men that ever lived.
This, my dear friend (*to* MOONEY),—is the noble
stranger.

MR. MOONEY.

A ha!

MR. STARGAZER.

Who arrived, punctual to his time, this afternoon.

MR. MOONEY.

O ho !

MR. STARGAZER.

Welcome him, my friend,—give him your hand.
(MR. MOONEY *appears confused and raises his leg.*)
No—no, that's your foot. So absent, Mr. Grig, in
his gigantic meditations that very often he doesn't
know one from the other. Yes, that's your hand,
very good, my dear friend, very good (*pats* MOONEY
on the back, as he and TOM *shake hands, the latter
at arm's length*).

MR. STARGAZER.

Have you made any more discoveries during my
absence ?

MR. MOONEY.

Nothing particular.

MR. STARGAZER.

Do you think—do you think, my dear friend,
that we shall arrive at any great stage in our
labours, anything at all approaching to their final
consummation in the course of the night ?

MR. MOONEY.

I cannot take upon myself to say.

MR. STARGAZER.

What are your opinions upon the subject ?

MR. MOONEY.

I haven't any opinions upon any subject what-
soever.

MR. STARGAZER.

Wonderful man! Here's a mind, Mr. Grig.

TOM.

Yes, his conversation's very improving indeed. But what's he staring so hard at me for?

MR. STARGAZER.

Something occurs to him. Don't speak,—don't disturb the current of his reflections upon any account.

> [MR. MOONEY *walks solemnly up to* TOM, *who retreats before him; taking off his hat turns it over and over with a thoughtful countenance, and finally puts it upon his own head.*

MR. STARGAZER.

Eccentric man!

TOM.

I say, I hope he don't mean to keep that, because if he does, his eccentricity is unpleasant. Give him another shock and knock it off, will you?

MR. STARGAZER.

Hush! hush! not a word.

> [MR. MOONEY, *keeping his eyes fixed on* TOM, *slowly returns to* MR. STARGAZER *and whispers in his ear.*

MR. STARGAZER.

Surely; by all means. I took the date of his birth, and all other information necessary for the purpose just now. (*To* TOM.) Mr. Mooney suggests that we should cast your nativity without delay, in order that we may communicate to you your future destiny.

MR. MOONEY.

Let us retire for that purpose.

MR. STARGAZER.

Certainly, wait here for a few moments, Mr. Grig: we are only going into the little laboratory and will return immediately. Now, my illustrious friend.

> [*He takes up a lamp and leads the way to one of the doors. As* MR. MOONEY *follows,* TOM *steals behind him and regains his hat.* MR. MOONEY *turns round, stares, and exit through door.*

TOM.

Well, that's the queerest genius I ever came across,—rather a singular person for a little smoking party. (*Looks into the crucible.*) This is the saucepan, I suppose, where they're boiling the philosopher's stone down to the proper consistency. I hope it's nearly done ; when it's quite ready, I'll send out for sixpenn'orth of sprats, and turn 'em into gold fish for a first experiment. 'Cod ! it'll be a comfortable thing though to have no end to one's riches. I'll have a country house and a park, and I'll plant a bit of it with a double

row of gas-lamps a mile long, and go out with a
French polished mahogany ladder, and two servants
in livery behind me, to light 'em with my own
hands every night.   What's to be seen here?
(*Looks through telescope.*) Nothing particular, the
stopper being on at the other end.   The little boy
with three heads (*looking towards the case*).   What
a comfort he must have been to his parents!—
Halloa! (*taking up a large knife*) this is a dis-
agreeable-looking instrument,—something too large
for bread and cheese, or oysters, and not of a bad
shape for sticking live persons in the ribs.   A very
dismal place this,—I wish they'd come back.   Ah!
—(*coming upon the skeleton*) here's a ghastly
object,—what does the writing say?—(*reads a label
upon the case*) " Skeleton of a gentleman prepared
by Mr. Mooney."   I hope Mr. Mooney may not
be in the habit of inviting gentlemen here, and
making 'em into such preparations without their
own consent.   Here's a book, now.   What's all
this about, I wonder?   The letters look as if a
steam-engine had printed 'em by accident.

[*Turns over the leaves, spelling to himself.*

GALILEO *enters softly, unseen by* TOM, *who has his
back towards him.*

GALILEO (*aside*).

Oh, you're there, are you?   If I could but

suffocate him, not for life, but only till I am one-
and-twenty, and then revive him, what a comfort
and convenience it would be! I overheard my
cousin Fanny talking to Betsy about coming here.
What can she want here? If she can be false,—
false to *me ;*—it seems impossible, but if she is ?—
well, well, we shall see. If I can reach that lumber-
room unseen, Fanny Brown,—beware.

> [*He steals toward the door on the* L.—*opens
> it, and exit cautiously into the room. As
> he does so,* TOM *turns the other way.*

TOM (closing the book).

It's very pretty Greek, I think. What a time
they are!

MR. STARGAZER and MOONEY enter from room.

MOONEY.

Tell the noble gentleman of his irrevocable
destiny.

MR. STARGAZER (with emotion).

No,—no, prepare him first.

TOM (aside).

Prepare him! "prepared by Mr. Mooney."—
This is a case of kidnapping and slaughter. (*To
them.*) Let him attempt to prepare me at his peril!

MR. STARGAZER.

Mr. Grig, why this demonstration?

TOM.

Oh, don't talk to me of demonstrations;—you ain't going to demonstrate me, and so I tell you.

MR. STARGAZER.

Alas! (*Crossing to him.*) The truth we have to communicate requires but little demonstration from our feeble lips. We have calculated upon your nativity.

MOONEY.

Yes, we have, we have.

MR. STARGAZER.

Tender-hearted man! (MOONEY *weeps*.) See there, Mr. Grig, isn't that affecting?

TOM.

What is he piping his boiled gooseberry eye for, sir? How should I know whether it's affecting or not?

MR. STARGAZER.

For you, for you. We find that you will expire tomorrow two months, at thirty minutes—wasn't it thirty minutes, my friend?

MOONEY.

Thirty-five minutes, twenty-seven seconds and five-sixths of a second. Oh! (*Groans.*)

MR. STARGAZER.

Thirty-five minutes, twenty-seven seconds, and five-sixths of a second past nine o'clock.

MOONEY.

A.M. [*They both wipe their eyes.*

TOM (*alarmed*).

Don't tell me, you 've made a mistake somewhere;
—I won't believe it.

MOONEY.

No, it is all correct, we worked it all in the most
satisfactory manner.—Oh! (*Groans again.*)

TOM.

Satisfactory, sir! Your notions of the satisfactory
are of an extraordinary nature.

MR. STARGAZER (*producing a pamphlet*).

It is confirmed by the prophetic almanack. Here
is the prediction for tomorrow two months,—" The
decease of a great person may be looked for about
this time."

TOM (*dropping into his chair*).

That 's me! It 's all up! inter me decently, my
friends.

MR. STARGAZER (*shaking his hand*).

Your wishes shall be attended to. We must
have the marriage with my niece at once, in order
that your distinguished race may be transmitted to
posterity. Condole with him, my Mooney, while

I compose my feelings, and settle the preliminaries
of the marriage in solitude.

> [*Takes up lamp and exit into room* R. MOONEY
> *draws up a chair in a line with* TOM, *a
> long way off. They both sigh heavily.*
> GALILEO *opens the lumber-room door. As
> he does so the room door opens and* BETSY
> *steals softly in, beckoning to* EMMA *and*
> FANNY *who follow. He retires again
> abruptly.*

BETSY (*aside*).

Now, young ladies, if you take heart only for
one minute, you may frighten Mr. Mooney out of
being married at once.

EMMA.

But if he has serious thoughts?

BETSY.

Nonsense, miss, he hasn't any thoughts. Your
papa says to him, " Will you marry my daughter?"
and he says, " Yes, I will " ; and he would and will
if you ain't bold, but bless you, he never turned it
over in his mind for a minute. If you, Miss (*to*
EMMA), pretend to hate him and love a rival, and
you, Miss (*to* FANNY), to love him to distraction,
you 'll frighten him so betwixt you that he 'll
declare off directly, I warrant. The love will
frighten him quite as much as the hate. He never
saw a woman in a passion, and as to one in love, I

don't believe that anybody but his mother ever kissed that grumpy old face of his in all his born days. Now, do try him, ladies. Come, we 're losing time.

[*She conceals herself behind the skeleton case. *EMMA *rushes up to* TOM GRIG *and embraces him, while* FANNY *clasps* MOONEY *round the neck.* GALILEO *appears at his door in an attitude of amazement, and* MR. STARGAZER *at his, after running in again with the lamp, which before he sees what is going forward he had in his hand.* TOM *and* MOONEY *in great astonishment.*

FANNY (*to* MOONEY). } Hush! hush!
EMMA (*to* GRIG). }

[TOM GRIG *and* MOONEY *get their heads sufficiently out of the embrace to exchange a look of wonder.*

EMMA.

Dear Mr. Grig, I know you must consider this strange, extraordinary, unaccountable conduct.

TOM.

Why, ma'am, without explanation, it does appear singular.

EMMA.

Yes, yes, I know it does, I know it will, but the urgency of the case must plead my excuse. Too fascinating Mr. Grig, I have seen you once and only once, but the impression of that maddening interview can never be effaced. I love you to distraction. (*Falls upon his shoulder.*)

TOM.

You're extremely obliging, ma'am, it's a flattering sort of thing,—or it would be (*aside*) if I was going to live a little longer,—but you're not the one, ma'am;—it's the other lady that the stars have——

FANNY (*to* MOONEY).

Nay, wonderful being, hear me—this is not a time for false conventional delicacy. Wrapt in your sublime visions, you have not [perceived]* the silent tokens of a woman's first and all-absorbing attachment, which have been, I fear, but too perceptible in the eyes of others ; but now I must speak out. I hate this odious man. You are my first and only love. Oh! speak to me.

MOONEY.

I haven't anything appropriate to say, young woman. I think I had better go. (*Attempting to get away.*)

FANNY.

Oh! no, no, no (*detaining him*). Give me some encouragement. Not one kind word ? not one look of love ?

---

* The word in brackets is wanting in the manuscript, and is here supplied conjecturally to complete the sense. See, however, *The Lamplighter's Story* (*infra*, p. 399, line 1).—ED.

MOONEY.

I don't know how to look a look of love.—I 'm,
I 'm frightened.

TOM.

So am I! I don't understand this. I tell you,
Miss, that the other lady is my destined wife.
Upon my word you mustn't hug me, you 'll make
her jealous.

FANNY.

Jealous! of you! Hear me (*to* MOONEY). I
renounce all claim or title to the hand of that or
any other man and vow to be eternally and wholly
yours.

MOONEY.

No, don't, you can't be mine,—nobody can be
mine.—I don't want anybody—I—I——

EMMA.

If you will not hear her—hear *me*, detested
monster.—Hear me declare that sooner than be
your bride, with this deep passion for another
rooted in my heart,—I——

MOONEY.

You need not make any declaration on the
subject, young woman.

MR. STARGAZER (*coming forward*).

She sha'n't,—she sha'n't. That 's right, don't
hear her. She shall marry you whether she likes it
or not,—she shall marry you to-morrow morning,—

and you, Miss (*to* FANNY), shall marry Mr. Grig if I trundle you to church in a wheelbarrow.

GALILEO (*coming forward*).

So she shall! so she may! Let her! let her! I give her leave.

MR. STARGAZER.

You give her leave, you young dog! Who the devil cares whether *you* give her leave or not? and what are you spinning about in that way for?

GALILEO.

I'm fierce, I'm furious,—don't talk to me,—I shall do somebody a mischief;—I'll never marry anybody after this, never, never, it isn't safe. I'll live and die a bachelor!—there—a bachelor! a bachelor!

> [*He goes up and encounters* BETSY. *She talks to him apart, and his wrath seems gradually to subside.*

MOONEY.

The little boy, albeit of tender years, has spoken wisdom. I have been led to the contemplation of womankind. I find their love is too violent for my staid habits. I would rather not venture upon the troubled waters of matrimony.

MR. STARGAZER.

You don't mean to marry my daughter? Not

if I say she *shall* have you ? (MOONEY *shakes his head solemnly.*) Mr. Grig, you have not changed your mind because of a little girlish folly?

TOM.

To-morrow two months! I may as well get through as much gold as I can in the meantime. Why, sir, if the pot nearly boils (*pointing to the crucible*),—if you 're pretty near the philosopher's stone,——

MR. STARGAZER.

Pretty near ! We 're sure of it—certain ; it 's as good as money in the Bank.

[GALILEO *and* BETSY, *who have been listening attentively, bustle about, fanning the fire, and throwing in sundry powders from the bottles on the table, then cautiously retire to a distance.*

TOM.

If that 's the case, sir, I am ready to keep faith with the planets. I 'll take her, sir. I 'll take her.

MR. STARGAZER.

Then here 's her hand, Mr. Grig,—no resistance, Miss (*drawing* FANNY *forward*). It 's of no use, so you may as well do it with a good grace. Take her hand, Mr. Grig.

[*The crucible blows up with a loud crash; they all start.*

24 *

MR. STARGAZER.

What!—the labour of fifteen years destroyed in an instant!

MOONEY (*stooping over the fragments*).

That's the only disappointment I have experienced in this process since I was first engaged in it when I was a boy. It always blows up when it's on the point of succeeding.

TOM.

Is the philosopher's stone gone?

MOONEY.

No.

TOM.

Not gone, sir?

MOONEY.

No—it never came!

MR. STARGAZER.

But we'll get it, Mr. Grig. Don't be cast down, we shall discover it in less than fifteen years this time, I dare say.

TOM (*relinquishing* FANNY's *hand*).

Ah! Were the stars very positive about this union?

MR. STÁRGAZER.

They had not a doubt about it. They said it *was* to be, and it must be. They were peremptory.

TOM.

I am sorry for that, because they have been very civil to me in the way of showing a light now and then, and I really regret disappointing 'em. But under the peculiar circumstances of the case, it can't be.

MR. STARGAZER.

Can't be, Mr. Grig! What can't be?

TOM.

The marriage, sir. I forbid the banns. (*Retires and sits down.*)

MR. STARGAZER.

Impossible! such a prediction unfulfilled! Why, the consequences would be as fatal as those of a concussion between the comet and this globe. Can't be! it must be, shall be.

BETSY (*coming forward, followed by* GALILEO).

If you please, sir, may I say a word?

MR. STARGAZER.

What have you got to say?—speak, woman!

BETSY.

Why, sir, I don't think Mr. Grig is the right man.

MR. STARGAZER.

What!

BETSY.

Don't you recollect, sir, that just as the house-clock struck the first stroke of five, you gave Mr. Galileo a thump on the head with the butt end of your telescope, and told him to get out of the way.

MR. STARGAZER.

Well, if I did, what of that?

BETSY.

Why, then, sir, I say, and I would say it if I was to be killed for it, that he's the young gentleman that ought to marry Miss Fanny, and that the stars never meant anything else.

MR. STARGAZER.

He! Why, he's a little boy.

GALILEO.

I ain't. I'm one-and-twenty next Lady-day.

MR. STARGAZER.

Eh! Eighteen hundred and—why, so he is, I declare. He's quite a stranger to me, certainly. I never thought about his age since he was fourteen, and I remember that birthday, because he'd a new suit of clothes then. But the noble family——

BETSY.

Lor, sir! ain't it being of a noble family to be the son of such a clever man as you?

MR. STARGAZER.

That's true. And my mother's father would have been Lord Mayor, only he died of turtle the year before.

BETSY.

Oh, it's quite clear.

MR. STARGAZER.

The only question is about the time, because the church struck afterwards. But I should think the stars, taking so much interest in my house, would most likely go by the house-clock,—eh! Mooney?

MOONEY.

Decidedly,—yes.

MR. STARGAZER.

Then you may have her, my son. Her father was a great astronomer; so I hope that, though you *are* a blockhead, your children may be scientific. There! (*Joins their hands.*)

EMMA.

Am I free to marry who I like, papa?

MR. STARGAZER.

Won't you, Mooney? Won't you?

MOONEY.

If anybody asks me to again I'll run away, and never come back any more.

MR. STARGAZER.

Then we must drop the subject. Yes, your choice is now unfettered.

EMMA.

Thank you, dear papa. Then I'll look about for somebody who will suit me without the delay of an instant longer than is absolutely necessary.

MR. STARGAZER.

How very dutiful!

FANNY.

And, as my being here just now with Emma was a little trick of Betsy's, I hope you'll forgive her, uncle.

EMMA.
GALILEO. } Oh, yes, do.

FANNY.

And even reward her, uncle, for being instrumental in fulfilling the prediction.

EMMA.
GALILEO. } Oh, yes ; do reward her—do.

FANNY.

Perhaps you could find a husband for her, uncle, you know. Don't you understand ?

BETSY.

Pray don't mention it, Miss. I told you at first, Miss, that I had not the least wish or inclination to

have Mr. Grig to myself. I couldn't abear that
Mr. Grig should think I wanted him to marry me;
oh no, Miss, not on any account.

MR. STARGAZER.

Oh, that's pretty intelligible. Here, Mr. Grig.
(*They fall back from his chair.*) Have you any
objection to take this young woman for better, for
worse?

BETSY.

Lor, sir! how ondelicate!

MR. STARGAZER.

I'll add a portion of ten pounds for your loss of
time here to-night. What do you say, Mr. Grig?

TOM.

It don't much matter. I ain't long for this
world. Eight weeks of marriage might reconcile
me to my fate. I should go off, I think, more
resigned and peaceful. Yes, I'll take her, as a
reparation. Come to my arms! (*He embraces her
with a dismal face.*)

MR. STARGAZER (*taking a paper from his pocket*).

Egad! that reminds me of what I came back to
say, which all this bustle drove out of my head.
There's a figure wrong in the nativity (*handing the
paper to* MOONEY). He'll live to a green old age.

TOM (*looking up*).

Eh! What?

MOONEY.

So he will. Eighty-two years and twelve days will be the lowest.

TOM (*disengaging himself*).

Eh! here! (*calling off.*)   Hallo, you, sir! bring in that ladder and lantern.

A SERVANT *enters in great haste, and hands them to* TOM.

SERVANT.

There's such a row in the street,—none of the gas-lamps lit, and all the people calling for the lamplighter. *Such* a row! (*Rubbing his hands with great glee.*)

TOM.

Is there, my fine fellow?   Then I'll go and light 'em.   And as, under existing circumstances, and with the prospect of a green old age before me, I'd rather *not* be married, Miss Martin, I beg to assure the ratepayers present that in future I shall pay the strictest attention to my professional duties, and do my best for the contractor; and that I shall be found upon my beat as long as they condescend to patronize the Lamplighter.

[*Runs off.* MISS MARTIN *faints in the arms of* MOONEY.

CURTAIN.

APPENDIX.

THE LAMPLIGHTER'S STORY.*

" If you talk of Murphy and Francis Moore, gentlemen,"
said the lamplighter who was in the chair, "I mean to
say that neither of 'em ever had any more to do with
the stars than Tom Grig had."

" And what had *he* to do with 'em? " asked the lamplighter who officiated as vice.

" Nothing at all," replied the other; "just exactly
nothing at all."

" Do you mean to say you don't believe in Murphy,
then? " demanded the lamplighter who had opened the
discussion.

" I mean to say that I believe in Tom Grig," replied
the chairman. " Whether I believe in Murphy, or not,
is a matter between me and my conscience; and whether
Murphy believes in himself, or not, is a matter between
him and *his* conscience. Gentlemen, I drink your healths."

The lamplighter who did the company this honour, was
seated in the chimney corner of a certain tavern, which
has been, time out of mind, the lamplighters' house of
call. He sat in the midst of a circle of lamplighters,
and was the cacique, or chief of the tribe.

---

* From *The Picnic Papers, by various hands, edited by Charles Dickens,*
Esq. London: Henry Colburn, 1841, vol. i. pp. 1–32.

If any of our readers have had the good fortune to behold a lamplighter's funeral, they will not be surprised to learn that lamplighters are a strange and primitive people; that they rigidly adhere to old ceremonies and customs which have been handed down among them from father to son since the first public lamp was lighted out of doors; that they intermarry, and betroth their children in infancy; that they enter into no plots or conspiracies (for who ever heard of a traitorous lamplighter?); that they commit no crimes against the laws of their country (there being no instance of a murderous or burglarious lamplighter); that they are, in short, notwithstanding their apparently volatile and restless character, a highly moral and reflective people: having among themselves as many traditional observances as the Jews, and being, as a body, if not as old as the hills, at least as old as the streets. It is an article of their creed that the first faint glimmering of true civilization shone in the first street light maintained at the public expense. They trace their existence and high position in the public esteem in a direct line to the heathen mythology, and hold that the history of Prometheus himself is but a pleasant fable, whereof the true hero is a lamplighter.

"Gentlemen," said the lamplighter in the chair, "I drink your healths."

"And perhaps, sir," said the vice, holding up his glass, and rising a little way off his seat and sitting down again, in token that he recognised and returned the compliment, "perhaps you will add to that condescension by telling us who Tom Grig was, and how he came to be connected in your mind with Francis Moore, physician."

"Hear, hear, hear!" cried the lamplighters generally.

"Tom Grig, gentlemen," said the chairman, "was one of us; and it happened to him as it don't often happen to a public character in our line, that he had his what-you-may-call-it cast."

"His head?" said the vice.

"No," replied the chairman, "not his head."

"His face, perhaps?" said the vice.

"No, not his face."

"His legs?"

"No, not his legs."

Nor yet his arms, nor his hands, nor his feet, nor his chest, all of which were severally suggested.

"His nativity, perhaps?"

"That's it," said the chairman, awakening from his thoughtful attitude at the suggestion. "His nativity. That's what Tom had cast, gentlemen."

"In plaster?" asked the vice.

"I don't rightly know how it's done," returned the chairman, "but I suppose it was."

And there he stopped as if that were all he had to say; whereupon there arose a murmur among the company, which at length resolved itself into a request, conveyed through the vice, that he would go on. This being exactly what the chairman wanted, he mused for a little time, performed that agreeable ceremony which is popularly termed wetting one's whistle, and went on thus:—

"Tom Grig, gentlemen, was, as I have said, one of us; and I may go further, and say he was an ornament to us, and such a one as only the good old times of oil and cotton could have produced. Tom's family, gentlemen, were all lamplighters."

"Not the ladies, I hope? " asked the vice.

"They had talent enough for it, sir," rejoined the chairman, "and would have been, but for the prejudices of society. Let women have their rights, sir, and the females of Tom's family would have been every one of 'em in office. But that emancipation hasn't come yet, and hadn't then, and consequently they confined themselves to the bosoms of their families, cooked the dinners, mended the clothes, minded the children, comforted their husbands, and attended to the housekeeping generally. It 's a hard thing upon the women, gentlemen, that they are limited to such a sphere of action as this ; very hard.

"I happen to know all about Tom, gentlemen, from the circumstance of his uncle by the mother's side having been my particular friend. His (that 's Tom's uncle's) fate was a melancholy one. Gas was the death of him. When it was first talked of, he laughed. He wasn't angry ; he laughed at the credulity of human nature. 'They might as well talk,' he says, ' of laying on an ever-lasting succession of glow-worms ' ; and then he laughed again, partly at his joke, and partly at poor humanity.

"In course of time, however, the thing got ground, the experiment was made, and they lighted up Pall Mall. Tom's uncle went to see it. I 've heard that he fell off his ladder fourteen times that night from weakness, and that he would certainly have gone on falling till he killed himself, if his last tumble hadn't been into a wheelbarrow which was going his way, and humanely took him home. ' I foresee in this,' says Tom's uncle faintly, and taking to his bed as he spoke—'I foresee in this,' he says, 'the breaking up of our profession. There's no more going the rounds to trim by daylight, no more dribbling down of the oil on the hats and bonnets of ladies and gentlemen when one feels in spirits. Any low fellow can light a gas-lamp. And it's all up.' In this state of mind he petitioned the government for—I want a word again, gentlemen,—what do you call that which they give to people when it's found out, at last, that they've never been of any use, and have been paid too much for doing nothing?"

"Compensation?" suggested the vice.

"That's it," said the chairman. "Compensation. They didn't give it him though, and then he got very fond of his country all at once, and went about saying that gas was a death-blow to his native land, and that it was a plot of the Radicals to ruin the country and destroy the oil and cotton trade for ever, and that the whales would go and kill themselves privately, out of sheer spite and vexation at not being caught. At last he got right-down cracked; called his tobacco-pipe a gas-pipe; thought his tears were lamp-oil; and went on with all manner of nonsense of that sort, till one night he hung himself on a lamp-iron in Saint Martin's Lane, and there was an end of *him*.

"Tom loved him, gentlemen, but he survived it. He shed a tear over his grave, got very drunk, spoke a funeral oration that night in the watch-house, and was fined five shillings for it in the morning. Some men are none the worse for this sort of thing. Tom was one of 'em. He went that very afternoon on a new beat, as clear in his head, and as free from fever, as Father Mathew himself.

"Tom's new beat, gentlemen, was—I can't exactly say where, for that he'd never tell; but I know it was in a quiet part of town, where there were some queer old houses. I have always had it in my head that it must have been somewhere near Canonbury Tower in Islington, but that's a matter of opinion. Wherever it was, he went upon it, with a brand-new ladder, a white hat, a brown holland jacket and trowsers, a blue neck-kerchief, and a sprig of full-blown double wall-flower in his buttonhole. Tom was always genteel in his appearance, and I have heard from the best judges, that if he had left his ladder at home that afternoon, you might have took him for a lord.

"He was always merry, was Tom, and such a singer, that if there was any encouragement for native talent, he'd have been at the opera. He was on his ladder, lighting his first lamp, and singing to himself in a manner more easily to be conceived than described, when he hears the clock strike five, and suddenly sees an old gentleman, with a telescope in his hand, throw up a window and look at him very hard.

"Tom didn't know what could be passing in this old gentleman's mind. He thought it likely enough that he might be saying within himself, 'Here's a new lamplighter,—a good-looking young fellow,—shall I stand something to drink?' Thinking this possible, he keeps quite still, pretending to be very particular about the wick, and looks at the old gentleman sideways, seeming to take no notice of him.

"Gentlemen, he was one of the strangest and most mysterious-looking files that ever Tom clapped his eyes on. He was dressed all slovenly and untidy, in a great gown of a kind of bed-furniture pattern, with a cap of the same on his head ; and a long old flapped waistcoat; with no braces, no strings, very few buttons ;—in short, with hardly any of those artificial contrivances that hold society together. Tom knew by these signs, and by his not being shaved, and by his not being over-clean, and by a sort of wisdom not quite awake, in his face, that he was a scientific old gentleman. He often told me that if he could have conceived the possibility of the whole Royal Society being boiled down into one man, he should have said the old gentleman's body was that Body.

"The old gentleman claps the telescope to his eye, looks all round, sees nobody else in sight, stares at Tom again, and cries out very loud :

"' Hol-loa ! '

"' Holloa, sir,' says Tom from the ladder; ' and holloa again, if you come to that.'

"' Here 's an extraordinary fulfilment,' says the old gentleman, ' of a prediction of the planets.'

"' Is there ? ' says Tom, ' I 'm very glad to hear it.'

"' Young man,' says the old gentleman, ' you don't know me.'

"' Sir,' says Tom, ' I have not that honour; but I shall be happy to drink your health, notwithstanding.'

"' I read,' cries the old gentleman, without taking any notice of this politeness on Tom's part,—' I read what 's going to happen in the stars.'

"Tom thanked him for the information, and begged

25 *

to know if anything particular was going to happen in
the stars, in the course of a week or so; but the old
gentleman, correcting him, explained that he read in the
stars what was going to happen on dry land, and that he
was acquainted with all the celestial bodies.

"'I hope they're all well, sir,' says Tom, - 'every body.'

"'Hush!' cries the old gentleman. 'I have consulted
the book of Fate with rare and wonderful success. I am
versed in the great sciences of astrology and astronomy.
In my house here I have every description of apparatus
for observing the course and motion of the planets. Six
months ago I derived from this source the knowledge
that precisely as the clock struck five this afternoon, a
stranger would present himself,—the destined husband of
my young and lovely niece,—in reality of illustrious and
high descent, but whose birth would be enveloped in
uncertainty and mystery. Don't tell me yours isn't,'
says the old gentleman, who was in such a hurry to speak
that he couldn't get the words out fast enough, 'for I
know better.'

"Gentlemen, Tom was so astonished when he heard
him say this, that he could hardly keep his footing on the
ladder, and found it necessary to hold on by the lamp-
post. There *was* a mystery about his birth. His mother
had always admitted it. Tom had never known who was
his father, and some people had gone so far as to say that
even *she* was in doubt.

"While he was in this state of amazement, the old
gentleman leaves the window, bursts out of the house-
door, shakes the ladder, and Tom, like a ripe pumpkin,
comes sliding down into his arms.

"'Let me embrace you,' he says, folding his arms about him, and nearly lighting up his old bed-furniture gown at Tom's link. 'You're a man of noble aspect. Everything combines to prove the accuracy of my observations. You have had mysterious promptings within you,' he says; 'I know you have had whisperings of greatness, eh?' he says.

"'I think I have,' says Tom,—Tom was one of those who can persuade themselves to anything they like,—'I have often thought I wasn't the small beer I was taken for.'

"'You were right,' cries the old gentleman, hugging him again. 'Come in. My niece awaits us.'

"'Is the young lady tolerable good-looking, sir?' says Tom, hanging fire rather, as he thought of her playing the piano, and knowing French, and being up to all manner of accomplishments.

"'She's beautiful!' cries the old gentleman, who was in such a terrible bustle that he was all in a perspiration. 'She has a graceful carriage, an exquisite shape, a sweet voice, a countenance beaming with animation and expression, and the eye,' he says, rubbing his hands, 'of a startled fawn.'

"Tom supposed this might mean, what was called among his circle of acquaintance, 'a game eye'; and, with a view to this defect, inquired whether the young lady had any cash.

"'She has five thousand pounds,' cries the old gentleman. 'But what of that? what of that? A word in your ear. I'm in search of the philosopher's stone. I have very nearly found it,—not quite. It turns everything to gold; that's its property.'

"Tom naturally thought it must have a deal of property, and said that when the old gentleman did get it, he hoped he'd be careful to keep it in the family.

"'Certainly,' he says, 'of course. Five thousand pounds! What's five thousand pounds to us? What's five million?' he says. 'What's five thousand million? Money will be nothing to us. We shall never be able to spend it fast enough.'

"'We'll try what we can do, sir,' says Tom.

"'We will,' says the old gentleman. 'Your name?'

"'Grig,' says Tom.

"The old gentleman embraced him again, very tight; and without speaking another word, dragged him into the house in such an excited manner, that it was as much as Tom could do to take his link and ladder with him, and put them down in the passage.

"Gentlemen, if Tom hadn't been always remarkable for his love of truth, I think you would still have believed him when he said that all this was like a dream. There is no better way for a man to find out whether he really is asleep or awake, than calling for something to eat. If he's in a dream, gentlemen, he'll find something wanting in the flavour, depend upon it.

"Tom explained his doubts to the old gentleman, and said that if there was any cold meat in the house, it would ease his mind very much to test himself at once. The old gentleman ordered up a venison pie, a small ham, and a bottle of very old Madeira. At the first mouthful of pie, and the first glass of wine, Tom smacks his lips and cries out, 'I'm awake,—wide awake'; and to prove that he was so, gentlemen, he made an end of 'em both.

"When Tom had finished his meal (which he never spoke of afterwards without tears in his eyes), the old gentleman hugs him again, and says, ' Noble stranger! let us visit my young and lovely niece.' Tom, who was a little elevated with the wine, replies, ' The noble stranger is agreeable.' At which words the old gentleman took him by the hand, and led him to the parlour ; crying as he opened the door, ' Here is Mr. Grig, the favourite of the planets ! '

" I will not attempt a description of female beauty, gentlemen, for every one of us has a model of his own that suits his own taste best. In this parlour that I 'm speaking of, there were two young ladies ; and if every gentleman present will imagine two models of his own in their places, and will be kind enough to polish 'em up to the very highest ̄pitch of perfection, he will then have a faint conception of their uncommon radiance.

" Besides these two young ladies there was their waiting-woman, that under any other circumstances Tom would have looked upon as a Venus ; and besides her there was a tall, thin, dismal-faced young gentleman, half man and half boy, dressed in a childish suit of clothes very much too short in the legs and arms, and looking, according to Tom's comparison, like one of the wax juveniles from a tailor's door, grown up and run to seed. Now, this youngster stamped his foot upon the ground and looked very fierce at Tom, and Tom looked fierce at him ;—for, to tell the truth, gentlemen, Tom more than half suspected that when they entered the room he was kissing one of the young ladies ; and for anything Tom knew, you observe, it might be *his* young lady,—which was not pleasant.

"'Sir,' says Tom, 'before we proceed any further, will you have the kindness to inform me who this young Salamander'—Tom called him that for aggravation, you perceive, gentlemen,—'who this young Salamander may be?'

"'That, Mr. Grig,' says the old gentleman, 'is my little boy. He was christened Galileo Isaac Newton Flamstead. Don't mind him. He's a mere child.'

"'A very fine child, too,' says Tom—still aggravating, you'll observe,—'of his age, and as good as fine, I have no doubt. How do you do, my man?'—with which kind and patronising expressions, Tom reached up to pat him on the head, and quoted two lines about little boys, from Doctor Watts's hymns, which he had learnt at a Sunday school.

"It was very easy to see, gentlemen, by this youngster's frowning, and by the waiting-maid's tossing her head and turning up her nose, and by the young ladies turning their backs and talking together at the other end of the room, that nobody but the old gentleman took very kindly to the noble stranger. Indeed, Tom plainly heard the waiting-woman say of her master, that so far from being able to read the stars as he pretended, she didn't believe he knew his letters in 'em, or at best that he had got no further than words in one syllable; but Tom, not minding this (for he was in spirits after the Madeira), looks with an agreeable air towards the young ladies, and, kissing his hand to both, says to the old gentleman, 'Which is which?'

"'This,' says the old gentleman, leading out the handsomest, if one of 'em could possibly be said to be handsomer than the other—'this is my niece, Miss Fanny Barker.'

"'If you'll permit me, miss,' says Tom, 'being a noble stranger and a favourite of the planets, I will conduct myself as such.' With these words, he kisses the young lady in a very affable way, turns to the old gentleman, slaps him on the back, and says, 'When's it to come off, my buck?'

"The young lady coloured so deep, and her lip trembled so much, gentlemen, that Tom really thought she was going to cry. But she kept her feelings down, and turning to the old gentlemen, says, 'Dear uncle, though you have the absolute disposal of my hand and fortune, and though you mean well in disposing of 'em thus, I ask you whether you don't think this is a mistake? Don't you think, dear uncle,' she says, 'that the stars must be in error? Is it not possible that the comet may have put 'em out?'

"'The stars,' says the old gentleman, 'couldn't make a mistake if they tried. Emma,' he says to the other young lady.

"'Yes, papa,' says she.

"'The same day that makes your cousin Mrs. Grig, will unite you to the gifted Mooney. No remonstrance —no tears. Now Mr. Grig, let me conduct you to that hallowed ground, that philosophical retreat, where my friend and partner, the gifted Mooney of whom I have just now spoken, is even now pursuing those discoveries which shall enrich us with the precious metal, and make us masters of the world. Come, Mr. Grig,' he says.

"'With all my heart, sir,' replies Tom; 'and luck to

the gifted Mooney, say I,—not so much on his account as for our worthy selves!' With this sentiment, Tom kissed his hand to the ladies again, and followed him out; having the gratification to perceive, as he looked back, that they were all hanging on by the arms and legs of Galileo Isaac Newton Flamstead, to prevent him from following the noble stranger and tearing him to pieces.

"Gentlemen, Tom's father-in-law that was to be, took him by the hand, and having lighted a little lamp, led him across a paved courtyard at the back of the house, into a very large, dark, gloomy room: filled with all manner of bottles, globes, books, telescopes, crocodiles, alligators, and other scientific instruments of every kind. In the centre of this room was a stove or furnace, with what Tom called a pot, but which in my opinion was a crucible, in full boil. In one corner was a sort of ladder leading through the roof; and up this ladder the old gentleman pointed, as he said in a whisper:·

"'The observatory. Mr. Mooney is even now watching for the precise time at which we are to come into all the riches of the earth. It will be necessary for he and I, alone in that silent place, to cast your nativity before the hour arrives. Put the day and minute of your birth on this piece of paper, and leave the rest to me.'

"'You don't mean to say,' says Tom, doing as he was told and giving him back the paper, 'that I'm to wait here long, do you? It's a precious dismal place.'

"'Hush!' says the old gentleman, 'it's hallowed ground. Farewell!'

"'Stop a minute,' says Tom, 'what a hurry you're in. What's in that large bottle yonder?'

"'It's a child with three heads,' says the old gentleman; 'and everything else in proportion.'

"'Why don't you throw him away?' says Tom. What do you keep such unpleasant things here for?'

"'Throw him away!' cries the old gentleman. 'We use him constantly in astrology. He's a charm.'

"'I shouldn't have thought it,' says Tom, 'from his appearance. *Must* you go, I say?'

"The old gentleman makes him no answer, but climbs up the ladder in a greater bustle than ever. Tom looked after his legs till there was nothing of him left, and then sat down to wait; feeling (so he used to say) as comfortable as if he was going to be made a freemason, and they were heating the pokers.

"Tom waited so long, gentlemen, that he began to think it must be getting on for midnight at least, and felt more dismal and lonely than ever he had done in all his life. He tried every means of wiling away the time, but it never had seemed to move so slow. First, he took a nearer view of the child with three heads, and thought what a comfort he must have been to his parents. Then he looked up a long telescope which was pointed out of the window, but saw nothing particular, in consequence of the stopper being on at the other end. Then he came to a skeleton in a glass case, labelled 'Skeleton of a Gentleman—prepared by Mr. Mooney,'—which made him hope that Mr. Mooney might not be in the habit of preparing gentlemen that way without their own consent. A hundred times, at least, he looked into the pot where they were boiling the philosopher's stone down to the proper consistency, and wondered whether it was nearly done.

'When it is,' thinks Tom, 'I'll send out for sixpenn'orth
of sprats and turn 'em into gold-fish for a first experiment.' Besides which, he made up his mind, gentlemen,
to have a country-house and a park, and to plant a bit of
it with a double row of gas-lamps a mile long, and go out
every night with a French-polished mahogany ladder, and
two servants in livery behind him, to light 'em for his own
pleasure.

"At length and at last the old gentleman's legs
appeared upon the steps leading through the roof, and he
came slowly down, bringing along with him the gifted
Mooney. This Mooney, gentlemen, was even more scientific in appearance than his friend; and had, as Tom
often declared upon his word and honour, the dirtiest
face we can possibly know of, in this imperfect state of
existence.

"Gentlemen, you are all aware that if a scientific man
isn't absent in his mind, he's of no good at all. Mr.
Mooney was so absent, that when the old gentleman
said to him, 'Shake hands with Mr. Grig,' he put out
his leg. 'Here's a mind, Mr. Grig!' cries the old
gentleman in a rapture. 'Here's philosophy! Here's
rumination! Don't disturb him,' he says, 'for this is
amazing!'

"Tom had no wish to disturb him, having nothing
particular to say; but he was so uncommonly amazing,
that the old gentleman got impatient, and determined to
give him an electric shock to bring him to;—'for you
must know, Mr. Grig,' he says, 'that we always keep a
strongly-charged battery, ready for that purpose.' These
means being resorted to, gentlemen, the gifted Mooney

revived with a loud roar, and he no sooner came to himself, than both he and the old gentleman looked at Tom with compassion, and shed tears abundantly.

" ' My dear friend,' says the old gentleman to the Gifted, ' prepare him.'

" ' I say,' cries Tom, falling back, ' none of that, you know. No preparing by Mr. Mooney, if you please.'

" ' Alas ! ' replies the old gentleman, ' you don't understand us. My friend, inform him of his fate,—I can't.'

" The Gifted mustered up his voice, after many efforts, and informed Tom that his nativity had been carefully cast, and he would expire at exactly thirty-five minutes, twenty-seven seconds, and five-sixths of a second past nine o'clock A.M., on that day two months.

" Gentlemen, I leave you to judge what were Tom's feelings at this announcement, on the eve of matrimony and endless riches. ' I think,' he says in a trembling way, ' there must be a mistake in the working of that sum. Will you do me the favour to cast it up again ? '— ' There is no mistake,' replies the old gentleman, ' it is confirmed by Francis Moore, physician. Here is the prediction for to-morrow two months.' And he showed him the page, where sure enough were these words—' The decease of a great person may be looked for, about this time.'

" ' Which,' says the old gentleman, ' is clearly you, Mr. Grig.'

" ' Too clearly,' cries Tom, sinking into a chair, and giving one hand to the old gentleman and one to the Gifted. ' The orb of day has set on Thomas Grig for ever ! '

"At this affecting remark the Gifted shed tears again, and the other two mingled their tears with his, in a kind —if I may use the expression—of Mooney and Co.'s entire. But the old gentleman, recovering first, observed that this was only a reason for hastening the marriage, in order that Tom's distinguished race might be transmitted to posterity; and requesting the Gifted to console Mr. Grig during his temporary absence, he withdrew to settle the preliminaries with his niece immediately.

"And now, gentlemen, a very extraordinary and remarkable occurrence took place; for as Tom sat in a melancholy way in one chair, and the Gifted sat in a melancholy way in another, a couple of doors were thrown violently open, the two young ladies rushed in, and one knelt down in a loving attitude at Tom's feet and the other at the Gifted's. So far, perhaps, as Tom was concerned,—as he used to say,—you will say there was nothing strange in this; but you will be of a different opinion when you understand that Tom's young lady was kneeling to the Gifted, and the Gifted's young lady was kneeling to Tom.

"'Holloa! stop a minute,' cries Tom; 'here's a mistake. I need condoling with by sympathising woman under my afflicting circumstances; but we're out in the figure. Change partners, Mooney.'

"'Monster!' cries Tom's young lady, clinging to the Gifted.

"'Miss!' says Tom. 'Is *that* your manners?'

"'I abjure thee!' cries Tom's young lady. 'I renounce thee. I never will be thine. Thou,' she says to the Gifted, 'art the object of my first and all-engrossing passion. Wrapt in thy sublime visions, thou hast not perceived my love; but, driven to despair, I now shake off the woman and avow it. Oh, cruel, cruel man!' With which reproach she laid her head upon the Gifted's breast, and put her arms about him in the tenderest manner possible, gentlemen.

"'And I,' says the other young lady, in a sort of ecstasy, that made Tom start,—'I hereby abjure my chosen husband too. Hear me, Goblin!'—this was to the Gifted,—'Hear me! I hold thee in the deepest detestation. The maddening interview of this one night has filled my soul with love—but not for thee. It is for thee, for thee, young man,' she cries to Tom. 'As Monk Lewis finely observes, Thomas, Thomas, I am thine, Thomas, Thomas, thou art mine: Thine for ever, mine for ever!' With which words, she became very tender likewise.

"Tom and the Gifted, gentlemen, as you may believe, looked at each other in a very awkward manner, and with thoughts not at all complimentary to the two young ladies. As to the Gifted, I have heard Tom say, often, that he was certain he was in a fit, and had it inwardly.

"'Speak to me! oh, speak to me!' cries Tom's young lady to the Gifted.

"'I don't want to speak to anybody,' he says, finding his voice at last, and trying to push her away. 'I think I had better go. I'm—I'm frightened,' he says, looking about as if he had lost something.

"'Not one look of love!' she cries. 'Hear me, while I declare——'

"'I don't know how to look a look of love,' he says, all in a maze. 'Don't declare anything. I don't want to hear anybody.'

"'That's right!' cries the old gentleman (who it seems had been listening). 'That's right! Don't hear her. Emma shall marry you to-morrow, my friend, whether she likes it or not, and *she* shall marry Mr. Grig.'

"Gentlemen, these words were no sooner out of his mouth than Galileo Isaac Newton Flamstead (who it seems had been listening too) darts in, and spinning round and round, like a young giant's top, cries, 'Let her. Let her. I'm fierce; I'm furious. I give her leave. I'll never marry anybody after this—never. It isn't safe. She is the falsest of the false,' he cries, tearing his hair and gnashing his teeth; 'and I'll live and die a bachelor!'

"'The little boy,' observed the Gifted gravely, 'albeit of tender years, has spoken wisdom. I have been led to the contemplation of womankind, and will not adventure on the troubled waters of matrimony.'

"'What!' says the old gentleman, 'not marry my daughter! Won't you, Mooney? Not if I make her? Won't you? Won't you?'

"'No,' says Mooney, 'I won't. And if anybody asks me any more, I'll run away, and never come back again.'

"'Mr. Grig,' says the old gentleman, 'the stars must be obeyed. You have not changed your mind because of a little girlish folly,—eh, Mr. Grig?'

"Tom, gentlemen, had had his eyes about him, and was pretty sure that all this was a device and trick of the waiting-maid, to put him off his inclination. He had seen her hiding and skipping about the two doors, and had observed that a very little whispering from her pacified the Salamander directly. 'So,' thinks Tom, 'this is a plot,—but it won't fit.'

" ' Eh, Mr. Grig ? ' says the old gentleman.

" ' Why, sir,' says Tom, pointing to the crucible, 'if the soup 's nearly ready——'

" ' Another hour beholds the consummation of our labours,' returned the old gentleman.

" ' Very good,' says Tom, with a mournful air. 'It 's only for two months, but I may as well be the richest man in the world even for that time. I 'm not particular. I 'll take her, sir. I 'll take her.'

" The old gentleman was in a rapture to find Tom still in the same mind, and drawing the young lady towards him by little and little, was joining their hands by main force, when all of a sudden, gentlemen, the crucible blows up with a great crash ; everybody screams ; the room is filled with smoke ; and Tom, not knowing what may happen next, throws himself into a fancy attitude, and says, ' Come on, if you 're a man ! ' without addressing himself to anybody in particular.

" ' The labours of fifteen years ! ' says the old gentleman, clasping his hands and looking down upon the Gifted, who was saving the pieces, ' are destroyed in an instant ! '
—And I am told, gentlemen, by-the-bye, that this same philosopher's stone would have been discovered a hundred times at least, to speak within bounds, if it wasn't for the one unfortunate circumstance that the apparatus always blows up, when it 's on the very point of succeeding.

"Tom turns pale when he hears the old gentleman expressing himself to this unpleasant effect, and stammers out that if it's quite agreeable to all parties, he would like to know exactly what has happened, and what change has really taken place in the prospects of that company.

"'We have failed for the present, Mr. Grig,' says the old gentleman, wiping his forehead, 'and I regret it the more, because I have in fact invested my niece's five thousand pounds in this glorious speculation. But don't be cast down,' he says, anxiously,—'in another fifteen years, Mr. Grig,——'

"'Oh!' cries Tom, letting the young lady's hand fall. 'Were the stars very positive about this union, sir?'

"'They were,' says the old gentleman.

"'I'm sorry to hear it,' Tom makes answer, 'for it's no go, sir.'

"'No what?' cries the old gentleman.

"'Go, sir,' says Tom, fiercely; 'I forbid the banns.' And with these words—which are the very words he used —he sat himself down in a chair, and, laying his head upon the table, thought with a secret grief of what was to come to pass on that day two months.

"Tom always said, gentlemen, that that waiting-maid was the artfullest minx he had ever seen; and he left it in writing in this country when he went to colonize abroad, that he was certain in his own mind she and the Salamander had blown up the philosopher's stone on purpose, and to cut him out of his property. I believe Tom was in the right, gentlemen: but whether or no, she comes forward at this point, and says, 'May I speak, sir?' and the old gentleman answering, 'Yes, you may,' she goes on to say that 'the stars are no doubt quite right in every respect, but Tom is not the man.' And she says, 'Don't you remember, sir, that when the clock struck five this afternoon, you gave Master Galileo a rap on the head with your telescope, and told him to get out of the way?' 'Yes, I do,' says the old gentleman. 'Then,' says the waiting-maid, 'I say he's the man, and the prophecy is fulfilled.' The old gentleman staggers at this, as if somebody had hit him a blow on the chest, and cries, 'He! why, he's a boy!' Upon that, gentlemen, the Salamander cries out that he'll be twenty-one next Lady-day; and complains that his father has always been so busy with the sun round which the earth revolves, that he has never taken any notice of the son that revolves round him; and that he hasn't had a new suit of clothes since he was fourteen; and that he wasn't even taken out of nankeen frocks and trowsers till he was quite unpleasant in 'em; and touches on a good many more family matters to the same purpose. To make short of a long story, gentlemen, they all talk together, and cry together, and remind the old gentleman that as to the noble family, his own grandfather would have been lord mayor if he hadn't died at a dinner the year before; and they show him by all kinds of arguments that if the cousins are married the prediction comes true every way. At last, the old gentleman, being quite convinced, gives in; and joins their hands; and leaves his daughter to marry anybody she likes; and they are all well pleased; and the Gifted as well as any of them.

"In the middle of this little family party, gentlemen,

sits Tom all the while, as miserable as you like. But, when everything else is arranged, the old gentleman's daughter says that their strange conduct was a little device of the waiting-maid's to disgust the lovers he had chosen for 'em, and will he forgive her? and if he will, perhaps he might even find her a husband,—and when she says that, she looks uncommon hard at Tom. Then the waiting-maid says that, oh dear! she couldn't abear Mr. Grig should think she wanted him to marry her; and that she had even gone so far as to refuse the last lamplighter, who was now a literary character (having set up as a bill-sticker); and that she hoped Mr. Grig would not suppose she was on her last legs by any means, for the baker was very strong in his attentions at that moment, and as to the butcher, he was frantic. And I don't know how much more she might have said, gentlemen (for, as you know, this kind of young women are rare ones to talk), if the old gentleman hadn't cut in suddenly, and asked Tom if he'd have her, with ten pounds to recompense him for his loss of time and disappointment, and as a kind of bribe to keep the story secret.

" 'It don't much matter, sir,' says Tom, 'I ain't long for this world. Eight weeks of marriage, especially with this young woman, might reconcile me to my fate. I think,' he says, 'I could go off easy, after that.' With which he embraces her with a very dismal face, and groans in a very dismal way that might move a heart of stone,—even of philosopher's stone.

" 'Egad,' says the old gentleman, 'that reminds me, —this bustle put it out of my head,—there was a figure wroug. He'll live to a green old age,—eighty-seven at least!'

"'How much, sir?' cries Tom.

"'Eighty-seven!' says the old gentleman.

"Without another word, Tom flings himself on the old gentleman's neck; throws up his hat; cuts a caper; defies the waiting-maid; and refers her to the butcher.

"'You won't marry her!' says the old gentleman, angrily.

"'And live after it!' says Tom. 'I'd sooner marry a mermaid, with a small-tooth comb and looking-glass.'

"'Then take the consequences,' says the other.

"With those words—I beg your kind attention here, gentlemen, for it's worth your notice,—the old gentleman wetted the forefinger of his right hand in some of. the liquor from the crucible that was spilt on the floor, and drew a small triangle on Tom's forehead. The room swam before his eyes, and he found himself in the watch-house."

"Found himself *where*?" cried the vice, on behalf of the company generally.

"In the watch-house," said the chairman. "It was late at night, and he found himself in the very watch-house from which he had been let out that morning."

"Did he go home?" asked the vice.

"The watch-house people rather objected to that," said the chairman; "so he stopped there that night, and went before the magistrate in the morning. 'Why, you're here again, are you?' says the magistrate, adding insult to injury; 'we'll trouble you for five shillings more, if you can conveniently spare the money.' Tom told him

he had been enchanted, but it was no use. He told the
contractors the same, but they wouldn't believe him.
It was very hard upon him, gentlemen, as he often said,
for was it likely he'd go and invent such a tale? They
shook their heads and told him he'd say anything but
his prayers,—·as indeed he would ; there's no doubt about
that. It was the only imputation on his moral character
that ever *I* heard of."

END OF VOL. I.